BROKEN FLOWERS

Kate McQuaile

Quercus

First published in Great Britain in 2020 by Quercus
This paperback edition published in 2020 by

Quercus Editions Ltd
Carmelite House
50 Victoria Embankment
London EC4Y 0DZ

An Hachette UK company

A CIP catalogue record for this book is available
from the British Library

PB ISBN 978 1 52940 3 978
EB ISBN 978 1 52940 3 961

10 9 8 7 6 5 4 3 2 1

Typeset by CC Book Production
Printed and bound in Great Britain by Clays Ltd, Elcograf S.p.A.

1

Now

Between lifting the poker and smashing it down on his head, there must have been a moment when I thought about what was going to happen, about the consequences of a heavy metal object making contact with flesh and bone. But if there was such a moment, I don't remember it. Nor do I remember having had any sense of a line about to be crossed, a line separating innocence and murder. The fact is that I have no memory whatsoever of that single moment – if it ever existed.

I've been good at shutting the memory of that night out of my mind – or, at least, good at slamming some cerebral door against it when it has pushed too far forward.

But there have been times when I've allowed the guilt to wash over me like a tidal wave until I think I'm going to drown. And there will be in the future. Maybe I'll see someone who reminds me of him, and for a fraction of a second my heart will pound faster and I'll feel my stomach churn. Or I'll hear a voice that sounds like his. And then there's that much deeper thing I dare not acknowledge. It lies below the surface. It will always be there.

I've rebuilt my life, reinvented myself. I've lied and I'm still lying. I no longer know the difference between what's true and what's false, what's real and unreal.

I know that I have rebuilt my life on an illusion, a pack of lies I told myself. I invented a new truth because it was the only way I was able to survive.

I realise that now as I walk down the short, narrow passageway that leads to the house I left four decades ago. The house where I became a murderer. Number 4 Paradise Place.

Earlier that day . . .

I'm sick with nerves and with longing. I haven't seen him for two years, two long years, and now I'm on my way to London to see him marry a woman I've never met. The conflicting emotions that threatened to drown me when I first drew the stiff white card out of the envelope are back. They batter my heart and my stomach as every swerve of the speeding train takes me closer to my son, my beautiful, angry son who walked out of my life on the day we buried his father.

He has found love, and I should be happy for him. But

I'm overwhelmed by a sense of grief and loss at having been excluded from all the events of the past two years that have led to his present happiness.

I wish I had been part of his getting to know this woman.

Over the years, I had glimpses into his romantic life. Sometimes he brought girlfriends to stay for weekends, and I saw several come and go. I liked most of them, and some of them I liked very much. But they rarely lasted longer than a few months and Chris and I began to wonder if we would ever see him settled.

The wedding invitation stands to attention in my open handbag. My hand slips into the bag and into the torn envelope. My fingers feel their way across the embossed wording that I now know by heart, the names that are etched into my brain. Arnaud and Alice Thomas. Marie-Laure Thomas.

Who are these people? How did Ben meet them? How much do they know about me? Has he told them why he hasn't spoken to me for two years? Perhaps he hasn't told them anything about me at all. My name is on the invitation, written in a hand I don't recognise.

I shiver and turn my face to the window, relieved that the seat booked for me is one of two facing the direction in which the train is travelling, and hoping the man sitting next to me won't notice that I'm crying.

He does notice, though.

'Are you all right?' he asks. His voice is quiet, kind.

This unexpected show of kindness from a stranger makes

me even more emotional. I can't speak because there's a great big lump in my throat and it's choking me. So I give my head a series of tiny shakes. They're meant to tell him that I'm fine and I don't need or want to talk. He produces a packet of tissues and hands them to me. Then he says something I don't hear properly because I'm blowing my nose loudly, and he disappears through the carriage. When he comes back a while later, he's carrying a small brown paper bag from which he takes two paper cups.

'I thought you might like some tea,' he says, putting both cups on to the tray in front of me and sitting back into his own seat. 'Milk and sugar, if you want them,' he adds, producing several small plastic containers of milk and a few paper tubes filled with sugar.

There's the hint of a soft country burr to his accent, though it's not very strong. It reminds me of Eddie – no, I *won't* allow myself to go there. I've been good at shutting out certain things, but every now and again something random breaks through my guard, so I concentrate on the tea, sipping it slowly. I smile occasionally at this kind stranger, whose rugged face and thick thatch of grey hair suggest he's somewhere in his mid-sixties. His eyes are a soft brown and when he smiles they shine brightly out beyond the wrinkled skin that frames them.

'Thanks,' I say. 'Things have been a bit difficult lately. It all got a bit too much for me back there, but I'm fine. I am, really.'

I don't mean to engage in any further conversation, but it's not easy to tell someone who has been so kind that I would prefer to put a barrier between the two of us for the remainder of the journey. So I let him talk away about his visit to Yorkshire to see his daughter and her family, and I smile and nod where I think it's appropriate, and after a while I begin to be grateful that he wants to talk to me, that he's giving me a respite from my own tormented thoughts. But the respite comes to an end all too quickly when he asks me why I'm going to London.

I could make something up, but I tell him I'm going to my son's wedding.

'Oh, very nice,' my travelling companion says.

I look at him, into his kind eyes, and I keep talking.

'To tell you the truth,' I tell this man I've never met before and will never see again, 'I'm not . . . in a good state about this wedding.'

Not in a good state is an understatement. I feel angry and sad at the same time. The first I knew of this wedding was when the invitation came in the post just a few weeks ago. I've been summoned. I haven't been consulted. I've been sent a train ticket and details of where I'm going to stay. My son has decided these things without speaking to me. He has decided I'm going to spend a week in London, presumably getting to know his fiancée and her parents and God knows who else. He isn't even going to be at the station to meet me; he can't be bothered. So he's sending a driver. The

5

instructions were delivered in a short, unsigned note that accompanied the invitation.

The man says nothing, but there's a sympathetic look on his face and in his eyes, and, in spite of the guardedness that I've preserved for so long, I find myself confiding in him. I don't tell him everything, of course. I don't tell him why Ben and I quarrelled. I skirt around that and he's too polite to ask questions. He just nods, occasionally pressing his lips together and widening them in an expression that seems to say he understands why I'm feeling anxious about the whole thing.

When the train eventually pulls in to King's Cross, the man stands up and takes his bag and coat down from the overhead rack. I'm almost tempted to remain in my seat and wait for the train to reverse and move north again.

The man has put his coat on and he's ready to go.

'I hope everything goes well,' he says.

'You've been very kind. It really has helped to talk to you.'

I walk through the gates towards a man in a dark suit who's holding up a big white piece of card with my name on it. All around me, passengers are hurling themselves into the arms of their lovers, their parents, their friends, their children. Desolation and grief overwhelm me.

How different it would be if I were walking through these barriers with Chris. It would be hard, but Chris would soothe and comfort me, promise that everything would be all right and that he would look after me as he had always looked after me. I had always been his priority, the most important thing in his life. Now I was no one's priority.

'Mrs Brown? Please come with me.'

I walk behind the driver to a street bordering the station. He has taken my wheelie case and is striding ahead of me. It's raining and I struggle to keep sight of him as I weave through a sea of umbrellas. Finally, seated in the back of the car, a large black Mercedes, I try to engage him in conversation. He's polite in that he answers my questions, but he's far from friendly. He tells me in short sentences that he's taking me to a hotel in Canary Wharf and that a different driver will collect me later this evening.

The hotel is ultra-modern. The staff on reception are sleek and fashionable. They seem friendly, too, but only on the surface; their smiles don't extend to their eyes. I'm sure they're looking down on me, because, in spite of my new clothes, I feel shabby, not quite good enough to stay in this place whose staff look like fashion models.

My room is what I suppose would be described as minimalist, with hardly any furniture apart from the huge bed, and the walls and carpet in shades of white, cream and grey. The only vibrant colour in the room bursts from the huge abstract paintings on the walls. I look at them closely and see that they're actual paintings rather than reproduction prints.

I have several hours to kill before the car picks me up. I could go for a walk, now that the rain has stopped and the weak winter sun seems to be trying to break through the grey clouds. I became a great walker after Chris died and I sold the garden centre. There was nothing else to do, no one to talk to. Not that I wanted to talk to anyone. So I walked and walked, for hours and hours, miles and miles. I was trying to walk away from myself and I'm still doing it. If I have a day without walking at least five miles I feel that things aren't quite right.

But I don't feel like walking through this part of London that seems like a grown-up version of Lego, only less friendly. When I lived in London for that short time in the late 1970s, I knew only West London and the West End, and I didn't even know those areas very well. I can't remember ever having visited the East End or even anywhere east of Tottenham Court Road.

I look out of my window on to an almost empty street, grey and bleak under the mass of cloud, and the granite-coloured water beyond it. I wonder whether Ben lives in this strange and sterile business kingdom, whether he looks out over the same stretch of the river from an apartment in one of those tall towers. Wherever I look, left or right or straight ahead, I see cranes reaching into the sky. I can't imagine him wanting to live in such a place.

And then, as if by magic, I begin to understand the beauty and drama of the shifting light on the water as the clouds part and come together again, creating pictures as stunning and beautiful as any moorland landscape. In the far distance, windmills stand out like giant angels keeping watch over a brave new world.

The next few hours drift by slowly. I think about visiting the hotel spa and having a massage and facial, but remembering how I felt so intimidated by the reception staff, opt instead for a long, slow bath. And then, although I don't mean to, I fall asleep on the huge bed.

When I wake up, the room is dark, save for a weak glow from the lights outside, and for a few moments I'm not quite sure where I am. I panic, afraid that I've slept through the evening, and that I won't see Ben, that he's going to be angry with me for missing the dinner. My panic subsides when I see the time shining eerily from the digital clock beside the bed. It's only six o'clock and the car isn't coming until seven. I have an hour to get ready.

You don't need a glamorous wardrobe when you live in the country and do the job I do, or, rather, the job I used to do. A couple of reasonably smart outfits and a pair of low-heeled shoes will see you through several years of social occasions. The rest of the time it's jeans, with jumpers and flat boots in the winter, T-shirts and trainers or plimsolls in the summer and wellingtons when it's raining, which is often.

I've had to buy new clothes for this trip to London, including a black dress that Ilaria made me buy. I lost a lot of weight when Chris died two years ago. Clothes that had once been snug now hang off me. The dress disguises my thinness. It even hints at curves I no longer have, despite my being a size ten, the size I was forty years ago. That's the only comparison between the eighteen-year-old girl I was then and the fifty-eight-year-old woman I am now. My hair, once the darkest brown, is now a bright silvery white.

I stopped colouring my hair when Chris died. I just didn't think about it. He lived for several days after the accident, drifting in and out of consciousness. I begged God to make him better, but his injuries were too much for him. The doctors said it was a miracle he'd lasted even those few days and that at least we'd been able to talk to him. By the time of the funeral, my grey and white roots ran along the top of my crown, an ugly stripe that showed how much I'd neglected myself.

Perhaps if Ben and I hadn't quarrelled I might have gone back to caring about my appearance. But we did quarrel and he walked away. And after that I had no interest in keeping up any kind of appearances. I looked old and worn and ragged, and as time passed I looked even older and more worn. I was depressed and sad. I'd lost my husband, and now my son was so angry with me that he wanted nothing to do with me.

People were kind. They rallied around, bringing cooked meals for which I had no appetite, leaving cards and notes to show their concern. But I couldn't confide in them. I couldn't tell them Ben had walked out. I left them to find out for themselves, and when they did they knew better than to ask me about it.

A few days after Ben left, Ilaria called me from Florence. We talked on the phone every so often. We saw each other every couple of years when she came to stay for a few days, sometimes with her husband, Matteo, sometimes by herself. Chris and I didn't travel. I hadn't told her about Chris's accident and death. I hadn't even *thought* of telling her because I was floundering and sinking in a pit of despair and had lost the track of my life.

'I'm coming tomorrow,' she said as soon as she heard what had happened.

She came for three weeks that time. And she came again, just a fortnight ago, to help me prepare for the wedding.

'I'm taking you to the hairdresser's,' she told me the day after she arrived. 'Get your coat on. We have an appointment at two in Leeds.'

'Leeds? What's wrong with here?'

'We have other things to do.'

The hairdresser chopped at my hair, which I'd allowed to grow so long that I now mostly wore it tied back and pinned in place here and there with clips. Ilaria gave me the odd anxious look, checking how I was coping as the scissors snipped away lock after lock of dull, ugly hair. If only she knew that I didn't care one iota, I thought at the time. The hairdresser could have shaved my head and I wouldn't have objected.

As we emerged from the salon hours later, Ilaria was overjoyed.

'*Bellissima!*' she exclaimed, bringing her hands together

with a clap and then throwing her arms around me. 'You look wonderful! She has taken years off you.'

I had to admit that I did look good. The hairdresser had practised her magic and my long, drab, multicoloured hair was now a silver pixie cut.

Over the next couple of hours, Ilaria dragged me into one boutique after another until she was satisfied that I had all the clothes I needed for London and the wedding.

'But I'll never wear these clothes and shoes again,' I protested after I had mentally totted up the amount of money I had spent. 'They're ridiculously expensive! You know I have no need for black cocktail dresses and high heels.'

'No matter,' Ilaria said, batting away my protests. 'You can afford it. These things are what you need for London, not your old-lady shoes and your safe little jackets and skirts and blouses and your jeans that are too big and too short and without any shape.'

She paused, pursed her lips and began to speak again.

'I don't want to be unkind, but you look, well, not very good. I think you have removed yourself from this life that is the only one you have. Chris would not want you to do that. So, please, even if it is only for a few days, make the most of yourself. Bring out that beautiful girl you were when I first knew you all those years ago, that beautiful girl you have locked away under your terrible clothes.'

I stared at her, shocked, not knowing what to say. She had never spoken to me in this way. Her words stung and stimulated at the same time. Why would I want to bring out the girl I was when we first knew each other in London? That girl had got me into trouble and I was well rid of her. And yet something in me responded to the idea that I could, even if just for a short while, be attractive, that I could dare to be what I no longer was. Attractive, feisty, brave.

Our last stop was at a department store, where the glamorous young woman on one of the make-up counters picked out a range of cosmetics to go with my new look and gave me a lesson in how to apply them. Another small fortune. She ran the various products we had bought through the till, but stopped when she came to the lipstick.

Looking at me with a very serious expression on her face and holding up the lipstick as if it were some kind of talisman, she said, 'The red lipstick. Very important for this new look of yours. If you're pushed for time, just go for the lipstick.'

So now, I'm waiting in my room for the call from reception that will tell me the car is here. I'm wearing my black dress and the silver earrings that go well with my silver hair. And I'm wearing my red lipstick like a badge of courage.

2

Then

It was the autumn of 1977, and Nan's life was beginning in earnest. She had grown up on the outskirts of a tiny village in the north of England and now she was in a different kind of village, one of those London villages that had joined seamlessly together to form a sprawling city. She was living in Notting Hill and she was overwhelmed by just about everything.

Pembridge Road on a Saturday afternoon was like Oxford Street, except that the steady but disorganised stream of mostly young people was heading for the second-hand clothes shops and stalls of Portobello rather than the Etams, Jane Normans and Chelsea Girls of the British high street. She revelled in joining the stream, happy to look like everyone else, the young people, the tourists, making their pilgrimage to one of the most famous streets in the world. But she felt special, because she knew she wasn't like the tourists, who stood out. She was *living* here, actually living in this place she had only read about in the papers and in magazines.

Punks were everywhere, some strangely glamorous, some just plain weird, jostling for space with the longer-established hippies. They seemed to have put a great deal of effort into the outfits they wore, although Nan suspected the electric kettle she saw one young woman carry as a handbag had been inspired by a sense of fun rather than a desire to be subversive. The hippies looked less contrived, less put together, in their floaty cheesecloth and cotton, their clogs and open-toed sandals and their long hair.

On Moscow Road, an artery of Greek restaurants and Middle Eastern cafés that joined Pembridge Square to Queensway, there were long queues outside a public telephone kiosk as word spread about the fault it had developed that meant cheap calls across the world; she usually called her parents from there because for just a few pennies she could talk for hours.

Annie Hall was showing at the Gate Cinema. Nan had already seen it twice, and, like almost everyone else she knew, she now peppered her sentences with *la-di-da*.

Everything was exciting. Everything was wonderful. It seemed as if nothing could go wrong. But Nan didn't know that everything was about to go wrong. Because 1977 wasn't just the year she began to live; it was also the year she began to fall apart.

A few weeks earlier . . .

Her father had insisted on driving her to London in his battered old Morris Traveller, a car that had carried as many sheep as people over the years. He swore quietly to himself every time he got lost, and he got lost many times once the car left the motorway and they were spewed into the London maze. The journey took a lot longer than it was supposed to, and when they finally reached Notting Hill and the hostel, the light was beginning to leave the sky. Nan stared out at the tall white houses, some with canopies made of wrought-iron and glass, that looked like mansions.

Her father parked the Morris and took Nan's case from the back, glancing nervously around him as if calculating the chances of some crazy person jumping out from behind a wall, intent on doing them harm. They climbed the steep flight of steps to the door and pressed the bell. A nun opened the door and welcomed them. Nan's father mumbled a few words to the nun and patted Nan on the shoulder in an awkward, almost embarrassed goodbye. He had never been the demonstrative type. And then he was off again, hurrying down the stone steps and across the road to the car, which, squashed into a space between a Jaguar and a Mercedes sports car, looked abandoned rather than parked. He was anxious to be back home where he knew every road like the back of his hand and could find his way across the fields in the dark on foot.

Nan waved goodbye, her heart aching because she understood that the life she had known until now was over. The next time she saw her parents, she would be different. London would change her; she knew this. And even though she wanted that change, even though she wanted to embrace whatever this new life would bring, she couldn't help feeling just a little bit sad. She willed away the tears that threatened as she watched the Morris disappear from sight.

The nun, who had introduced herself as Sister Maria, led her up several flights of stairs to a tiny room with a single bed, a little chest of drawers with a lamp, a wardrobe, a chair and a table. Sister Maria pointed to the jug of water and Clingfilm-covered plate of cold meat and salad on the table and explained that Nan had missed dinner. She went through the rules. Breakfast was from seven to nine and dinner from six to seven, provided as part of the £14 weekly rent, but girls had to buy their own lunch. The front door was locked at eleven o'clock on weeknights and at half past midnight on Saturdays.

The nun left and Nan hoisted her suitcase, a battered, ancient thing held shut by a leather belt, on to the bed. She was tired and she hadn't eaten for hours, but she knew that the first thing she had to do was unpack, to make the room hers. Only when her clothes were hanging in the wardrobe, her shoes standing abreast at the bottom of it and her underwear in the chest of drawers did she feel she could sit down and eat.

The cold roast beef was dry and tasteless and the salad consisted of a few lettuce leaves, a hard-boiled egg cut into quarters, a couple of spring onions and several slices of beet-root that leaked little puddles of deep pink vinegary liquid on to the plate. Under a paper napkin she found two slices of rubbery-looking white bread and a small foil-wrapped rectangle of butter. She was still hungry when she finished eating because the anticipation that had built all through the long drive from Yorkshire had sent her metabolism into overdrive. How was she going to sleep? She wished now that she hadn't discreetly left behind the bag filled with apples and cheese and ham and home-made bread her mother had packed for her. But her exhaustion after the long journey south turned out to be greater than her hunger, greater even than her excitement, and she was asleep almost as soon as she turned off the light.

3

Now

The car, another Mercedes, is black and sleek. The driver, who wears a dark suit, opens the door for me. I ask him where we're going but he says it's a surprise. I make several attempts to engage him in conversation but he answers in monosyllables, so I give up and spend the journey from the hotel looking out of the window. I keep an eye out for landmarks like the Post Office Tower, Marble Arch, Buckingham Palace, but I spot nothing, not even street names, because the car is moving too quickly for me to get a good look.

We've been driving for about twenty-five minutes when things start to look familiar. It's not that I recognise specific shops or buildings; it's more the shape of the streets, the way one turns into another or curves along a hill.

It's only when we turn into a road with a raised pavement and tiny shops on the left-hand side that I have a definite sense of having been here before. I'm trying to work out whether I really do know where I am when I catch sight of the pub. The Rising Sun. The shock is like electricity, jolting through my body. We are driving through the last place in the world I want to be: Notting Hill. And we are close to – I can hardly bear even to think of the name – Paradise Place. Involuntarily, I shiver, close my eyes and start to count – one, two, three, four, five . . . When I reach one hundred, we will have left these streets behind and I will be able to open my eyes again.

But all of a sudden I become aware that the car has purred to a halt. I hear the driver speaking on his phone but his voice seems far away. I don't know what he's saying. I wait, my eyes still closed. I'm trying to count but I can't. I feel a flutter of panic somewhere at the top of my chest.

A blast of cold air hits me and I open my eyes to see that the driver is holding the door open for me. I sit still, paralysed. I don't want to get out of the car, but the driver reaches towards me and takes my hand and there's nothing I can do but scramble inelegantly on to the pavement. The driver points towards a narrow passageway and tells me it's too narrow for the car and that I will have to walk the remaining few yards to the house, where someone will be waiting for me.

'I . . . I can't go in there . . . I can't . . .'

Fear squeezes my vocal cords and my voice dries up. The driver gives me a look that tells me he sees I'm in a state but he says he's sorry, he would come with me if he could but he can't leave the car because he has had to stop on a double yellow line.

Am I really back at the place I ran away from all those years ago? Is this real or am I imagining it? But the thumping of my heart and the sickening twist of what feels like a rope tightening around my stomach tell me that it's all too real. My instinct tells me to run, to run as fast as I can, away from that passageway I once knew so well. But something else tells me that if I'm going to see Ben I will have to walk along that dark passageway to the house beyond. So I stumble along the cobbled, dimly lit passageway, the cold wet wind in my eyes, trying to convince myself that the fact I am here, walking towards the house I fled four decades ago, is all just a coincidence.

Suddenly, I stop. My mouth is dry. Even my heart feels as if it's no longer beating. In the darkness, I think I hear someone say my name. Unnerved, I whip around. But there's no one there. I exhale in a short burst of relief. It was my imagination. And then I hear it again, my name spoken so quietly that it could be a whisper on the wind. I turn around again and this time I see a human shape. But this can't be happening. It can't.

Because he's dead.

Because I killed him.

I close my eyes and take several deep breaths, in and out, in and out. But when I open my eyes again, he's still there. And he's watching me, his arms folded, a half-smile on his face.

'It's been a long time, Nan.'

The shock of seeing him, hearing his voice, overwhelms me. I would know that voice anywhere. It hasn't changed. Sonorous, mellifluous. And he still speaks in that languid drawl I once found so attractive, so exotic, so dreamy and hypnotic. No hint of estuary has crept into his accent.

He looks the same, too, although that patrician look is even more pronounced four decades on. The deep-set grey eyes, the slightly flared nostrils, the wide, almost perfectly shaped mouth. His once-dark hair has faded into shades of grey, but it's the same hair, thick and wavy.

I feel as if there's a vice inside me, squeezing my stomach so hard that I don't know whether I'm in pain or whether I'm going to be sick. I try to convince myself that he's not real, that the guilt I've tried to suppress over the years has burst through with a vengeance and conjured him up. He doesn't exist because he's dead.

But then I feel him take my elbow in the palm of his hand and steer me to the end of the passageway towards the house I had hoped never to see again. Number 4 Paradise Place.

Surely this is all in my mind, all wrapped up in this unintended, unplanned return to London that is laying waste to my emotions. I'm not really walking into Paradise Place. There's no one beside me. There's no hand on my arm.

Nobody's footsteps are keeping time with the click-clacking of my heels on the cobbles.

We reach the stone steps and begin to climb towards the door that I know should be dark green but whose colour isn't easy to make out in the dark. It's only when I half-miss a step and almost fall that I realise there's no one beside me any more. I look around and behind me but, beyond the misty, inadequate light thrown by the single street lamp, there's only the darkness. Maybe there never was anyone. I have imagined him.

A vertical sliver of light appears ahead and for a fraction of a second I feel a sense of relief, because its strangeness convinces me that I have indeed been temporarily afflicted by emotional trauma.

But, just as quickly, I feel that sense of relief dissipate and turn to panic. The thin sliver of light becomes a blaze as a door opens wide to reveal a woman, a beautiful young woman who rushes forward, holding her arms out to me.

'Nan! I am Marie-Laure,' she says, wrapping her arms around me. 'I am so happy to meet you at last.'

I submit to the embrace in stupefied silence, my voice still caught somewhere inside me.

That's when I catch sight of Ben, hovering in the background. I detach myself from Marie-Laure and move towards him, wanting to throw my arms around him but not daring to because I'm so unsure of how he will respond. Just as I reach him, he puts both hands on my shoulders, holding me at a distance, signalling with a slight application of pressure from his fingers that I must not try to come too close. He kisses my cheek, so quickly and so awkwardly that my hand rises involuntarily to my face as if to check whether his lips have left any impression at all.

The lukewarm greeting from my son leaves me gutted. After two years that have torn me apart, this is all he is willing to give. But I hide my dismay, persuading myself that this peck on the cheek represents one more step towards reconciliation.

I look at Marie-Laure, whose face is a picture of happiness. Ben looks awkward. He hasn't said a word. Maybe he's as nervous as I am, worried about what will happen between us over the next few days.

I'm too overwhelmed to take in the house properly, to look for all the things that may have changed and all the things that may not. We are still in the hallway. I know there is a room to the right of it, but I don't dare to look towards it. I don't dare think about the things that happened in that room. I shiver involuntarily. Am I really back in this house or am I somehow going mad? Maybe I'm still at the hotel, in the middle of a dream that has turned into a nightmare.

'Oh, you're cold,' Marie-Laure says. 'Never mind, you will soon warm up.'

She's fussing around me, admiring my hair and my clothes, wittering on about how happy she is that I've come to London and how excited she is about getting to know me at last.

She's a lot younger than Ben – at least ten years younger,

maybe more, which surprises me. His previous girlfriends have all been his contemporaries. I wonder what, apart from her stunningly good looks, has brought them together. Perhaps he has simply reached the age at which he's ready to settle down and Marie-Laure happened to be around.

I have no doubt that she will have been attracted to my son not just because he's handsome, but also because of his qualities of kindness and decency (although I remind myself that I haven't seen any kindness from him in the past couple of years).

It occurs to me now that my future daughter-in-law rather than my son has been the driving force behind the invitation to attend their wedding. I wonder how much pressure from Marie-Laure was needed to get him to agree to invite me.

'I hope you like your hotel,' Marie-Laure is saying.

I nod and smile, still too overwhelmed to respond in words. *Will she ever stop talking?* In my head, I'm telling her to shut up, that the only voice I want to hear is that of my son. But Ben, who has retreated behind Marie-Laure, remains silent. For a moment, I think he looks like a shy toddler. He had been a quiet child. I remember how my father, no great talker himself, would ask him whether the cat had got his tongue. I try the question out in my head. *Cat got your tongue, Ben?* But I mustn't say anything like that to him, even if I dress it up as banter. I must be patient, let him come to me now that I've made this journey to him.

Two people materialise in front of us, a man and a woman.

'You must meet my parents,' Marie-Laure says, beaming. Her smile is wide, her teeth white and even. Her eyes are so lit up that her whole face seems to glow. She seems very young, too young to be getting married. 'Alice and Arnaud.' She elongates slightly the second syllable of her mother's name. *A-leece.*

'How lovely to meet you,' Alice, tall with casually but perfectly styled and highlighted shoulder-length blonde hair, says. She's wearing a navy dress that is so beautiful and yet so simple that it must have cost a fortune. She bends to kiss me on both cheeks. Her voice is warm and husky; she makes each word sound slightly exotic with her precise annunciation. She sounds almost English.

Arnaud, not quite as tall as his wife, comes forward and shakes my hand, giving the smallest of bows as he does so. He doesn't look very French. He reminds me a little bit of Vladimir Putin.

I have nothing to say to these people. How am I going to get through the evening, making small talk with strangers, when all I want is to be alone with Ben? I look around for him, but he's walking away from me. We all fall into place behind him, shuffling away from the entrance hall, and for a few seconds no one is talking to me. That's when what happened outside the house comes back into my mind. I shiver, remembering the voice, the pressure of that hand under my elbow. But he was never there, except in my imagination, was he?

4

Then

As far back as she could remember, Nan had drawn things. She had no memory of a time when she didn't have a pencil in her hand, sketching away. And she couldn't quite remember the point at which she had decided she would become an artist; she just always knew she would.

When she told her parents she wanted to go to art college, they didn't react well. Her mother and father, who had both been forced to leave school early to help out on their respective family farms, wanted something different for Nan. They wanted her to have a respectable career as a teacher or a nurse. She was bright, they told her. Why couldn't she be sensible and go to teacher-training or secretarial college, do something that would get her a job? Look how well her cousin Susan had done, they said. Susan, now twenty-five, had done a secretarial course, got a job in a big company in Leeds, married her boss and was now living with her husband

and two children in a huge house with a dishwasher and what Nan's mother described as all the mod cons.

Nan didn't want to be like Susan, who, once she had bagged a husband and started producing children, had become prematurely middle-aged. No, Nan was going to follow her dreams, wherever they might take her. And now, here she was, following her dreams with a vengeance and stopped in her tracks at least once a day by the sudden realisation that she was in London. *Here I am, on a Number 12 bus*, she would marvel. Or, *Here I am, walking along Oxford Street*.

That wasn't to say she didn't miss home – her mother's hearty cooking, those quiet evening walks with her father and the dogs in summer, the way the moorland changed colour under the shifting light and the passing of one season into another.

Her heart still felt a pinch when she thought about that last morning at home before her father had driven her down to London. Her mind buzzing with excitement and apprehension and her body alert, as if wired up to an electricity supply, she had lain awake for much of the previous night. And as the first signs of dawn had begun to push light through the tiny gap in the curtains, she had finally given up on sleep and set off to walk alone around the place that had formed her. It was as if she had needed to imprint its comforting familiarity indelibly on her mind, safeguard her memories of how it was before she left to begin a new life that would change everything.

She retrieved the memory easily. It had been glorious, that morning. The sunlight, pushing through the leaves of the trees, had created a stippling effect, making her think of an impressionist painting. The hedgerows had been a riot of pink wildflowers, and montbretia grew profusely, bursting from the ditches with its bright orange flowers sitting on top of long, elegant stems. At intervals, the trees parted to reveal fields rolling away from the other side of the stone wall, making clearer the sound of the brook far below and bringing the hills on the other side of the valley closer.

And there she'd been, willingly leaving it behind. Sometimes, as she'd walked, she had felt her resolve waver. She'd thought she could go back to the house and tell her parents she had changed her mind, and they would be glad. But those feelings of indecisiveness had lasted only moments. She was leaving. She had to leave, because she was pursuing a dream. That dream might turn out to be a nightmare, but she had to follow it, because she knew that if she didn't she would regret it for the rest of her days.

And now, a world away in London, she made a special effort to remember that final morning and all the colours of home, because they were already beginning to fade.

In Notting Hill, or at least in the part where she lived now, the colour that dominated was the white of the stucco on the tall villas that lined the streets and squares. These houses were beautiful but intimidating. There was no softness about them. Even the hostel looked imposing. But just a short distance away, behind the Gate and Coronet cinemas on the south side of Notting Hill Gate, were narrow streets of much smaller and prettier houses painted in light pastel colours. She walked along those streets every day to the Byam Shaw School of Art on Campden Street, wishing she could live in one of those pretty little houses.

The first few weeks hadn't been easy. She felt gauche and unworldly in comparison with some of her fellow students, many of whom had come from other countries to study there. She felt less talented, too, even though she had been accepted into the school on the strength of the portfolio she had assembled. In art class at her secondary school, she had stood out; her drawings and paintings were so much better than those of her classmates. Her art teacher, Miss Sheringham, had encouraged her to make the most of her 'special' gift and had insisted on paying for the foundation course at Byam Shaw.

'I have more money than I need,' Miss Sheringham had told Nan's parents, who had objected strongly to what they saw as an unnecessary act of charity. 'I see this as an investment,' she assured them.

Now, though, Nan felt she was nothing special at all. She looked at what other students were working on and she felt frustrated by her own attempts, which, in comparison, seemed so childish and lacking in originality.

She was beginning to realise that becoming an artist wasn't just about being able to draw and paint but was also about going through new experiences that would influence the way she thought and the way she saw things. She knew that her mind was already beginning to open and expand; she could feel it. But she had a sense of being so far behind everyone else in that respect and she was impatient to catch up.

She hadn't bonded with any of the other students yet; truth be told, she was a little in awe of them and their ideas and embarrassed by her lack of exposure to the kind of art they wanted to create in the future. All she wanted to do was draw well and paint well but that didn't seem to be enough. She was shy in their company. And the most they did was to acknowledge her presence with a nod. They hadn't made an effort to get to know her and why would they, she asked herself, be bothered with a mousy northern girl who had no right to be there?

She tried not to think about Miss Sheringham. She had written an eager letter to her former teacher about her first week at the school and had received a letter back. *I am immensely proud of you*, Miss Sheringham had written. *I hope with all my heart that you will develop into the artist I failed to become.* How could she live up to that hope, which, she was quickly realising, had been sorely misplaced?

Despite the shortcomings of the hostel, she felt comfortable there. It was a friendly place and she was becoming friends with girls from all over the world – Colombia, Italy, Spain, Iran. She loved listening to their stories of home, lapping them up eagerly. Most of these girls were in London to learn English. There were several English girls at the hostel, too, some studying and some newly arrived in London for work. But these English girls all seemed so sophisticated, so *knowing*, even though they were the same age as she was or slightly younger.

She liked Ilaria, an Italian girl, best of all. They were fast becoming best friends, which surprised her, because she had never really had a best friend before. She and a couple of local girls who lived nearby and went to the same school had palled around together at home. But it wasn't as if she had chosen them or they her; they had just fallen in together and, before Nan had even started to think about leaving, she and they had just as easily drifted apart. It was different with Ilaria. They might be from different countries and backgrounds, but Nan was beginning to feel as if she had known this girl with olive skin and jet-black hair all her life.

Ilaria was in London to learn English because she wanted to work in the Italian tourism industry. At some point, she would go back to Florence, but it wouldn't be for a long time, not for a year at least.

Nan, making the most of the short time she had been in London and enjoying hanging around with Ilaria, felt a bit guilty that she hadn't been home yet for a weekend. She cringed when she thought of the disappointment in her father's voice each time he asked her whether he should meet her at the station on the Friday evening and she lied and said she wasn't able to make it after all because she had extra classes over the weekend and she didn't want to miss them.

She felt especially guilty about Chris. He was at agricultural college in Cirencester but still managed to get home to Yorkshire most weekends. He rang her once a week and she waited at the coin-operated telephone on the ground floor of the hostel for his call, which he tried to make at seven o'clock on the dot every Wednesday. Sometimes the call came later because one of the other girls was on the phone and Chris hadn't been able to get through.

At first, she looked forward to hearing his voice and was happy when the telephone rang and there he was at the other end of the line. She couldn't wait to tell him about all that had happened since the last time they had spoken. And then, almost imperceptibly, the anticipation and the pleasure turned into something else that she couldn't quite identify, and the weekly call became a duty rather than a joy and a time to catch up with each other. The conversation was pretty much the same every week. He told her he missed her and couldn't wait to see her, and she told him she missed him too and she *would* get home for a weekend one of these days but she just *had* to attend those extra classes.

She had been talking to Chris now for what seemed like ages and she was starting to feel guilty about that too, because a girl was pacing around behind her, looking impatient and cross. The girl spread her arms and hands and lifted her shoulders and her eyebrows, as if to say, *Come on, finish your call and let someone else use the phone.*

'I'm sorry, but there's a queue for the phone,' she said in a whisper. 'I have to go. I'll talk to you next week.'

'Oh,' she heard him say, a sad-sounding *oh* that made her feel bad. And then he paused for a second before he said, 'I miss you.'

'I miss you too,' Nan said. And she felt even worse now, because she was discovering that she didn't really miss him very much at all. She felt uncomfortable about this. She hoped it was just the novelty of being in London and immersing herself in a new life. But she feared that it might be something more fundamental, and that was something she didn't want to think about.

Ilaria was waiting for her outside the front door. She was sitting on the top step, elbows on knees, smoking a cigarette. Nan held out her first and middle fingers in a vee and Ilaria stood up and gave her the cigarette. She hadn't told her parents or Chris that she had taken up smoking; she knew they wouldn't like it. They wouldn't like a lot of things she did now. Smoking was just one of them. Drinking was another.

'God, I need a drink,' she said, with a shudder.

They walked the short distance to The Rising Sun. Inside, Ilaria ordered a half of lager and Nan, who didn't think she would ever acquire a taste for any kind of beer, asked for a Dubonnet and lemonade. The barman smiled.

'Is that a Yorkshire accent?' he asked.

'I didn't think it was that obvious,' Nan said, with a laugh. But it was a slightly embarrassed laugh. She had been conscious of how different she sounded from the other students and had been trying to modify her accent.

'Well, you don't sound like Harvey Smith but I can tell you're from up that way,' he said, making her smile.

'You have a bit of an accent yourself,' she said.

'East Anglia,' he said. 'Norfolk.'

Ilaria paid for the drinks and they found somewhere to sit. Every now and again Nan looked around and met the barman's eyes. She looked away again quickly, but she always looked back and when she didn't catch his eye because he was serving someone she felt vaguely disappointed.

His eyes were green. He was tall and thin and quite nice looking. His longish, very straight fair hair kept falling in front of his eyes and he would brush it back behind his ear. She hadn't noticed him here before.

'Are you new?' she asked him when she went back to the bar for more drinks.

'No,' he said. 'I've been here for a few months. I've seen you in here before, though, I think.'

He asked her about herself as he poured the drinks. He wasn't flirty, not in an obvious way, but she could tell somehow that he found her attractive. She wondered whether he would ask her out and whether she would accept. Her guilty feelings about Chris niggled her. He was the only boyfriend she had ever had, and everyone, including Chris and herself, expected that the relationship, which had begun when they were both fifteen, would lead them down the aisle. But she was beginning to question that assumption, especially now as she stood eyeing up the barman.

Chris was – well, Chris was a farmer. He was good-looking in a rugged, farmer-ish way, with his brown curly hair and strong build. He would be seen as a catch in Yorkshire, not just because of his looks but because he came from a family of well-off farmers and the farm would eventually go to him and his brothers. But London was where she lived now, not Yorkshire, and she couldn't imagine him in London. She couldn't imagine him . . . She didn't really want to imagine him at all.

During this past summer, he had wanted them to sleep together. She had made excuses, the biggest one being that she couldn't risk becoming pregnant, not when she had art college ahead of her. She just wasn't ready to take such a big step, she had said. It might be 1977 but they were in Yorkshire, not swinging London. And, in any case, she had reminded him, her family was religious in a quiet, diligent way, even if she wasn't. Her father was a member of the parish council. Her mother was on the church-cleaning rota.

She knew already that her parents disapproved of sex before marriage because of remarks they had occasionally made, and she would feel bad about doing something that would upset them, even if they never found out. Chris had been all right about it, although he had kept trying to persuade her that it would be a wonderful thing for both of them.

Nan hadn't been persuaded. Maybe if she had felt more of a sense of urgency about it . . . But she hadn't felt anything like that at all. She went so far and no further, because she just never did start to experience all the feelings she had read about in magazines – the intensity, the sense of not being able to stop herself. Maybe those intense feelings would come later with Chris. She had read about that, too; how that could happen with someone you had known for years and take you by surprise. She and Chris had got together at a hop in the village hall, when he'd been the only boy who'd asked her to dance. He'd asked whether he could walk her home and she'd said yes. He hadn't tried to hold her hand or kiss her, but as he'd said goodnight and she'd thanked him for walking her home, he had suggested they might go for a walk the following day. And so they'd drifted slowly into a girlfriend–boyfriend relationship; it wasn't particularly exciting – she hadn't once thought she might lose control – but it had been quite nice.

She wondered now what it would be like to kiss the barman. He didn't ask her out, but he did ask her when she would be back in the pub.

'Oh, I don't know; maybe tomorrow evening if I'm not busy,' she told him, trying to sound casual.

But of course she would be back. She liked the attention he was paying her. She picked the drinks up slowly, turning her head away from the barman, showing him the side of her face she thought looked good in profile, giving him time to say something else.

'My name's Edward, by the way. But I also answer to Eddie.'

'My name's Anne, but everyone calls me Nan.'

'Nan,' he said, trying it out. 'Nan. I like it.'

And then he was gone, summoned by some old chap with a huge handlebar moustache who was loudly demanding, 'Any chance of a drink around here?'

Nan carried the drinks carefully to the table.

'I thought you were never coming back,' Ilaria said. 'Was he flirting with you? Did he ask you out on a date?'

'No,' Nan said. 'Well, not exactly.'

She tried to downplay the significance of her exchange with Eddie at the bar, but already she was thinking about what she would wear the following evening and how she would apply layer after layer of thick black mascara that would lengthen her eyelashes and make her blue eyes look even bluer. She would ask Ilaria, who had learned a thing or two from her hairdresser sister, to do her hair again, the way she'd done it last week when they'd gone to the disco down on Kensington High Street: piling it up on her head in such a way that when they were dancing some of it had become loose and tumbled down in auburn tresses to her shoulders. She remembered how she'd felt that night: pretty, beautiful even; she'd felt that for the first time in her life as she'd thrown herself into the beat of Donna Summer singing 'I Feel Love'.

Ilaria teased her about Eddie as they walked back to the hostel. 'You like him,' she said in a sing-song voice. 'I think you will want me to leave the window open for you tomorrow night. Or maybe you will sleep somewhere else . . .'

Ilaria shared a room on the ground floor with another Italian girl. When any of the girls were planning to stay out beyond the curfew, they told Ilaria and her roommate, and they would open the big window in their room so that the latecomers could climb in and sneak back to their rooms.

'Don't be silly! He's going to be working. And, anyway, you're coming with me, because I'm not going on my own,' Nan said. She was doing her best to sound nonchalant, as if going back to the pub the following evening would be just something amusing to do, as if she couldn't really care less. Secretly, though, she was building up a story in which something would happen between her and Eddie.

At that moment, Chris made a brief appearance in her mind and she squirmed.

Oh, why does it have to be so complicated?

5

Now

We file through the house into a large room at the back. There are French doors, beyond which I can see one of those modern urban outside spaces that, by dint of a few potted plants placed here and there on a paved surface, are called gardens.

Some of my anxiety falls away now, because I recognise nothing about this room or the instead-of-a-garden garden beyond it. The house has changed beyond recognition – at least this part of it has; the original kitchen has been extended and modernised. That we are all standing in it is a coincidence, no more than that. What happened outside, as I walked along the passageway towards the house, was my imagination running away with itself.

But even as I reassure myself, I begin to wonder again how Ben and Marie-Laure have come to live here. To my knowledge, Ben is still working full time as an architect and painting in his spare time. But this house must have cost a fortune and, even with Ben's architectural know-how, the refurbishment must have been expensive too. Perhaps Marie-Laure also has a job that pays good money. I feel uneasy, though. Of all the houses in London, how does Ben come to be here? How can it be just coincidence?

I'm deep in thought as Arnaud hands me a glass of white wine. I take the glass without thinking and look at it in confusion.

'If you are wondering whether it is one of my wines, I am afraid that it is not,' he says. 'We produce only red.'

'*Our* wines, *chéri*,' Alice interrupts.

Just as I begin to register the fact that my son's future in-laws are wine producers, Alice manoeuvres me away from Arnaud and we stand by the French doors. 'My darling husband is a typical man. He's happy to take all the credit when I'm the one who turned our business into a force to be reckoned with.'

She clinks her glass against mine.

'I . . . I'm sorry, but I don't drink,' I say apologetically. 'I hope you don't mind . . .'

Alice drains her glass and then takes the one I am holding so awkwardly. She raises it to her lips and sips.

'You don't drink wine or you don't drink any alcohol at all?'

'I don't drink at all,' I say.

She gives me a quizzical look and I feel obliged to give an explanation.

41

'It just . . . doesn't agree with me.'

'Such a shame. Your son is marrying into a wine-producing family and you won't be able to enjoy the obvious benefits.'

I don't want to discuss my teetotalism, so I tell Alice that her English is incredibly good.

'That's because I *am* English!' she exclaims with a lifting of her eyebrows, as if astonished by my failure to realise that she wasn't born in France. 'Oh, I know I've picked up a lot of French quirks in my accent and even sometimes in my grammar over the years, and these days I seem to think mostly in French, but I'm as English as you are. I'm a Manchester girl.'

'How – how did—'

'How did I end up married to Arnaud? When I was eighteen, I went to work for Arnaud's family as an au pair. Not looking after Arnaud himself, obviously – he has a much younger sister and I was employed to give her conversation practice in English. It was only supposed to be for the summer and then I would go to university back in England. But one thing led to another and, well, here we all are.'

I look across the room at Arnaud, who's talking to Ben and Marie-Laure. Measured against his wife, he seems so bland.

'We have become very fond of Ben,' she says softly, the French inflexions returning to her voice. 'We love him.'

'Thank you,' I say, my voice heavy with emotion and gratitude.

'And we hope you will love Marie-Laure. She really is a good girl. And she'll be a wonderful wife and mother.'

I feel a surge of emotion as I try to deal with the knowledge that Ben has a new family; that he is buying into a package consisting not only of the woman he loves but her parents too. Where do I fit in? Do I even have a place in the hierarchy of his nearest and dearest? I try to stop the tears that blur my vision but I'm only partly successful.

Alice puts her arms around me and holds me close for a moment.

'I'm sorry,' I mumble into her shoulder. 'It's all been a bit much for me.'

When she releases me and I straighten up, I become aware that the room has gone quiet. Ben, Marie-Laure and Arnaud are staring at us. Marie-Laure and Arnaud are wearing expressions of curious concern. But when I look into Ben's eyes I can't read them. What is he thinking?

Marie-Laure comes over, Ben in tow, and Alice steps back. I wish Marie-Laure would leave Ben with me and go away, but she hovers, beaming, looking from me to Ben and back again to me.

I can't take my eyes off Ben. He seems different, older. Maybe it's the light, but I think I can see thin blazes of grey running through his brown hair. I feel angry and sad at the same time for having been denied these two years during which the first signs of his mortality, those grey hairs, have appeared. How much of his life have I missed? Marie-Laure is just one part of it.

'It's lovely to see you, Ben,' I say.

Inside, I'm horrified to hear myself address my own son as if he were a distant relative or an acquaintance I hardly know. I'm hoping that he won't hear in my voice the nervousness I feel.

'And it's wonderful to meet Marie-Laure,' I add quickly, firmly, with a smile flashed in her direction. I know I may need to rely on her to help me rebuild my relationship with my son and I notice that the moment I mention her name his eyes seem to become brighter.

'It's . . . nice to see you too,' he says.

Nice. I digest this word in the silence that lasts a few seconds.

He looks away to meet Marie-Laure's eyes for a moment and when he looks at me again, he says, 'You look well.'

'Thank you.'

Oh, Ben, are we doomed to talk to each other like strangers for ever?

It's Marie-Laure who comes to the rescue. There won't be any awkward silences while she's in full flow.

'I am sure you would like to know how we met,' she says.

I smile and my head nods up and down in gratitude.

'Very much,' I say truthfully. I really do want to know how they met.

'It's *such* a romantic story. My godfather asked Ben to paint me! So, I sat for him many times and, as you say in

England, one thing led to another and – *voilà!* – we are getting married!'

She laughs her tinkling, trilling laugh.

Marie-Laure is in her element now. 'I knew at once,' she
declares. 'Bouff!' She clicks her fingers. 'Ben did too but he
was so professional.' She leans towards me in a conspiratorial
way and says, her mouth forming a little pout, 'He was *too*
professional. It took me a long time – two whole weeks – to
get him to admit that he was feeling the same.'

I wait for Ben to speak, to add his contribution to the
story, but he stands quietly, giving her free rein to tell me
the most intimate details of their romance. I don't want to
hear them. My gratitude for her timely intervention is rap-
idly turning into annoyance. Has she no sense of propriety?
She may be about to marry my son but I am meeting her
for the first time and I am uncomfortable with the way she
is speaking about him. And I can't understand why Ben is
listening to this and not saying a word, not stopping this girl
from embarrassing all of us. But I realise with a jolt that he
really must love her.

'I'd very much like to see the painting,' I say. 'I mean,
the painting that brought you together.'

'It's upstairs. I can show it to you very quickly,' Marie-
Laure says.

But Ben, looking even more uncomfortable now than at
the beginning of our conversation, glances at his watch and
says there isn't time.

45

'We should go to the restaurant. It's not far but we should leave now,' he tells us firmly.

He helps me into my coat, a small gesture that fills me with a mixture of joy and relief. We leave the house and I cast my eyes around, wondering whether *he* is there, lurking somewhere in the darkness. I see no one, hear no one. But the feeling of being watched pervades me. Maybe I really am going mad. For a long time, even before Chris died, I had a sense of a presence I could neither see nor hear. Chris tried to be reassuring, but he was worried that I was becoming increasingly unable to cope with the lies I had told. He tried to persuade me that it would be best for my mental health and, therefore, for all of us if I told the truth. *The truth*. Why do people hold up *The Truth* as something pure, something good and honourable? My truth is nothing like that; it's ugly and violent and shameful and no good can come of telling it.

We walk through the passageway on to Pembridge Road and then turn left into a curving street of tall white Victorian villas. Chepstow Crescent, another name that rings bells loudly. On the other side of Pembridge Road is the entrance to the square where the hostel had been; I wonder whether it still exists.

It hadn't been my choice to live there. My parents found it through the vicar, who called some clerics he knew in London and asked them whether they could recommend a student hostel that would be suitable for a young woman of good moral character.

I know now that I should have stayed there instead of moving to Paradise Place.

Even with that thought, I'm starting to feel a bit more relaxed. I reassure myself that Ben and I will find our way back to each other slowly but surely. That the strange experience I had earlier was all in my mind, the result of the shock of discovering that I was back in the part of London from which I had fled all those years ago. That my son and his fiancée have ended up living in Paradise Place is no more than a bizarre coincidence.

We're in Ledbury Road now, but it's not the slightly shabby street I remember. The white stucco on the houses looks fresh and there are upmarket designer boutiques on either side of the road. We turn into Westbourne Grove: more shops and boutiques. We come to a halt outside what looks like a very upmarket restaurant. I'm on the verge of exclaiming that everything is so different from what I remember, but I stop myself in time. They don't know about those months I spent in London. Not even my son knows. I've made sure of that.

As we enter the restaurant, Ben's phone rings and he steps back outside to answer it. Inside, Marie-Laure takes command of the seating. I count six chairs, wondering whether the restaurant has made a mistake or whether someone else will join us. But even as my nervousness begins to return, two waiters remove the sixth place-setting and chair. Ben comes in and says something to Marie-Laure and then to Alice and Arnaud.

'Nan, would you like to sit between Ben and my mother?' Marie-Laure says, and I smile gratefully at her.

It's a while before the group buzz dissipates. There's a lot of talk about the restaurant's starry reputation and whether to go for the tasting menu without the recommended wines or for the tasting menu with the wines. Alice weighs in with a suggestion – although it sounds more like an order – that we should leave everything, including the wine, to the restaurant. Everyone murmurs agreement except me – I don't dare say a word. This meal is going to cost a fortune.

'We were going to be six,' Marie-Laure tells me as she passes her menu to the waiter. 'My godfather insisted on taking us here but unfortunately he has had to go out of London on urgent business.'

'So bloody typical of him,' Alice says. 'I hope he's given them the number of his credit card to cover the bill.'

'Alice!' Arnaud says, clearly embarrassed.

'Don't worry, Alice, it's all been taken care of,' Ben says. He turns to me. 'It sounds quite old-fashioned but Marie-Laure's godfather is, effectively, my patron. If it hadn't been for him buying my stuff, I doubt I would have been able to make it as a painter, because it's thanks to him my name is getting around. And I wouldn't have met Marie-Laure.'

'Don't be silly,' Marie-Laure interjects. 'You had your paintings in Lucinda's gallery already, so your name was getting around. And I think we would have found each other even if we had not been introduced because it is very clear to me that we are meant to be together.'

'It's very clear to me, too,' Ben says, reaching across the table to touch her hand. Their eyes lock together and I look into both of their faces, forced by the obvious chemistry between them to acknowledge that something strong and unbreakable has bound them together.

At this, Arnaud asks us to raise our glasses to the happy couple. I have questions buzzing around in my head and churning up my guts, but I'm not going to ask them tonight. I'm torn between wanting to know more about this godfather of Marie-Laure's who has yet to materialise and my fear that I will learn something I don't want to know. I've convinced myself that what happened in Paradise Place as I made my way towards the house was some kind of emotion-induced apparition. Now I'm feeling less sure.

6

Hugo

It was a painting that led me to her.

For years, I had no idea where she was. And, as I'm sure anyone would understand on learning the extent to which I suffered, and for a very long time, I had every reason to look for her. I knew little about her beyond the fact that she came from Yorkshire. I rather suspect I never got around to asking her where exactly her family lived, but it's also possible that this was one of the pieces of information that was lost irretrievably when she tried to kill me. I can still see the expression on her face as she brought the poker down towards me and I still find it hard to describe. Fearful, furious, ugly. I had misread her completely.

When Eddie brought her to see the room, I saw a young and unsophisticated girl. She was a pretty little thing, I remember thinking. She might even become a beauty once her cheeks, which made me think of a pair of early autumn apples, lost their plumpness. She didn't conform to my type. She was on the short side, no more than five-three or -four, and a brunette. I've always liked blondes, the taller the better. Nevertheless, she had some quality I couldn't quite put my finger on, and I had no hesitation about taking her on as a tenant. It was obvious to me on that very first visit that she found me attractive. I also suspected that Eddie was either already involved with her or working up to it. So, having no wish to create tension among the three of us, I decided immediately that Nan Smith was off-limits.

There was also the matter of my other girlfriends. It was difficult enough making sure they didn't encounter one another as they filed in and out of the house; I didn't need the complications that would surely result from sleeping with someone, regardless of how enticing she might be, who lived in the room above mine.

Nevertheless, once she moved in, I found it increasingly difficult to ignore her charms. She was like a sponge, eager to soak up every experience that living in London, and in what she clearly saw as a Bohemian house, could bring. And, as she adapted to London and the kind of freedom that had not previously been available to her, I saw something else: a determination to get what she wanted and discard what she didn't want. I saw it in the way she dealt with Eddie, playing him like a yo-yo, reeling him in and then pushing him away. I saw it in the way she behaved after she split up with her boyfriend, miserable one minute and then looking at me as if she wanted to jump straight into bed with me the next.

It was, I realised only much later, inevitable that something would happen between us. But it was unfortunate that what did happen turned into something horrific that took away two years of my life and left me permanently scarred.

When I eventually recovered and was in a position to look for her, all I had was her name. There was no internet in those days, only telephone books and directory inquiries and I had no idea what her father's first name was. I went to the Post Office and asked for the Yorkshire directories. Of course, there were countless listings under the name Smith. I tried to remember whether she had mentioned a town or village; that would have narrowed things down somewhat. But I couldn't recall the name of a single place she had mentioned.

So I gave up and tried to get on with my life. Nevertheless, my anger and need for revenge remained inside me, close enough to the surface that when I became aware many years later of the existence of such things as the internet and Facebook, I tried searching for her. I found plenty of women called Nan Smith but she wasn't among them. She had no online presence whatsoever. And so I gave up again.

And then I came across the painting. I was persuaded by a gallery-owner friend with a reputation for launching the careers of many big-name artists that her latest protégé was the real thing and that I should consider buying a couple

52

of his paintings before he became expensive. It would be a very good investment, she said. Lucinda knew her stuff and was particularly good at spotting up-and-coming talent; she saw it as her mission. I had taken her advice in the past, buying several paintings from her over the years and, once their value had risen, had subsequently resold them through her for quite a profit.

I wasn't particularly looking to invest in art at that time, but I reckoned that it would do no harm to have a look at these paintings she was so keen for me to see. I also had an ulterior motive. Lucinda, an extremely attractive woman, was in the middle of a divorce from her American banker husband and I was working up towards a spot of leg-over with her. I decided that I would turn up at her gallery in Cork Street, check out her up-and-coming paint-thrower but avoid committing myself to a purchase. I would then suggest dinner around the corner at Cecconi's, after which she would be more than happy to hop into a taxi with me for some further fun at my place.

Lucinda had six paintings to show me and as soon as I laid eyes on the first, I knew she was right. This Ben Brown had something. I couldn't quite put my finger on whatever it was, because he wasn't doing anything remarkable or different – not to my eye, at least. If anything, his paintings were rather on the old-fashioned side: landscapes in which the sky was a colour you might expect a sky to be and the grass green and not some bilious shade of yellow or orange or God knows what. Although they were landscapes, they had an architectural quality to them. They were good. They were very, very good.

I examined each of them in turn and then came to an unexpected portrait of a woman. I don't particularly like portraits unless they're of my own ancestors, and even then I would think twice about handing over good money for one, especially one by a virtually unknown artist. But there was something about this one that drew me in. I stared at it for a long time, trying to make sense of the ripple I felt in my stomach. It didn't particularly look like her, but perhaps it transmitted something of her that my subconscious picked up. It was only when I leaned forward and saw the title on the label that I knew for certain that I had finally found her.

Nan Mending.

I could barely contain my excitement, which, happily, Lucinda took to be related entirely to the talent of her new artist.

'Tell me about this fellow,' I said. 'Where he's from, where he trained.'

'He's from Yorkshire,' she said. 'He didn't actually go to art college. He has quite a good career as . . .'

I stopped listening at that point. I didn't care what he had done for a living before becoming a painter or whether he still had a full-time job. The most important thing was that he had painted a portrait of a woman called Nan – my Nan. And he was from Yorkshire.

'I'll take them,' I said, pulling out my chequebook.

'All six?' Lucinda asked, doing her best to sound as non-chalant and breezy as if I was buying a few postcards and not six paintings that were probably overpriced. I hadn't even tried to bargain with her.

'All six. And I'm interested in anything else of his you can get.'

'He's not madly prolific, but I can ask him.'

She must have thought all her Christmases had come at once.

We never made it to Cecconi's. Lucinda, in a state of high excitement over the amount of money I was handing over to her with hardly a thought and anticipating further sales, brought out a bottle of champagne she kept in a fridge for such occasions. And . . . well, suffice it to say that we brought the evening to a highly satisfying climax.

7

Then

Did Eddie fancy her or not? He hadn't tried to kiss her or even touch her. He had made no attempt to hold her hand, despite her having given him plenty of opportunities. Yet she felt there was *something* developing between them. The question was *what* exactly? Several weeks had passed since the night he had chatted her up in the pub and they were spending a lot of time together when she wasn't at the school and he wasn't working, which was usually during the day because he worked behind the bar most evenings.

They went for walks around Holland Park, stopping to feed the squirrels or join the small groups of people who watched enthralled when one of the peacocks spread its fan. They usually stopped at the little café, taking their drinks outside to the tables that sat just out of sight of the Dutch garden.

He had told her a little bit about himself, but not very much. He was from a place in Norfolk that was so tiny it barely qualified as a village, though it had two pubs. One of the pubs had been in his family for years.

'Is that where you learned how to pull pints?' Nan asked.

'Yeah. My dad had me and my sister helping out behind the bar of The Florin as soon as we were tall enough to reach the pumps.'

'Are you going to take over when your dad retires?'

'No way. It's the middle of nowhere and there's a big world out there that I wouldn't mind seeing. Anyway, if my dad doesn't sell it, he'll probably give it to Ellen. My sister. She's practically running it now.'

'You didn't fancy university, then?'

'I tried it. I did a couple of years in Norwich but – well, I wasn't getting anything out of it, so I dropped out.'

'What were you studying?'

'History. But I didn't want to be a teacher and what else would that qualify me for? Anyway, that's all in the past and I'm fed up of the past. It's the future I'm interested in.'

She asked him what kind of future he was planning.

'Planning? I'm not planning anything. I'm going to take things as they come. You know that saying, the best-laid plans of mice and men? I can't remember the rest of it but the meaning is that if you make plans you can be sure they'll go wrong.'

Nan wondered whether he had already seen his plans founder. Maybe he had had some big love affair that had left him hurt and disappointed and that was why he wasn't in a rush to take things further with her. Or maybe he just liked to take things slowly. He certainly wasn't shy; it was he who had chatted her up that time in the pub, not the other way around. Or maybe he just liked her platonically and didn't fancy her at all, though she had a feeling that this wasn't the case.

Anyway, Eddie's slowness suited her fine, because, deep down, she was beginning to understand that the real romance she was experiencing was with herself, the discovery of her own power. She was experimenting with new ways of wearing clothes and with the way she looked. She could feel herself becoming more confident.

She complained to Eddie about the ridiculously early curfew at the hostel and he laughed and said, 'It will keep you out of trouble.' But one Sunday, when the pub was closed for the afternoon and they were walking around Holland Park, he told her there was a room going in the house where he lived, just around the corner. It was thirteen pounds a week and included electricity and gas.

Her initial excitement on hearing this dribbled away as she began to calculate what leaving the hostel would mean. The rent Eddie had mentioned was two pounds less than she was paying now. But for those extra two pounds she got breakfast and dinner every day at the hostel, even at weekends. How would she cover the additional cost of food? She would have to ask her parents for more money. She would have to explain to them why she was leaving the hostel and they wouldn't like it. And what would she say to Chris? He would want to know more about who else was living in the house and she would have to tell him that she knew this person called Eddie and then Chris would probably wonder why she hadn't mentioned Eddie until now.

'I'm not sure,' Nan said. 'I mean, I'm not sure I'm ready for a move from the hostel yet.'

'Why don't you have a look at the room? There's no harm in seeing it. You might hate it anyway,' Eddie said. He looked at his watch. 'You can see it now, if you like. I've still got time before the pub opens again.'

Eddie was right; there was no harm in seeing the room. She was beginning to find the hostel claustrophobic. She had even suggested to Ilaria that they might look for a flat to share, but Ilaria wasn't interested because it would cost too much. In any case, Ilaria would be going back to Italy for good the following summer.

'All right. Let's go, then,' Nan said, and she noticed that Eddie looked quite pleased. She wasn't sure what moving into Eddie's house might mean, whether it suggested that he wanted their friendship to develop into something more intimate or whether it showed that he thought of her just as a friend. But there was no point in speculating at this point, especially when uppermost in her thoughts right now was the prospect of living in a real house and not in an all-female student hostel run by nuns.

The house was only a few minutes' walk from the pub,

just off Pembridge Road. She had known roughly where Eddie lived – 'up the road' was how he had put it – but she hadn't been there, mainly because he hadn't actually invited her. Funny, she thought now, how she had never noticed the odd little passageway that led to Paradise Place. Maybe that was because it was set at a peculiar angle and because it was so unexpected. She and Eddie walked along the narrow-cobbled lane that was bordered on either side by high walls. Seconds later, they emerged into a small square – except that it wasn't quite a square because there were houses only on three sides, two facing the passageway and one on either side. It was more like a courtyard, in which the cobbles had given way to uneven flagstones.

'Oh! This is gorgeous!'

Eddie smiled. 'It's quiet, anyway. The people living in the other houses are all ancient. You don't hear a peep from them. You can hear a pin drop once you leave the main road. Here we are, it's this one,' he said, pointing to the house to the right.

As she walked across the flagstones she felt as if she was travelling back several centuries.

These houses were different from the other big and mostly white houses and villas that were typical of this part of Notting Hill. They were tall – she counted three storeys – but narrow and made of small dark red bricks that seemed to crowd and press into one another.

Eddie turned a key in the lock and opened the green door into a dark-red-and-white tiled hallway.

'Hang on, I'll see if Hugo's here. He owns the house.'

Eddie left her in the hallway and came back almost immediately, followed by the best-looking man she had ever seen.

She had never met anyone called Hugo before. It was the
kind of name you would expect to find in a romantic novel
set in the Middle Ages. She had assumed Eddie's landlord was
someone quite a lot older, because of the fact that he owned
a house. But this man was young, probably twenty-four or
twenty-five at the very most.

'Hello,' he said.

His voice made her think of James Mason, her mother's
favourite actor, but it was slightly deeper, slightly lazier. It
was gorgeous and it made her go weak at the knees. The
way he said *hello* was the most seductive sound she had ever
heard, as if on the way up from his chest it had picked up
some huskiness from his throat. *He* was gorgeous, with dark
eyes and dark, slightly untidy hair that was neither short nor
long. He looked like a poet. He was wearing a loose, collarless
white shirt; it was the kind of shirt her grandfather would
have worn, but on Hugo it looked romantic. Under his light-
grey linen trousers he was barefoot, and she couldn't help
but stare at his long toes. A blush stole uncomfortably on
to her cheeks, and she raised her hand to her face and then
to her hair, as if brushing away a stray lock.

'Nan,' she croaked, just about able to speak, the flame in
her cheeks burning even more intensely under his appraising
gaze.

'Why don't you take Nan upstairs and show her the room, Eddie, and I'll make a pot of tea? Or perhaps Nan would like a glass of wine?'

He was looking directly at her now and she was burning in the warmth of the look, mesmerised by the way his mouth moved and the way he said her name, the *a* vowel lengthened slightly as if he was playing with it, savouring it. She could watch and listen to him for ever.

He inclined his head to one side, lifted his eyebrows slightly, and she realised he was waiting for her to answer.

'Oh, thanks. I'd love a glass of wine,' she said, adding quickly, 'But only if you have a bottle open already.'

Hugo smiled. 'There's always a bottle of wine open in this house.'

Nan followed Eddie to the stairs.

The room was at the top of the house. The walls were painted turquoise and the floorboards were stained dark brown, a startling and wonderful colour scheme she could never have imagined might work, despite her love of paint and colour. The ceiling was low and the room was on the small side, but it was bigger than her room at the hostel. She noticed that the bed was big too, a double. She had never slept in a double bed before. Not since she was a child and had crept into her parents' bed when she had nightmares. The bed had been stripped and she wondered whether she would have to buy sheets and pillowcases and a bedspread or quilt if she took the room.

As if reading her thoughts, Eddie gestured behind him with his thumb. 'There's a big cupboard out on the landing. Maybe you saw it. That's where the sheets and blankets and things are kept.'

She put her hand on the mattress and pressed. It was surprisingly firm. Much better than the one at the hostel and heaps better than her old mattress at home, which had an old door underneath it to stop it sinking into the loose metal springs of the ancient iron bedstead.

At the hostel, storage had been limited to a wardrobe. Here, there was not only a wardrobe and a bedside table but also a big chest of drawers. Idly, she opened the drawers one by one. She almost missed the photograph, which was partly concealed under the base of a lamp. It was a shot taken from a distance, but Nan could see that the girl was very attractive, with long fair hair.

'Who's this?' she asked.

'Oh,' Eddie said. He looked at it and Nan noticed that he was frowning. 'It's just the girl who had your room before. Do you want to come next door and see my room? There's just the two of us up here. Hugo's room is on the first floor. That's where the bathroom is.'

She peeked into Eddie's room. It had the same stained floorboards, but the walls were red, not turquoise; a deep, dark red.

'The girl who had my room before . . .' she began, and she realised that she had said *my room*, that she had already made up her mind. 'Was she here for long?'

'I can't really remember how long she was here,' he said. 'Do you think you'll take the room?'

'I think so . . . yes, I will.'

Back downstairs, Hugo was removing the cork from a bottle of red wine in the kitchen. His mouth widened into a broad smile as Nan and Eddie approached and he poured the wine into the biggest wine glasses Nan had ever seen. The three of them took their glasses and Nan and Eddie followed Hugo into a room at the front of the house, where he invited them to sit down on old but rather grand sofas. The walls were painted green and covered in framed landscapes and portraits that were obviously old.

Nan had never been in a house like this, a room like this. It wasn't a big house, but everything about it spoke of old money and privilege. It made her think of those stately homes whose aristocratic owners charged ordinary people like herself and her parents money for the privilege of seeing inside them.

She wondered whether the paintings were what her parents would call 'real' and not just copies, but she couldn't really ask Hugo that.

While Nan had been looking around the room, Hugo had put on a record. He told her that the music had been written in the early seventeenth century for the Sistine Chapel in Rome by a composer called Allegri.

Nan listened, entranced by the soaring voices.

'It's wonderful,' she said. She had never heard anything like it.

Hugo smiled, a beautiful, wide, sensual smile that made her body melt.

'It is, isn't it? In fact, it's so wonderful that the Vatican wouldn't let it be performed or published anywhere else. It's Mozart we have to thank for the fact that we can hear it now. He heard it just once and was able to write it down,' he said. 'Well, that's how the story goes. Whether it's true is another question entirely.'

She was listening to him so intently that she noticed only in the nick of time that she was holding her glass at a precarious angle. She hoped to God she hadn't spilt any of the wine on the sofa or on the Persian rug, which looked as if it might be very old and valuable.

Hugo didn't appear to have noticed her near miss with the wine. He was still talking about the music.

'I would never describe myself as religious but I'm inclined to think that if there is a heaven beyond the clouds, there must be music like this in it,' he said. 'Or, to put it another way, if there's proof of the existence of God it has to be this.'

There was something slightly blasphemous about this, Nan thought, wondering what her parents would say if they knew she was participating in a conversation that mentioned God in such a light way.

But she realised that she didn't actually care what her parents would think. She was listening to what Hugo was saying, but she was also hearing the way the sound of his voice was somehow in harmony with this strange and glorious music that seemed to come from another dimension, seeping into every conscious part of her.

Her eyes drifted again to the paintings that covered the walls in the room, several smallish landscapes and a couple of big portraits. Yes, they were 'real' paintings, oils and water-colours, not the cheap prints of girls with jet-black hair and huge eyes and single tears falling from the eyes that her mother was partial to.

'Nan's an art student,' Eddie said.

'Ah. Where are you studying?' Hugo asked.

'Byam Shaw,' she said proudly.

Hugo lifted his eyebrows in recognition. Then he went back to the record player, removed the *Miserere* and put it back in its sleeve, and selected another record which he placed on the turntable.

'You'll know this then,' he said. And then, he added quickly, 'Or perhaps not.'

She recognised the voice immediately. It was Kathleen Ferrier, beloved of her parents and whose record of folk songs they played every Sunday evening. She knew every song on that record and could sing 'Blow the Wind Southerly' in her sleep, but she didn't know this one.

As she listened, she felt her heart turn heavy with sadness for everything she had left behind and, at the same time, with longing for what she had yet to know. She felt her body infused with desire for Hugo. *He is perfect*, she thought to herself.

'It's ... so beautiful,' she said quietly when the song ended. She could barely put words together, so strong were the emotions that coursed through her.

Hugo turned off the record player and handed her the sleeve, which showed a Pre-Raphaelite painting she should probably have known but didn't recognise.

'"Silent Noon", words by Dante Gabriel Rossetti, music by Ralph Vaughan Williams, painting by Byam Shaw,' Hugo said. 'You can see the painting at Leighton House. Full of Pre-Raphaelite stuff, if you like that sort of thing. I do happen to like it, but it's not to everyone's taste. You know where it is, don't you? You can walk down through Holland Park, but do check that it's open.'

Hugo had clearly assumed that she would want to take the room. She waited for him to explain how the house worked, what the rules were, but he just told her she could move in whenever she was ready. He didn't even mention the rent.

'I'll sort out a key and give it to Eddie for you,' he said.

Eddie glanced at his watch and said he had better get back to the pub. Nan didn't get up immediately. The music was still playing and Hugo was still sitting languidly on his sofa. She hadn't finished her wine either, and she wondered whether Hugo would invite her to stay longer so that she could drink it. She waited for him to issue the invitation, but he didn't.

She shouldn't have been surprised, really, she thought, wondering at the same time how she was going to get up from the sofa without looking awkward. He had no interest in prolonging her visit; she was mistaking good manners for something else. Socially, he was well above her. Obviously rolling in money. And so good-looking. He could have anyone he wanted. And he was that bit older, too. Only by a few years, but old enough not to be interested in an eighteen-year-old girl from Yorkshire. He probably saw her as a kid, a country kid lacking any sophistication whatsoever. She wished she had dressed up a bit before the visit to the house, but Eddie had sprung it on her.

Reluctantly, she rose to her feet, said goodbye to Hugo and followed Eddie out of the house. She glanced back several times before they entered the passageway, just in case Hugo might be watching through a window.

'I love the room,' she told Eddie eagerly, sweeping away her disappointment at seeing the empty window frames. 'And the house is fabulous. Does he – Hugo – really own it? What does he do for a living?'

'It's his family's. But I don't know if it's *his*, like, if his name is on the deeds.'

He hadn't answered her second question so she asked it again.

'I don't know what he does,' Eddie said, a touch of irritation in his voice. 'I don't think he does anything very much. He doesn't need to, anyway. His family has loads of money.'

'I don't think I've ever met anyone so cultured,' Nan said. 'He knows so much about art and music and—'

'Yeah, well, it's easy to be cultured when you don't have to work. I'll remind you of what you said when you complain about him playing bloody Beethoven at full blast at nine o'clock on a Sunday morning when you're trying to sleep.'

'Oh, I don't think I'll mind,' she said.

He stopped and gave her an odd look. Then he started walking again.

'He has a lot of women,' he said. He threw her another odd, sideways look. 'Just so you know'

Nan wasn't sure what to make of what Eddie was telling her. Was he giving her sound advice or was he revealing something else, something about himself? The tone of his voice persuaded her that it was the latter.

He was jealous of her obvious attraction to Hugo.

She felt a slight touch of apprehension about moving into the house. She had given Eddie the impression that she was interested in him. And she *had* been interested in him but he hadn't done anything about it. If he had finally woken up to her, it was too late, because now she had seen Hugo. She felt something stir inside her as she remembered the effect Hugo had had on her the moment she had laid eyes on him. Physical, visceral, primitive, like nothing she had ever felt before, and she felt it again now. And, it seemed, Eddie knew it too.

It was only as an afterthought that Chris came into her mind, and that was when she knew she was playing with fire. The flirtation with Eddie had been one thing, but this overwhelming attraction she had for Hugo was different. Was she ready to risk her relationship with Chris? Maybe she should tell Eddie to tell Hugo that she had changed her mind and wasn't going to take the room after all.

But she knew she wasn't going to do that. She was going to move into Hugo's house and suffer the consequences. She wasn't a child any more. She had come to London not just because she wanted to study art but because she wanted a new life. She wanted excitement and she wanted change and, she began to understand with a mixed sense of guilt and inevitability, Chris might not be part of that change.

She banished these troubling thoughts and her mind shot back to Hugo.

'You haven't told me his surname,' she said.

'Bennett,' he said. 'Hugo Bennett.'

Later, in her room at the hostel, she wrote out his name in swirling letters. *Hugo Bennett.* And then, even though she knew she was being ridiculously childish and silly, she wrote *Hugo and Nan Bennett. Mrs Hugo Bennett.*

8

Now

We leave the restaurant and walk back towards Paradise Place, Alice and Marie-Laure talking enthusiastically about the food and Arnaud throwing in the occasional comment. Ben and I follow quietly. He's a lot more relaxed than he was at the beginning of the evening. I manage to get him to ease back well behind the others and tell him how lovely Marie-Laure is and how glad I am that he has found her.

His face lights up and I know for certain that my route back into his heart is through Marie-Laure.

'I've never met anyone like her. She's beautiful and she's kind and clever – you know she works for a human rights charity? – and I knew – I don't know how – but I knew the moment I saw her that I was going to marry her. This is going to sound crazy, but it was as if I'd come home.' He pauses for a moment. 'I wish Dad could have met her.'

'I wish that too,' I say. 'Look, Ben, about Dad and . . . and everything . . . I'm trying to find a way to talk to you about it, but I need to get my head around it all. I know you'll think I've had enough time to think about it, but something has happened . . . that I need to get to grips with. Can you bear with me for just a little bit longer? Please?'

'What do you mean, something happened? What happened?'

'I . . . I can't really talk about it. Not yet.'

He frowns. 'Is it something to do with your health?'

'No, no, honestly, it's not a health thing. But it's . . .' I trail off, searching for the words that will make my excuse not to talk more plausible.

'You're doing it again,' Ben says. His voice sounds weary. 'Clamming up. It's what you've always done. You did it to Dad and you did it to me and you're still doing it. Jesus!'

'Ben, I . . . I'm sorry. I really am. I promise things will be different. But, please, just let me have a little bit longer.'

'How long is a little bit longer?'

'A few days? Please? I can't tell you why just now, but give me just a little more time. I promise.'

He shrugs, says nothing.

There are only inches of space between us as we walk side by side but our short conversation has driven us so far apart that those few inches seem to have turned into a wide, deep chasm.

I can't bear this silence. I need to get him to talk again, so I ask him about the wedding. When I first opened the invitation, the fact that my son was getting married to someone I didn't know knocked me for six. Then something else sprang out at me, the name of the venue, *Leighton House*, but I managed to dismiss it as a coincidence. It was simply a venue, and a venue probably relevant to Ben in that a well-known Victorian painter had lived there. After everything that has happened in the past few hours, though, I can't help wondering whether it's more than a coincidence.

I think about that first time I went to Leighton House. The memory of it is still as vivid as the visit itself. It was more of a pilgrimage than a visit, a need to see a painting that I would never have wanted to see had I not been beguiled by Hugo.

The memory is strong now of that dark and rainy afternoon. I walked down there through the park and by the time I reached what looked like a dull Victorian mausoleum I was soaked through and almost ready to turn around and go back to the hostel. But when I went inside, I was captivated by the extraordinary tiles and fountain and golden dome of the Arab Hall. I felt that day as if I was in Damascus or Baghdad rather than in a big old house in a quiet street in Kensington. But I hadn't gone there simply out of curiosity. I wasn't a fan of the Pre-Raphaelites. I just wanted to see the Byam Shaw painting, *Silent Noon*, because Hugo had told me I should see it.

And I see it now in my mind. The girl lying on the grass in her voluminous yellow-green dress, her auburn hair spread out around and behind her head, an apple in her hand. And gazing at her, the young man with his mop of dark, dark hair, propped up on the elbow of his right arm, a lyre in his left. And I hear the emotive voice of Kathleen Ferrier singing 'Silent Noon'.

A couple of days after that first visit to Leighton House, just before I moved into Paradise Place, I bought a packet of henna and Ilaria put it on my hair.

Ben has no idea that I know Leighton House like the back of my hand, so I mention it now, telling him I looked it up on the internet.

'It looks wonderful. Did you choose it because of it being an art museum?'

But it turns out that, just like the expensive restaurant, Leighton House is primarily the choice of Marie-Laure's godfather, who is also insisting on paying for the reception.

I pick up a hint of embarrassment in Ben's voice as he tells me this.

'I'd rather just go down to the nearest registry office and then have a small lunch at a decent restaurant,' he says. 'But Hugo is insisting on nothing but the best for his only goddaughter and Alice and Arnaud are happy to go along with it because they're not having to pay.'

Hugo! I feel unsteady, as if I might topple over. So I hadn't been wrong. I hadn't imagined what happened in the passageway. All through the evening, I had tried to convince myself that my imagination had been working overtime. I had hoped no one would say his name so that I could continue to convince myself that my nervousness about seeing Ben again and finding myself in front of Paradise Place had conjured Hugo up. And even now, as I hear Ben say his name, I want to think I have misheard him. But there was no mistaking that voice, and there's no mistaking it now as I hear it in my head.

I should feel relief, because if it's the same Hugo, it means I didn't kill him.

I'm not a murderer.

And yet I feel no relief, only a deepening fear.

'Are you all right?' Ben asks. 'You're as white as a sheet. You *are* ill, aren't you? Tell me the truth.'

'No, I'm not ill. Honestly, I'm fine. It's just all the excitement. You know, meeting Marie-Laure and her parents, seeing you, the wedding. I just wish . . .'

I don't say it, that I wish with all my heart that Chris could be here. Because if Chris hadn't had the accident, hadn't died, maybe none of us would be here, not even Ben.

Ben says nothing and in the silence between us I can hear my heart beating fast.

'So . . . how long have you and Marie-Laure been living in the house?' I ask, anxious to hear him speak again. 'It's . . . quite amazing.'

'Oh, we don't live there. Paradise Place belongs to Hugo. He's lived there for decades, I think since the mid-seventies. Alice and Arnaud are staying there this week. When we get them back to the house, Marie-Laure and I will take you to

Canary Wharf – that's where we live, not too far from your hotel. We would have picked you up this evening but we were busy all day with Alice and Arnaud. Actually, Hugo suggested that you should stay in the house too, but there are only three bedrooms and you'd be on the top floor in the room next to Alice and Arnaud, and there's only one bathroom. I thought you might feel a bit overwhelmed. I hope you don't mind. I mean, if you'd rather stay at Paradise Place, I can—'

'No!' I say, rather too quickly and forcefully, my stomach churning at the thought of being back on that top floor, maybe even in the room that was once mine. Ben turns his head sharply to look at me. 'What I mean is . . . I'm sure it would be lovely to stay there but you were right to think I'd prefer the hotel – which is very nice. I like it.'

Just as I'm about to ask him how he came to meet Hugo, we turn the corner and find the others waiting for us at the entrance to Paradise Place.

'You'll come in for a nightcap, won't you, Nan?' Alice says. 'Who knows, perhaps the elusive Hugo will make it home to join us.'

There's a hint of resentment, maybe even of aggression, in her voice, and all of a sudden I wonder whether there's something between her and Hugo. Nothing would surprise me now. And I remember also the change in Ben's tone when he spoke about Leighton House being Hugo's choice of venue. Maybe *he* feels resentment towards Hugo too, but for different reasons.

I feel pressure building in my head.

I don't want to go back inside that house, but I have no choice. My son is already leading me into Paradise Place and I will follow him to the ends of the earth and beyond. Ben looks at his watch.

'It's not too late for you, is it? You can come in for a bit and then Marie-Laure and I will take you back to the hotel.'

This time, Alice leads us into the room at the front of the house. There's no escape. I can't refuse to enter that room. My eyes go straight to the fireplace, to the embers still burning in the grate, and to the cast-iron fire tools hanging on their stand. I wince, and for a few moments that seem to go on for ever I relive that terrible night. I see them both, Hugo and Eddie, against the glowing flames. I hear the sound of metal on flesh. I see the dark blood, can even smell the tang of it. My stomach squeezes and, involuntarily, my eyes close.

'It's so beautiful, isn't it?' Marie-Laure says, coming to stand beside me. 'It must bring back such lovely memories.'

Her voice hauls me back to the present. I stare at her, shocked and confused. How can she know I've been here before?

'I love this very much,' she says. 'I hope I will see the place for myself very soon.'

Relief floods through me as I realise that she's talking about the painting that hangs above the fireplace. I recognise it as one of Ben's, a view of the Calder Valley from a point just above Heptonstall. I remember the excitement in his voice when he rang to say that a well-thought-of London gallery was going to show some of his paintings.

'That's marvellous!' I said.

'Maybe you'll come down to see them in the gallery?'

I remember the pleading in his voice, remember that I said, yes, yes, of course I would. But I was lying. I had made him a promise that I had no intention of keeping.

It's painful now to look around that room, even though it has been softened by the replacement of those old landscapes and portraits with more modern and mostly abstract art.

Marie-Laure's voice interrupts my thoughts again.

'Oh, I almost forgot – you wanted to see the painting. Ben's painting of me. Shall we go upstairs now?'

I steady myself, smile, and follow her up the stairs to the first floor. She throws open the door of the bathroom, and as I'm wondering why she's doing that I realise that I'm looking into what now seems to be a study, with a desk, modern-looking office chair, several low-height filing units made of light-coloured wood and a light grey sofa.

For a moment, I'm able to convince myself again that it's all just coincidence. The Hugo I knew would never have changed the character of this house by knocking down walls and building new ones. The light-coloured varnishes of the desk and units tell me another version of the same story: the Hugo I knew liked dark brown furniture, old furniture. The kind of furniture someone of his class appreciated.

But Ben says the Hugo he knows has lived in the house since the seventies. Maybe I imagined him saying that. Maybe I'm imagining everything.

And the man I thought I saw earlier this evening was the product of my imagination.

But my moment of calm reasoning is quickly shattered when my field of vision widens.

Two paintings hang on the wall. One is the portrait of Marie-Laure that she wants me to see and admire. But it's the other painting that stops me in my tracks. I stare at it, horrified by the fact that it is hanging in this room, in this house. I recognise it the moment I lay eyes on it. I never sat for that painting. Ben did it when he first left home to study architecture in London. He used an old photograph taken by Chris when I was sewing a button on a shirt and unaware that the camera was pointing at me until I heard the click.

'To remind me of you, Mum,' Ben said on the phone when he told me what he was working on. And I had laughed, telling him I hoped he would never need reminding. He tried to persuade me to travel down to London to see it, explaining that it was too big to carry up to Yorkshire on a crowded train. But I couldn't face going to London – it was torment enough that my son was there – and so Ben took a photograph of the painting and sent it to me.

I hadn't thought about that painting for years. I must have taken it for granted that he had held on to it. I could never have imagined, even when he walked away after Chris's funeral, that he would sell it or give it away. Yet here it is, hanging in Hugo's study.

Marie-Laure's voice interrupts my thoughts.

'Oh, my goodness, you must be very surprised to see this. I had almost forgotten that it was here. I should have told you.'

'How . . .?' I have no words to form the question I want to ask. The shock of seeing it, in this house, is too great.

'Hugo was very persuasive. When you meet him, you will understand why it's so hard to refuse him anything. He wanted it for a long time, since he first saw Ben's paintings in the gallery, before he even met Ben. He thought it was the best, although he loved all the paintings, but Ben wouldn't sell it.' She shrugs and smiles. 'But, as I told you, Hugo is very persuasive. And he offered a lot of money. It was difficult for Ben to refuse.'

It was difficult for Ben to refuse.

How difficult can it be to say, *No, I'm not letting you have this painting because it's a painting of my mother and it's personal*?

But, of course, I know why he let the painting go, and I don't even have to ask Marie-Laure when exactly he sold it to Hugo. That knowledge cuts me to the quick.

'I'm a little bit overwhelmed. I hadn't expected to see this here,' I tell Marie-Laure, whose expression of mild alarm suggests she has seen the effect of the painting on me. 'I'm sorry . . . it's upsetting to think that Ben didn't want to keep it.'

'Oh, Nan, please don't be upset! Let me talk to Hugo . . .

and to Ben, too. It was not that he wanted to sell it. It was just that Hugo—'

'Can be very persuasive,' I say with bitter sarcasm. 'You've said that.' I compose myself. 'When exactly did Hugo come across Ben?'

'It must have been nearly three years ago. I'm not quite sure of the exact date. He saw his paintings in a gallery and met Ben soon after that.'

'And he saw that painting of me before he met Ben?'

'Yes.'

'Did he know who I was?'

'What do you mean?'

'Did he recognise me from the painting? Is that why he wanted it?'

Even before she answers, I know I've asked the wrong questions.

'No, of course not.' She looks puzzled. 'How could he recognise you or know who you were? He didn't even know who Ben was at the time, or who his mother was. He just loved Ben's work the moment he saw it and he thought the painting of you was very fine.'

'What I meant was . . . did he know I was Ben's mother, and you've answered that. But, please, Marie-Laure, tell me exactly how you came to meet Ben. And when.'

She pauses for a few seconds, as if she's having trouble piecing together all the elements of the story.

'But I told you earlier how we met.'

'No, you told me Hugo commissioned Ben to paint you. That's all. I want to know everything. I want to know why he wanted Ben to paint you.'

Her face is a knot of worry, her lips pursed, her eyebrows almost meeting.

'Nan, you're making me . . . a little bit worried. There is no mystery. Hugo is my godfather. He has been very important in my life. He thinks of me almost as a daughter. He is closer to me than to his brother's sons. Is it so strange that he would ask his favourite painter to paint me?'

I say nothing. I wait for her to continue.

'I met Ben last year. Hugo told me he had asked Ben to do the painting and that I should call him to arrange the first sitting. And so I did that, and there were lots of sittings and we started to know each other. I fell in love with him very quickly – for both of us, it was love at first sight, a *coup de foudre*.'

'What about Hugo? Did he encourage you to . . .' I stop short of using the word that has come into my head: *ensnare*, '. . . to be in a relationship with Ben?'

She looks at me as if I'm insane. And then, softening her voice as if speaking to a child, she says, 'Why would he do that? I am a lot younger than Ben. And I had a boyfriend then. A very nice boyfriend. Hugo liked him. He was very surprised when I left Valentin for Ben.'

She makes it all sound so plausible, so coincidental. It's Hugo who worries me. He *was* there this evening, waiting for me in the dark. He appeared and then retreated into the shadows. What does he want? Why didn't he come into the house? And where is he now?

For so long, I've been able to put what happened in this house all those years ago behind me. I broke off contact with everyone I knew then in London, even Ilaria. When she eventually found me, married to Chris and the mother of a child, I told her a small part of my story. I had had a nervous breakdown, I told her. That was true, but it wasn't the whole truth.

I had disappeared, escaped back to Yorkshire where I eventually slipped into a quiet, comfortable life. I made a cocoon for myself and my little family. At the back of my mind for so long had been the fear of the knock on the door that would destroy my sheltered world. But the knock never came. I thought I was safe.

But I don't feel safe any more. Not even from myself. Because what I have kept buried somewhere deep inside me is clawing its way to the surface and I'm powerless to stop it.

And among the ghosts of the past, I see Eddie. Eddie, who brought me here in the autumn of 1977. Eddie, who saw what I did.

Funny, I struggle now to remember what he looked like, the details of his face, his eyes, his hair.

The last time I saw his face was—

'Nan? Nan?'

Marie-Laure is touching my arm, bringing me back to the present.

'Sorry. It was just a bit of a shock, seeing that painting of me. Shall we go back downstairs?'

'Of course.'

She smiles at me, but it's a cautious smile. I wonder whether she thinks I'm mad. Maybe she's right; maybe I *am* mad and becoming madder by the hour.

9

Hugo

My initial assumption when I saw the title of the painting was that she had married someone called Mending. Nan *Mending*. I still laugh when I recall that foolish moment. She was, of course, sewing something, with a needle and thread. I have spent many hours in the company of that painting. I have stared at it, trying to gain a sense of the woman she has become, asking myself whether the *Mending* of the title is no more than a description of the activity in which she is engaged or whether it hints at some need of hers to mend things – hearts and souls, perhaps, as well as torn shirts and trousers – as reparation for what she did.

What kind of mother had she been? The painting was undoubtedly a loving one. Everything about it – the softness of the colours, the use of light and shade, the overall gentleness of it, testified to that.

I had given up on the idea of finding her, only to have

her come to me in the form of a painting. I spent hours thinking about how I would approach her, what I would say, what I would do. But first I had to have that painting in my house, where I could spend time with it, studying it, studying her, learning how she had changed. You can imagine my dismay, therefore, when Lucinda dropped her bombshell. *Nan Mending* wasn't for sale, after all. Including it had been a mistake and Ben Brown was withdrawing it, she said apologetically. She would refund the money I had paid for it.

I have never – even as a child – been given to tantrums, but when I heard this I threw the nearest thing to one and told Lucinda, who was extremely surprised by my insistence on having this particular painting, to tell Ben Brown that I would take all six paintings that hung in the gallery or none at all. I expected her to come back and tell me that he had agreed. But he stood his ground.

I was astonished. My inclination was to tell Lucinda that the deal was off and that she should refund the entire sum of my cheque. But I had to admire, albeit grudgingly, Ben's refusal to part with the painting of his mother. So I went ahead with the purchase of the other five paintings. After all, Lucinda had presented them to me as an investment and I would hold on to them until I was ready to sell them at a decent profit. And, I reminded myself, whether or not I owned the portrait, I had achieved what I had been seeking for so many years: I had found Nan. I did, however, wonder why, if Ben wasn't willing to sell the painting, he had included it in the exhibition at the gallery and had allowed Lucinda to give it a price tag. Lucinda suggested that either he hadn't expected anyone to want to buy it or he had only realised when I insisted on buying all six paintings how attached he was to it.

'Sons and mothers,' she said in a matter-of-fact tone, as if that explained everything. It didn't.

Lucinda and I were now seeing each other on a regular basis, although I maintained other liaisons she knew nothing about. Her supreme talent for extracting information from people – cultivated, perhaps, as a tool of the trade in a highly competitive environment – came in handy. And, being in regular contact with Ben Brown, she was able to tell me much of what I needed to know, a particularly important piece of information being the fact that his family owned a garden centre near Hebden Bridge in Yorkshire.

The painting was secondary to that information, and yet it stirred up so much in me. When I thought about her, I saw in my mind images of her all those years ago. But the painting had managed to hint at something ineffable, something my own memories acknowledged but couldn't quite express.

It's mine now. Ben agreed to sell it to me shortly after his father died. I asked him why he was finally willing to let me have it when hitherto he had so steadfastly refused. He shrugged, I recall. Things had changed, he said.

It was clear to me that something had indeed changed in

Ben's relationship with his mother since he painted that portrait. He never spoke of her. Whenever I tried to encourage him to talk about her, he changed the subject. Had she, I wondered, turned on him as she had turned on me?

He still hadn't admitted to me that the woman in the painting was his mother. And even, later, when we began to plan the wedding and draw up the guest list, he didn't allude to the fact that the *Nan* in the painting that now hung in my study was the Nan Brown, his mother, who was being invited to London to watch her son marry my goddaughter. I let it go. Even with the questions gathering in my head, I felt elated. After all, I would see her again very soon.

10

Then

Nan's parents weren't too happy when she called to break the news about her move from the hostel, or about having to send her some extra money to cover the additional expenses she would have. She didn't tell them that the reason she was leaving was that there were too many restrictions. Instead, she explained that she often had to stay late at the college or go to evening lectures, which meant that she missed the main meal at the hostel and then had to buy food outside. Moving to the house in Paradise Place would probably turn out to be cheaper in the long run because she would be able to cook her own meals, she told them.

Her parents said they didn't like the fact that she was going to be living in a house with two men and that at least they knew she was safe in the hostel. She reassured them with the lie that Ilaria was moving with her and that they would be sharing the room.

She heard the disappointment and worry in their voices, but she heard something else that she couldn't quite put her finger on, maybe their sense of the inevitability of the change she was making, as if it had come as no real surprise to them. Perhaps they had expected this all along, to lose her to London, while hoping and praying at the same time that their fears would not be realised.

She didn't tell them that she felt apprehensive too. She welcomed the changes this new life was bringing, but it was hard to let go of the certainties of the old life; her move to Paradise Place would push them even further away. The old life sent her unexpected reminders that rose up from somewhere deep within her, images of her parents going about their quiet, uneventful lives, of evening walks under a rising moon and dew settling on grass and heather, of new lambs born early amid heavy falls of snow. Somehow, moving out of the hostel and into a room in a house was an even deeper acknowledgement of a farewell to home and a permanent commitment to London.

Telling Chris about the move was harder. She stumbled through the reasons she was leaving the hostel and at first he seemed to understand them. She told him the same lies she had told her parents. He asked her about the other people in the house and how she had met them. He assumed that the others were girls and when she told him that they weren't and that she had met one of them in the pub down the road he was confused and angry.

'It's like you've had this other life going all along and I don't know anything about it,' he complained. 'You never mentioned this Eddie bloke once until now. Or the other one.'

'I've met lots of people since I've been here,' she retorted. 'I didn't think I had to tell you the name of every single one of them. And anyway, I'm telling you now. Eddie is just a friend. The other one just owns the house. He's older than us and he's not a friend. He's the landlord.'

'Are you going out with Eddie? Because if you are—'

'No! I'm not going out with anyone.'

'You're supposed to be going out with me.'

'What I meant was that you're the only one I'm going out with.'

'I just get the feeling that ... that things are different between you and me,' Chris said. 'Maybe you'd rather we didn't see each other any more.' He sounded sad and defeated and that made her feel terrible.

'Nothing has changed. Honestly,' she said. 'It's just that I've had to get used to the way things work down here. And I promise I'll go home soon for a weekend.'

'I don't know, Nan. You keep saying we're going to see each other soon but I haven't seen you for ages. I manage to go home at least every second weekend, but you haven't made it home once and it doesn't sound as if you're going to. All you have to do is go to the station and buy a ticket and change at Leeds. If you need the money, I'll send it to you. And if you want to end it with me, just tell me. I'd rather know for sure than keep wondering what the hell is going on.'

This was the point at which she should have told him that maybe they ought to have a break for a while. She was besotted with Hugo, but hadn't seen him since the day she had visited Paradise Place for the first time. Maybe it was just a crush that would burn itself out, just as her initial interest in Eddie had begun to fade when he hadn't followed through on what she had thought might happen.

She didn't want to lose Chris.

Not really.

Not now, anyway.

She thought about how easy it had always been to be with him. The change had come when she'd moved to London. Maybe it was a natural thing, a temporary abandoning of everything that had been a normal part of her previous life as she adjusted to this new life in a capital city. Maybe she just needed to get through the infatuation with Hugo and then she would be ready to get her relationship with Chris back on an even keel.

So she told him again that she wasn't seeing anyone else. And she insisted that she didn't want to break off their relationship.

Chris asked her for the telephone number at Paradise Place.

'Oh, I'll call you with it when I move in. I haven't got it yet,' she said.

This was true; it hadn't occurred to her to ask for the number. But something else hadn't occurred to her until now: what if Chris were to ring and she wasn't there, and he asked for Ilaria? He had never spoken to Ilaria, but if he was suspicious and anxious, it wasn't impossible that he would. And if Hugo answered the phone, he would say Ilaria didn't live there. She would have to think about this. She could rope Eddie in, but she wasn't sure she wanted to involve Hugo, who would probably think of her, at best, as being childish.

'When are you moving in?' Chris asked.

'Not for a week. I'll call you with the number as soon as I move in. I promise.'

She had made the two dreaded but necessary calls, and as she replaced the receiver and pressed button B to return the coins she hadn't used up she felt a current of relief flow through her with such force that she had to sit down on the bottom stair and allow a long sigh to escape.

Ilaria and Eddie, in between his shifts in the pub, helped her to move in. She had accumulated quite a lot of things in the short time she'd been in London. And, in preparation for her move to Paradise Place, she had been wandering around the stalls and bric-à-brac shops on Portobello. She was particularly pleased with the richly patterned rug in shades of red and brown – it was called a *kelim* – she had bought from a tall, red-haired man who wore a crimson beret and an Afghan coat over pink corduroy trousers and peculiar leather slippers with toes so pointed that they were starting to curl. She would place it in the middle of her room. From a woman on another stall she had bought a large macramé wall hanging. The colour was nondescript, a dull shade of brownish-beige, but she knew as soon as she saw it that it would stand out against the turquoise wall. The woman also sold her a lamp, throwing in for free a large piece of pink gauzy fabric that she said should be draped over the lamp so that the light would cast a warm glow across the room.

And now, here they were on a rainy autumnal Sunday afternoon, Nan, Ilaria and Eddie, bathed in the pink light that emanated from both lamps and sitting on huge cushions bought by Ilaria as a moving-in present. Nan had opened a bottle of Mateus Rosé and was pouring the wine into cheap glasses she had bought at Woolworths on Portobello; she didn't feel she could use Hugo's expensive-looking glasses, although he had told her to use anything she liked. The Mateus bottle, once emptied and rinsed, could become a base for a candle.

She was beginning to feel like a real Londoner now, but there was something missing; the thrill of moving into Paradise Place had been dampened by Hugo's absence. She hadn't caught sight of him all weekend.

'Is Hugo away then?' she asked Eddie, trying to make her voice sound bright and nonchalant, as if she didn't care.

'He could be. I have no idea,' Eddie said, and Nan fancied

she saw his mouth curl into a scowl. 'He doesn't tell me when he's not going to be here. We're not his friends, you know. We just rent rooms in his house.'

Chastened, Nan lowered her head for a moment. He was right, of course. She and Eddie were just Hugo's tenants, no more than that. Hugo wasn't interested in either of them or in their little lives, and especially not in hers. She needed to grow up. But she was hurt by the tone in Eddie's voice and she wanted to hurt him back. So, because she remembered how, just a week before, he hadn't wanted to talk about the previous occupant of the room, she brought her up again.

'The girl who had this room before me,' she said. 'What was she like? Why did she leave?'

As she hurled out the questions, she watched Eddie's face and was rewarded by a darkening of his expression.

'I don't know why you're so obsessed with her. She was already here when I came and she left not long afterwards. She kept herself to herself and I don't know where she went, because she didn't tell me. Oh, I almost forgot – her name was Olivia Locke and she had a job in some office. Are you satisfied now?' he said. And then his face lightened and he lifted his hands, palms upward. 'Honestly, Nan, there's no mystery here. This is London. People move around all the time. But if you're so curious about her, why don't you ask Hugo?'

Later, after Eddie had left for his shift at the pub and Ilaria had gone back to the hostel, she put up her Jimi Hendrix poster on the back of the door, fastening it with Blu-tack. She couldn't get Olivia out of her mind. Maybe she and Eddie had had a fling and it had ended badly. But all she could think about was the way Eddie had told her that if she wanted to know more about Olivia she should ask Hugo. She wondered whether Olivia and Hugo had been sleeping together and whether Eddie had been jealous. And the more she thought about it, the more jealous she became too.

11

Now

Just as I walk into my room at the hotel, my mobile pings. It's a text from Ilaria, asking how things have gone so far and telling me that if I need to talk to her I can phone her any time, day or night.

I'm fine. Everything is going well. I press SEND.

How can I explain to her what happened this evening when I'm still trying to make sense of it myself?

There's so much I've never told Ilaria, even when she agreed to became part of the lie. After I fled London I had no thought of contacting her, despite having her address and telephone number in Italy. She, like Eddie, was part of the past I wanted and needed to forget. But Ilaria, it turned out, had no intention of forgetting me.

Ben was just a few weeks old and sleeping quietly in my arms when the phone rang. I would have ignored it, let it ring out until it stopped. But Ben started to stir and I rushed to the phone to stop the racket it was making. At the same moment that I answered the phone, making no attempt to disguise the irritation in my voice as I barked 'Hello', Ben let out a wail.

'Nan, is it you?'

I couldn't speak. I was paralysed by all the emotions that her voice brought out in me – anguish, relief, fear and a host of others I couldn't name.

'Nan, it's me, Ilaria. Please talk to me. I've been so worried about you. It has taken me so long to find you.'

She had called the telephone number at Paradise Place many times but no one had picked up. She had written to me there but had received no reply. When she called The Rising Sun and asked for Eddie, she was told he no longer worked there. She had got on with her life, finding a job as a tourist guide in Florence. But eventually, when she was able to take a few days' leave, she had flown to London, hoping to corner one of us at the house.

'But it was locked up, empty. No one was there. I asked the old woman who lives in the house next door but I think she is beginning to lose her mind. She kept shaking her head. So I went to the hostel and the office was able to give me the phone number of your parents. They remembered my name but I had to persuade them to give me your number. What happened? Have you been sick?'

Sick? Yes, you could say that, I thought.

'I had a . . . a nervous breakdown. I'm fine now. And . . . and . . .'

Ben wailed again.

'And I'm married . . . to Chris. We have a baby.'

She took the train up from London the following day and met my little family. I asked her then not to mention Hugo or Eddie or even London in front of Chris.

'It's a time of my life I want to forget,' I said. 'We . . . we don't talk about any of it.'

'But how did we meet? What shall I tell your son if he asks me some day?'

'You came to Yorkshire as a tourist and we got talking in a café?'

She shrugged. 'If that's what you want, sure. But—'

'It's what I want.'

She never questioned me about my nervous breakdown, never probed, never brought up the past. She never once mentioned Hugo. Nor did she ask how I had rekindled my romance with Chris. Perhaps she just assumed that it had never really ended and that my breakdown had brought us closer. Which was true. It was only when I thought I had lost everything that I came to understand how kind and loyal and true Chris was. That was when I began to love him properly, and over the years that love deepened. As he grew older and more rugged, he became more handsome, too. We were happy, so happy.

I take Chris's photograph from the hard-backed envelope

in the pocket of my suitcase and tell him about the evening. I tell him about Marie-Laure, what she looks like, how her voice sounds. I tell him she's a little bit annoying but that she has a good heart, that I think I will grow to like her and that I'm sure she will be good for Ben. I tell him he would probably fancy Alice something rotten but that he might find Arnaud a bit of a cold fish. I don't tell him about Hugo or what happened outside the house. He would worry.

I still curse him for abandoning me.

For the first few weeks after he died, I kissed his photograph every night before I went to bed. Then I punched it. I punched it again and again and again before throwing it away from me, cursing him for leaving me. And finally, pummelled by grief, I picked it up from the floor and kissed it again before placing it under my pillow. I don't do that any more. I've almost become accustomed to being alone. Nowadays, I just touch Chris's face every night before I sleep. I do it now. I kiss his face and I put the photo back in the envelope and then I lie back and wait for sleep to come.

But tonight, like every other night, sleep takes its time in coming and I lie awake, reliving the night of the accident.

It didn't even occur to me to be worried when I looked at the clock and realised Chris was later than he had said he would be. He had driven to Ilkley to discuss ideas for a garden project with a new client. He had planned to drop in to see his father, who now lived in a care home in Keighley, on the way back. I just assumed that the visit to the client had over-run or that he had stayed with his father, who was in the late stages of dementia, a little longer than usual. As I hadn't heard from him, I expected him to be home in time for dinner. I didn't call him; I knew that if he was going to be very late, he would let me know.

Eventually, the flash of car lights in the distance and then the change in the intensity of the beam as they came closer told me that Chris had turned from the road into the lane leading up to the house. I was lifting the casserole from the oven when the front doorbell rang.

That was the first sign that something was wrong, but I understood that only in retrospect. At the time, I remember, I wondered who was at the front door, because I knew it wasn't Chris, who always came in through the back. Even if he had decided, for whatever reason, to use the front door, he would have used his key. The sense of an unseen presence had been plaguing me for some time and my hackles rose at the sound of the doorbell. I'm ashamed to say that my concern at that moment was for myself, not for my husband. It didn't occur to me, not even for a fraction of a second, that anything had happened to Chris.

Still wearing the oven mitt, I went cautiously to the front door, but I didn't open it straight away.

'Who is it?' I called out.

'Mrs Brown?' a man's voice said. 'It's the police. We need to talk to you.'

My first thought was that I was going to be arrested and

charged with murder. I leaned back against the wall, my breath coming in gasps.

And then the voice spoke again.

'Mrs Brown? Are you all right? It's your husband. I'm sorry but he's had an accident.'

I pulled the door open and saw two police officers. They said they hadn't been at the scene of the accident. All they could tell me was that his vehicle had come off the road and had overturned. There were no witnesses and no indication that another vehicle had been involved. A passing driver had seen the wreckage and alerted the emergency services.

'Is he . . . alive?' I asked, and when they told me he was, I exhaled loudly and said, 'Thank God.'

That bloody jeep, I swore silently on the journey to the hospital in the police car. Chris had had a lot of problems with it over the past few years and I had been nagging at him to replace it. But he was very attached to it, and every time he collected it from the garage after its latest repair he was overjoyed when it was pronounced good for at least another year and its next MOT. 'Or its next breakdown,' was my usual response. He could be very stubborn about holding on to the things he loved. Just a week or so earlier he had shelled out yet more money on two brand-new tyres to replace a punctured front wheel and a spare that had hung on the back of the jeep for years without having to be called into action but which had turned out to be unusable because it had degraded.

I resolved to put my foot down once he was out of hospital. The jeep had to go. He could keep it in the garage as a sort of mechanical pet if he couldn't bear to part with it but I would forbid him even to think of driving it out through the gate. Money wasn't tight but it wasn't plentiful either. I was determined that we were going to replace that bloody jeep. I felt a bit better, more positive, as I concentrated on this plan.

But Chris never came home. When we got to the hospital, a doctor took me into a room and told me he'd sustained severe internal injuries and that they were doing all they could for him. I listened to them, aghast. This couldn't be happening.

'I want to see him,' I said.

He was in a room by himself. From the doorway, my first impression was that he looked peaceful, as if he were sleeping. But then I saw all the wires and the beeping machines, and I saw his poor, battered and cut face, and I burst into sobs.

It took him four days to die. He lapsed in and out of consciousness, each period of consciousness becoming shorter and shorter until the final day, when he didn't once open his eyes. I don't remember leaving his bedside during that time, but I must have done. I must have slept. I must have eaten. I must have gone to the toilet.

And Ben must have spent time with him. Of course, Ben must have spent time with him, because . . .

The anguish I felt then has barely diminished. And it has been compounded by the distress of Ben cutting me off. Now

I have the opportunity to make things right with my son. He knows something, because he told me what Chris had said to him. But he doesn't know everything; if he did our relationship would be even worse than it is now. How can I tell him the truth, knowing that he will never forgive me?

When I was a child, my mother used to say, 'Tell the truth or someone else will tell it for you.' There are only two other people who know what happened that night: Hugo and, wherever he is, Eddie. But their version of the truth may be different from mine. And they don't know all of it.

Maybe I can tell Ben what I told Ilaria, that I had once spent time in London, that I had had a nervous breakdown and had returned home to Yorkshire. But that will invite questions – where did I live in London? Why did I keep it such a secret? And he will wonder what else I am keeping from him.

At some point, exhausted, I fall asleep. But there's no respite from the past. I dream of Eddie. He's looking at me questioningly, almost mournfully. I wait for him to speak. But he says nothing, just keeps his eyes fixed on me. And although I try, I'm unable to look away. It's a version of a dream I've had many times over the years. I've been able to control the daytime, use everything in my power to keep bad memories buried. But the night is different. That's when Eddie comes to me to remind me of what I've done.

12

Then

Her first few days at Paradise Place were wonderful and frustrating at the same time. She loved turning the key in the front door, knowing that she could come and go when she pleased. There were no rules, no curfews. It was heaven. She loved her room, which she had filled with esoteric treasures from the market, and the big bed that was so comfortable. But she was disappointed that she hadn't once caught sight of Hugo. She had heard classical music – sometimes loud and crashing, sometimes soft and lyrical – from the room at the front of the house, but when he was in there he kept the door closed and she didn't dare make an entrance that he might not welcome.

She had entertained the notion that she and Hugo would get to know each other as they coincided in the kitchen, and that they would soon be sharing meals together, washed down with a bottle of wine that he would take from the wine rack in the kitchen or even fetch from his cellar. She hadn't been down there, but Eddie said Hugo used it to store his more expensive wine. The door to the cellar was kept locked; perhaps Hugo was afraid his tenants would help themselves too often.

She found herself obsessing about where Hugo might be, and with whom. Ilaria, who thought Nan was wasting her time, rolled her eyes whenever Hugo's name was mentioned.

One afternoon, in life-drawing class, Nan was working on a sketch of the young, fair-haired man posing just a few feet away from her, but it was Hugo's face that emerged as she moved the pencil around. The tutor stood behind her and praised her representation of the model's general anatomy, although he suggested that she might think about studying the bone structure of his face more closely. She blushed, embarrassed by the stark way in which her obsession with Hugo had shown itself. She had not set out to draw Hugo's face. She had not even been consciously thinking of him during the class.

On her first proper Sunday morning at Paradise Place, the end of her first full week in the house, she slept until eleven o'clock, something she had rarely done at the hostel because sleeping late meant no breakfast. She was starving now after so many hours in bed and could think of nothing but food, so she threw a big jumper over her pyjamas and bounded down the stairs.

She was inside the kitchen before she realised that Hugo

was there. And he wasn't alone. Sitting with him at the table, drinking coffee and eating toast, was a girl. A slender and ravishingly beautiful blonde girl who was wearing a shirt that was too big for her – *it must be one of his* – and not much else. The shock of it was too much for her; the sight of the two of them cosily having breakfast, the realisation that they had spent the night together, in his room, in his bed, crushed her. But she was stuck to the spot, standing like an idiot in her silly brushed-cotton pyjamas, her face still creased from sleep and her hair like a bird's nest.

'Nan, come and have some coffee,' Hugo said in his velvety drawl. 'And meet Caroline. Caroline, would you be a darling and get a mug for Nan while I cut some more bread for the toaster?'

Nan would much rather have turned on her heels and fled back upstairs, but she couldn't think of any excuse to do that. In any case, she was in the grip of some terrible, masochistic need to torture herself by observing how Hugo and Caroline were with each other. She sat down at the table. Caroline was reaching up into a cupboard for a mug and Nan couldn't help but stare at her, at the silky hair that looked almost silver in the cold stream of light coming in through the window, at the long bare legs that gave her a coltish quality. *This girl comes from a different drawer*, Nan thought, repeating silently the phrase her mother had always used for people who came from a higher social order, and for a second she entertained in her mind an image of a drawer opening and this beautiful creature springing out of it. How could she compare with someone like this?

Caroline poured coffee into the mug and slid it towards Nan, who was just about able to mumble a 'thank you'. Seconds later, Hugo was back with toast. The two of them fussed over her: would she like marmalade or honey? Perhaps she would like a boiled egg, or would she prefer it poached? It was as if she and not Caroline was the guest in the house and it made her feel uncomfortable. At that moment, she wished she hadn't been so eager to leave the hostel.

It wasn't as if Caroline was snooty or unlikeable. Far from it. She was *nice*. Friendly and open, welcoming. It was just that with every word she uttered she was making Nan realise how far beyond her reach Hugo was. *Of course* Hugo was going to be attracted to someone as beautiful as himself, someone who spoke in that same aristocratic drawl, rather than to a Yorkshire girl whose accent was impossible to disguise and which broke through all her efforts to dilute it.

'Have you changed your hair colour?' Hugo asked, indicating her hennaed locks with a nod. And then he turned to Caroline. 'Nan is at the Byam Shaw. Don't you think she looks like one of those girls you see in Pre-Raphaelite paintings?'

Nan blushed and her heart jumped in her chest. Did this mean that he thought she was attractive, even pretty? After all, she remembered, he did say he liked the Pre-Raphaelites. Although . . . did liking Pre-Raphaelite paintings mean that he liked girls with mad red hair?

'Yes, very like one of those girls with long auburn hair. That look really suits you, Nan,' Caroline said. 'How interesting that you're at the Byam Shaw. My grandmother has a house almost next door to it. You must meet her. Which reminds me, Hugo: I really must pop along later to see her. Will you come with me? You know how fond she is of you.'

Hugo, who had just placed two slices of toast in the rack, emitted a groan. 'Must I? I see enough of the old bat every Christmas,' he said. And then he put his hand behind Caroline's head, stroked her hair and said, 'Of course I'll go with you.'

Nan's heart sank further as her brain processed all these pieces of information. Hugo and Caroline hadn't just spent one night together; they were an established couple. He knew her family. He spent Christmas with them every year, probably in some mansion or castle in the middle of nowhere. How stupid she had been even to dream that someone like him might be interested in her. He would laugh if he knew. And here she was now, having to act as if this was just a normal morning and that her heart wasn't hurting like mad.

'How are you settling in, Nan? Have you got everything you need?' Hugo asked.

'Yes,' she mumbled through a mouthful of toast. 'The room is very nice.'

And then she heard a sound and turned around to see Eddie.

'Eddie!' Caroline exclaimed. 'How lovely to see you. You

never seem to be around when I'm here. Are you going to have some breakfast?'

'Hello, Caroline, nice to see you too. Yeah, I'll have some coffee.'

Eddie sat down next to Nan and slid easily into the conversation.

'What are you up to these days, Caroline?' he asked, helping himself to a slice of toast and covering it in copious amounts of butter before spooning marmalade on top.

'Oh, this and that,' Caroline answered vaguely. Nan took this to mean that Caroline didn't do very much at all. But of course she didn't. She was like Hugo, born with a silver spoon in her mouth. She probably had her own flat, bought by her rich father, who was probably a duke or a lord. And she probably had an allowance that came every month without fail.

Eddie chatted away to Caroline and Hugo, completely at home with these beautiful creatures. Sometimes, he turned sideways to look at Nan, including her in the conversation. But all she thought she could see every time she met his eyes was a look that told her he *knew* and had known all along that she wanted Hugo and that she could never have him. She felt sick and embarrassed.

Later, back in her room, she tried to muster up enthusiasm for the letter she was trying to compose to Miss Sheringham, but her disappointment hovered like a dark cloud over every word she wrote.

13

Now

I'm still asleep when the room telephone rings. I answer it, expecting it to be the front desk. But it's Alice, reminding me that we agreed to meet for lunch and that she's calling to confirm. I recall some kind of chat about a programme for today, but I hadn't realised at the time that it was going to be just Alice and me together for lunch.

'I've booked a table at Wisteria. On Kensington High Street,' she says. 'Half past twelve.'

'Wisteria,' I repeat, committing it to memory. 'Can you give me the address?'

'It's just across the road from the tube station. I keep forgetting you don't know London. Just take a taxi. The driver will know it.'

I check the time; I have just an hour and a half to take a shower, get dressed and travel across town to the restaurant. I'm slightly apprehensive at the thought of how much a taxi will cost from Canary Wharf and when I ask the concierge for an approximation, I'm shocked when he tells me that, depending on traffic, it's likely to be the best part of fifty pounds.

I take the tube, which turns out to be easy and quick; the Jubilee Line, which didn't exist in the late seventies, takes me to Westminster, where I change to the Circle Line and get out at High Street Kensington. The underground feels so different from the way it was forty years ago. The carriages are cleaner and smoking is banned. My nostrils curl as I remember the awful fug of those smoke-filled carriages.

There are other differences, too. At Canary Wharf and Westminster, the glass barriers and automatic doors on the Jubilee Line platforms make it impossible for people to jump in front of a train. During the few months I lived in London, I had always been afraid to stand too close to the platform edge, terrified that I would lose my balance or, worse, that some crazy person would push me on to the track. The glass barriers are reassuring.

But there's no such reassurance when I reach the Circle Line platform, no glass walls separating the platform from the tracks. I stand back, well away from the edge of the platform, looking anxiously around me and wondering whether any of the seemingly harmless people milling on the platform pose a danger. But the train arrives and I get on, choosing a standing position from which I can see all around me. I look for Hugo. Is he somewhere on the train, following me, watching every move I make?

All through the journey I think about the questions I want to ask Alice. How do she and Arnaud know Hugo? Why did they ask him to be godfather to Marie-Laure? I want to know everything she can tell me about him. But I mustn't seem too interested or she may wonder why. And I must be careful not to let slip that I know Notting Hill and Kensington, that I have been here before.

I'm still thinking about this as the train pulls in to High Street Kensington and the doors open. There are a lot of passengers getting out and the process is slow. I lower my foot on to the platform but just as I'm shifting my weight on to it, I feel myself pitching forward. Someone has pushed me from behind. I manage to prevent myself from crashing to the ground. It all happened in an instant, but it was an instant too long for me to see who had pushed me. I look at the people moving towards the steps and back at the people still coming from behind. A small and stocky middle-aged woman immediately behind me is staring at me with what I can only describe as vehemence.

'Get a move on. You're holding everyone up,' she snarls.

'Was it you who pushed me off the train?'

She ignores my question and walks past me, racing up the steps with the kind of energy I would not have expected in someone of her age. It must have been her. *But what if it wasn't?*

I emerge from the tube station with just a couple of minutes to spare and rush across the road to the restaurant. Alice is already at the table, a large glass of white wine in front of her. She rises to embrace me, and as we sit down a waiter materialises in front of us, asking what I would like to drink.

'Just water, please.'

'Still or sparkling?'

'Bring a large bottle of still,' Alice tells him before I can answer. I would have chosen sparkling. 'Now, Nan, what's with this abstinence thing? What would you really like to drink?'

I laugh nervously. 'I just don't drink alcohol,' I say.

'Bring me another glass of Chablis,' Alice commands the waiter and as he goes off to fetch the wine, she turns to me.

'This is a very special occasion, the mothers of the bride and groom getting to know each other. Did you ever think, when you were young, that you'd be this old? I didn't. I still think I'm twenty-five and *immortelle*.'

She gabbles on like this for a while, and I wonder how much she has had to drink before my arrival.

I'm nervous about making conversation, afraid that she will respond unpleasantly to whatever I say. And there's definitely no point asking questions about Hugo. But I can't just sit here saying nothing. Just as I'm thinking through all this, Alice homes in on the one thing I don't want to talk about – why Ben and I have such a strained relationship.

'So, Nan, what's the story with you and Ben? What

happened between you to make you so awkward with each other?'

'Is it that obvious?' I ask, taken by surprise. And then I immediately regret that I've opened myself up to an interrogation from her.

'Yes, it is. Neither of you looked exactly comfortable with each other last night. And I could tell before you arrived that Ben was nervous.'

I stare at my nearly empty water glass.

'Oh, come on, I know the two of you haven't been talking to each other for ages. Marie-Laure says something happened at your husband's funeral, or before it, or whenever, but even she doesn't know the full story. Or, if she does know it, she's not telling me out of loyalty to Ben.'

'She doesn't need to know. It doesn't affect her.'

'Doesn't affect her? Of course it affects her! She's marrying into your bloody family. What affects Ben affects her. And because I'm her mother, it affects me too.'

'It's nothing. A family thing. It's . . . private. Between Ben and me and we'll get over it. We're getting over it already.'

I'm speaking quietly, hoping she will lower her voice, which has already attracted a few looks from other diners.

'Nan,' she says, deliberately opening her eyes as wide as they can go and adopting a look of incredulity, 'until last night, you hadn't spoken to each other for two years. I'd hardly call that *getting over it*.'

'I'm here, aren't I? He wants me at his wedding.'

Alice snorts and lifts her glass to her lips.

'Sure he does. After Marie-Laure threatened to cancel the wedding if he didn't invite you.'

I stare at her, shocked into stillness by what she has just told me. I had assumed that Marie-Laure had worked on Ben to invite me, but I hadn't for a moment imagined that he had given in only because she had threated to call off the wedding.

'Oh, dear me. You're upset. Shouldn't have said that. There, I've slapped my wrist. Naughty Alice.'

'But it's true, isn't it?' I say, defeated and on the verge of tears. 'Ben only invited me because Marie-Laure gave him an ultimatum.'

Alice shrugs, takes another sip from her glass.

'You're a strange woman, Nan. I like you. I really do. There's something about you that makes me want to give you a big hug and look after you. But I'd like to give you a good shake at the same time because there's something so . . . so bloody withheld about you.'

She pauses for another sip.

'And there's so much we don't know about you,' she continues.

'There's nothing to know. My husband died. I was falling apart. Ben and I . . . we said things we shouldn't have said. And now I'm trying to come to terms with it all and get my life back to normal. Whatever normal is. That's all.'

I pick up my water glass and drink from it, hoping she'll

get the message that I can't, *won't*, talk about what happened between Ben and me.

'Maybe you'll explain something to me, in that case.'

'What?'

'Why Hugo has that painting of you in his study.'

Her words, unexpected, hit me like a missile.

'I . . . I have no idea. I suppose he must have liked it.'

'Really? I can't imagine why. Oh, don't misunderstand me. It's a very good painting. Obviously done a few years ago, given that your hair was dark in it. If anything, you look even better now in the flesh than you do in the painting. But I'm beginning to find it all very strange. It never occurred to me to question it before, because I just supposed that Hugo had taken a particular fancy to one of Ben's paintings. But Marie-Laure told me about your reaction to it when you saw it last night. And now I keep asking myself two questions over and over. First question: who on Earth buys a portrait of someone he doesn't know from Adam, even if he knows the painter? Do you know, Nan? Because I certainly don't. And the second question is why the subject of the portrait asked my daughter some very strange questions last night.'

She pauses and narrows her eyes. I know what's coming next.

'Are you sure you've never met Hugo?'

I try to look incredulous, surprised and amused by her question.

'Of course I'm sure. How would I have met him?'

I'm trying to sound confident, convincing. Alice doesn't look convinced.

'All very odd,' she says. 'Maybe we'll ask him when he turns up, whenever that's going to be, what he liked so much about the painting of a woman he'd never met – still hasn't met – that he pestered her son to sell it to him.'

I can't take any more of this. I fold my napkin and put it on the table.

'I'm sorry, Alice. I can't deal with . . . with this. I have to go,' I say, picking up my bag.

She says nothing as she watches me get up from the table. As I start to walk away, she raises her glass in a mock salute.

I'm too angry and upset to go straight to the tube, so I walk through Kensington Gardens and Hyde Park towards Knightsbridge, trying to calm down. I'm out of my depth among these people. I have no control over what's happening. Last night, Alice was nice to me. Today, she's horrible and cruel.

I came to London hoping for a reconciliation with Ben. Instead, I feel as if I've wandered on to the set of a horror film.

There will be a dinner tonight at Paradise Place. I've been told that Hugo is going to do his best to be there.

I shudder. And it's not just because of the cold wind that's blowing from the east.

14

Hugo

I have often wondered how different my life might have been had I never met Eddie Martin and Nan Smith. Or, as she calls herself these days, Nan Brown.

I was twenty-three when Eddie brought her to the house. I hadn't needed to take in lodgers; my parents gave me a reasonable allowance and the house was mine, inherited from a great-uncle whose favourite nephew I was. Nevertheless, the rent money did come in handy, because it enabled me to maintain my interest in fine wine, an indulgence I could not have afforded on my allowance alone.

Perhaps I should explain at this point how my interest in fine wine came about. It certainly wasn't through my parents, who were creatures of habit and who had been ordering the same claret from the same supplier for years. My great-uncle, on the other hand, was something of a connoisseur, and when I finally took possession of the house I discovered the remains of what must have been an extraordinary collection. Most of the bottles were empty; rather eccentrically, my uncle had replaced them on the shelves after drinking their contents. But there were about forty unopened bottles left, dotted here and there among the ghostly empties. It didn't take me long to get through them.

Once the wine had all been drunk, I had a dilemma: go back to drinking cheap plonk, which was all I could afford on my allowance, or find a way of making enough money to buy decent stuff. I asked my parents to increase my allowance. My father exploded, telling me to get a proper bloody job in London or return to Leicestershire to work on the estate in preparation for taking it on when the time came.

I wasn't against the idea of a job; the problem was that nothing particularly interested me, and my classics degree, albeit from Oxford, hadn't qualified me for much beyond academia – which would require further study and a level of discipline I doubted I could sustain – or teaching. I shuddered at the thought of teaching and I saw little point in amassing a collection of degrees.

What Oxford had given me, however, was an entry into the world of high culture, a world that would be closed to me if I returned to Leicestershire and the estate. I was neither a musician nor an artist, but I wanted to be part of that higher world. At Oxford, I had joined my college choir, which, unlike many, did not audition prospective members. The choirmaster was very encouraging about my voice, describing it as 'a pleasant light baritone' that could do with nurturing. And so I set about nurturing it to the extent that when I left Oxford and came to London I was deluded enough to think that I might become a professional singer.

I had visions of engagements all over the world, at the Met in New York, La Scala in Milan, Covent Garden here in London. I was a light baritone now, but I convinced myself that some day I would sing Scarpia in Puccini's *Tosca*, Iago in Verdi's *Otello*. My ambition knew no limits.

I took singing lessons from one of the top teachers in London and, after a year of study, began to audition for opera companies and professional choirs. They all rejected me and I had to accept that, despite the expensive lessons, I simply was not good enough to sing professionally. I also had to accept that, even with my allowance, I had been living beyond my means.

It was Caroline who suggested that I might think about letting one or even two rooms in my house. The more I thought about her suggestion, the more I liked it. Caroline offered to spread the news that I was looking for lodgers, but I told her firmly that I had no intention of taking in friends or friends of friends, who might not always be forthcoming with the rent, and that I preferred to keep my prospective tenants at a distance. So I put a notice in the newsagent's at the bottom of Pembridge Road and within a day had my first lodgers.

Renting out the two rooms fulfilled a second need – to

keep girlfriends at a remove. Several, having spent a few nights in the house, had dropped hints about moving in. I ignored them, pretended I hadn't heard. Even Caroline, who shared a flat with two other girls just off Sloane Square, had mooted the idea of coming to live at Paradise Place, pointing out that she would be closer to her grandmother if she did so. I said as drily as I could that if she really wanted to be closer to the old bat she should think about moving in with her. She didn't bring up the subject again.

Eddie came through his predecessor, who was moving out of London and who drank at the pub down the road where Eddie had just got himself a job as a barman. I didn't recognise him immediately but he knew who I was straight away, reminding me that his uncle had worked as a gardener-cum-handyman at my boarding school in Norfolk. I vaguely remembered the quiet, intense boy who could be seen regularly working alongside his uncle. It wasn't surprising that he had recognised me. I was older by a few years and was quite prominent in the school, mainly as a member of the first cricket eleven, although I was pretty good at most sports.

As a lodger, he was clean and quiet; sometimes I hardly knew he was in the house. But, a far cry now from the timid boy who had helped his uncle in the gardens at my boarding school, he was confident in his skin and anything but in awe of people he might once have considered to be, to quote an old phrase, *above his station*. He was unapologetic about his presence when I had overnight guests. Some previous tenants, seeing Caroline or someone else in the kitchen or coming out of the bathroom, would scurry away and keep their distance. Not Eddie. He was completely relaxed and confident in his right to use all parts of the house. I liked that about him.

He had clearly overcome his humble beginnings to become a confident young man. He told me he had dropped out of university because he wanted to travel and, if I didn't mind, he probably wouldn't stay at Paradise Place for more than three or four months. I told him that was fine by me. As it turned out, he ended up staying for rather longer than either of us expected.

He was, despite his general cheerfulness, given to occasional moods. When I look back now, I wonder whether he could be described as 'passive-aggressive'. But that term was not commonplace in the nineteen seventies – or if it was I certainly was not aware of it. As for Nan – not for a moment could I have imagined the sweet little thing who had appeared in my house wanting to rent a room as being capable of such violence.

It was obvious when Eddie brought her to see the room that his interest in her was more than platonic. I confess that I felt slightly sorry for him; I could tell at once that Nan was hungry for adventure and that if Eddie was going to succeed in getting her into his bed he wouldn't have her there for long. I made a bet with myself that she wouldn't last more than a couple of months and would go the same way as Olivia.

Eddie's problem was that he just couldn't have a normal, casual relationship with a girl. I had seen him in action with Olivia (although *action* wasn't exactly the right word in his case): getting interested in her, hanging around her like a lost puppy and then, when she did succumb to his charms, becoming too intense too quickly and scaring her off. In fact, he scared her straight into my bed. Olivia was more like Caroline, still a free spirit. She liked sex, even reported that Eddie wasn't bad at it, but said that his intensity terrified her. He had even begun to talk about staying in London after all and the two of them perhaps getting a flat together. When she left, she told me not to give him her new address, a bedsit in West Norwood – about as far from Notting Hill and Eddie as it was possible to be and still have a London postcode. 'I'm sure he'll make someone a great husband but it won't be me,' I recall her saying.

Caroline was quite fond of Eddie and thought he was rather good-looking. She also felt a little sorry for him. He really needed to lighten up, she said.

'Perhaps I should sleep with him,' she said one night as, enjoying a post-coital ciggie in my bedroom, we heard Eddie return from the pub. 'You wouldn't mind, would you?'

'Not at all, my sweet,' I said. I blew a ring of smoke into the air. 'As long as you don't mind if I sleep with Nan.'

At that point I had no intention of sleeping with my newest

lodger because, as I had already decided, I had no wish to disturb the balance of the house. My words had flowed easily in response to what Caroline had said. But maybe it was at that moment that some unconscious intention was triggered. I slept with a lot of girls and I particularly liked sleeping with Caroline, who was not only adventurous but also not in the slightest bit possessive. She had other boyfriends and knew I had other girlfriends.

Caroline and I were equals. Our families, who had known each other for generations, had already begun to assume that a marriage was inevitable. I wasn't averse to the idea; she and I would make an ideal husband-and-wife team. But that wasn't going to come about any time soon – if it ever did. We were far too young to get married, and far too young to stop sleeping with other people.

Nan, I thought, even as I teased Caroline, would almost certainly be the clingy type.

'Oooooh, so you're thinking of breaking in little Nan,' Caroline said. 'Well, she's very pretty and very sweet.'

'I have your blessing, then?' I said, dragging on the cigarette again and watching the smoke curl into the air.

She leaned across me to bite my neck, rather more viciously than I would have liked. I moaned in a mixture of pain and pleasure, ready for what I knew would follow. But then she stopped, raised her head and looked directly into my eyes.

'Just be careful, Hugo. She's not like us.'

'Now when have I not been careful?' I said, teasingly.

It was not, perhaps, the right thing to say given that Caroline had had an abortion earlier in the year. She hadn't told me who the father was but had insisted that the baby wasn't mine.

'That's not what I meant,' she growled, returning to the business of biting my neck.

How right Caroline was. It was very simple. Nan was simply *not like us*. I should indeed have been more careful. If I had heeded her words I would not have lost two years of my life in a brain-damaged fugue. I would not have done the things I've had to do. But I refuse to blame myself for those things. Nan ruined my life and I want her to know it. I want her to know everything I went through, the pain and torment I suffered. I want her to pay for all of it.

And yet something in me still responds to her, even now after everything that happened.

That delicious feeling of excitement as she walked towards my house is still with me. I'm reliving it now, watching myself standing in the shadows in Paradise Place, hoping no one in the house would spot me. No one did. So many feelings, mixed feelings, stirred within me as I watched her. They were almost enough to make me retreat and leave her to her reunion with her son, disappear until after the wedding and back out of her life.

I could see that she was already in something of a state. Perhaps, as she walked into Paradise Place, she too was reliving every moment of that night forty years ago. Perhaps she felt sorry for what she had done to me.

But even as I thought this, the memory of her face when she heard and saw me returned with a sharp stab. I had said her name quietly, not really intending that she should hear. But she did hear me, and, even in the dark, I saw the startled, terrified look that crept across her face. I stood back and watched her stumble. That was when I moved out from the shadows and took her arm to steady her.

'It's been a long time, Nan,' I said.

She didn't answer. The shock of seeing me had rendered her incapable of speech. I saw the fear and disbelief in her face. I felt her arm tremble as I put my hand below her elbow. That gave me a sense of satisfaction. But as I moved away from her, back into the shadows, I was left with a feeling of disquiet, because it wasn't just fear I saw on her face. It was revulsion, too.

15

Now

My phone rings as I walk out on to Canada Square from the tube station. I look at the screen and see the number 121. Someone has left a message. I lift the phone to my ear, hoping to hear Ben's voice. But it's Alice.

'Nan, I'm – I'm sorry, really sorry. I behaved very badly. I drank a bit too much. To be honest, I drink a bit too much most of the time. I just hope you can forgive me. I promise—'

I touch the red button and put the phone back in my bag. I'll call her later. Right now, the only person I want to talk to is Ben. I look around me, at the tall buildings that seem so unreal, like toy buildings for grown-ups. Ben lives somewhere among these buildings, but I don't know where. I don't even know his phone number. I'm overwhelmed by a need to find him, and as I enter the lobby of my hotel, I have an idea.

I approach the front desk, trying to make my smile as hapless-looking as possible.

'I wonder whether you can help me . . .' I begin.

The young woman behind the desk smiles and waits for me to tell her what I want.

'I'm afraid I've lost my telephone, and it's a bit of a disaster because I need to call my son urgently and I haven't got his number in my head.'

She looks at me blankly, as if to ask how she can possibly help.

'The thing is, he booked me into the hotel and I wonder whether you can check the booking details, just in case his number is there.'

'I'm not sure I can do that, Mrs . . .?'

'Brown. I'm in room 352.'

'Mrs Brown,' she says, 'there are rules about data protection.'

'Oh, for goodness' sake! He's my son!'

My voice is so loud that a couple of people standing at the far end of the desk turn to stare at me. I open my bag and start pulling things out of it – my key card, my driving licence, my passport – and slamming them down on the counter.

'Look, check me out in your system. My name's Nan Brown. My son is Ben Brown. All I need is his phone number because I've lost my phone.'

'Let me check,' she says quickly. After a few moments, she tells me she has found a telephone number associated with the booking but that, because of data protection issues, she cannot give it to me. Just as I'm about to burst into tears of anger and frustration, she says that what she can do is call the number and ask if the person will speak to me.

'Would you like me to do that, Mrs Brown?'

I nod.

'Can you wait for five minutes, until I'm back in my room?'

'Of course.'

I wait for what seems like ages. At least ten minutes.

When the room phone eventually rings, I rush to grab it.

'Ben!'

But it's not Ben.

'Nan.'

My breath stops as I hear the way the voice caresses the first N before letting it slip on to the vowel, the endlessly long vowel.

'It really has been a long time, hasn't it? We have rather a lot of catching up to do. But you'll forgive me, won't you, if we don't do it right now? We have plenty of time. After all, what's another day or two when forty years have gone by?'

'What's going on, Hugo?' I ask when I am finally able to find my voice. 'What do you want from me?'

He doesn't answer and I wait. The silence on the line makes me wonder whether he's still there, whether he has been there at all and I have imagined him.

'I'm still thinking about that, Nan,' he says eventually.

And then I hear the click that ends the call and I start to shake.

The room phone rings again. I pick up the handset, hold it to my ear and listen.

'Nan, it's me. Alice. Are you there? Are you all right?'

'I'm fine.'

'Look, I know I behaved badly. I left a message on your phone saying I was sorry. Did you get it?'

'Yes, I got it. I was going to call you.'

'Please, let me make it up to you. I *am* sorry, I really am. Can we talk?'

'We're talking now.'

'I mean, talk in person. I'm downstairs in the lobby.'

'Give me a few minutes. I'll come down.'

I wash my face in the bathroom and apply a new layer of make-up: foundation, eye shadow, mascara. And the red lipstick. I tell myself that I'm in control now. *I* have the upper hand because Alice has come to see *me*, to beg my forgiveness for the cruel things she said in the restaurant. But I don't feel as though I'm in control of anything. Especially not now, not after that phone call from Hugo.

Alice looks contrite. As soon as she sees me walking towards her, she leaps to her feet and rushes forward. But she doesn't embrace me; perhaps she has seen from my face that it would be the wrong thing to do.

'I wanted to talk to you, just the two of us, before we all

get together this evening,' she says. 'I don't want there to be any animosity between us. I don't want Marie-Laure and Ben to be upset in any way.'

I suggest that we go to the coffee shop in the hotel. At least here I can pretend that I'm in charge of the proceedings, even if I feel anything but.

A waitress asks what we would like to order. I expect Alice to order a glass of wine, but she asks for tea. Her demeanour is different now. All the belligerence has gone.

'I don't understand why you were so . . . so cruel to me, Alice,' I say as the waitress retreats.

Her face twists in pain. My words have hit home. I have wounded her. But I feel no triumph as she looks away.

'I don't know why either . . . Well, maybe I do. Maybe I'm—' She breaks off. She looks embarrassed.

Maybe she's going to tell me she's an alcoholic. That won't exactly be a surprise.

'Maybe I'm jealous of you.'

'Jealous? As you've pointed out so clearly, I have a strained relationship – if I have a relationship at all – with my son. You have a daughter who, as far as I can tell, adores you. And you have a husband.'

'A husband I don't love, who doesn't love me and who bores me to tears.'

'That's hardly a tragedy. But you must have loved him once.'

'Sure I did. I loved him and everything he represented.

After growing up on a council estate in Manchester, living in France with Arnaud and his family was like living in Paradise. I bought into a package, a beautifully wrapped package called the Thomas family and their vineyards. I didn't realise it at the time, but that's what I did.'

'You have Marie-Laure,' I remind her gently. I feel sorry for her now. 'Even if your marriage has become boring, isn't she worth it all?'

Her face softens and she makes an attempt at a smile.

'Yes, she's worth every moment of it. But . . . No, you're right. She *is* worth everything.'

'Are you thinking about a divorce?'

'Oh, it's far too late. There would be no point, because the only man I want – the only man I've ever wanted – seems to be far more interested in you than he is in me.'

My mouth drops open in a mixture of shock and horror. Am I hearing things? Is Alice telling me she's in love with Hugo? Has she spoken to Hugo about me? What has he told her?

I shake my head in confusion. 'What do you mean?'

'Well, he certainly doesn't have a painting of *me* in his study,' she says. 'Oh, it's a long story and you probably don't want to hear it. You've got enough to deal with.' She hesitates, then goes on, 'But . . . if you don't mind, I'd like to tell you about it, because . . . well, I've never told anyone before.'

'It's all right. I – I don't mind.'

'We met Hugo when he came to buy wine from us. You know he has a wine business?'

'No, but I—' Just in time, I stop myself from finishing what I was going to say, that I know he has always had a keen interest in wine. I give a small cough, and apologise. 'Sorry, I hope I'm not getting a cold. No, I didn't know that. I don't know anything about him.'

'It's small, very exclusive and very successful. You won't have heard of it. He doesn't advertise because he doesn't have to – he's blessed with a lot of luck and, as you'll discover for yourself, a great deal of charm. He supplies some boutique hotels and upmarket restaurants, for example, but he also has a client list of seriously rich people who rely on him to stock up their cellars.'

I nod, taking this in.

'He's been taking our top wine for years. It's a good arrangement that benefits both him and us. But ... well, it hasn't been the only arrangement between us. I mean, between Hugo and me.'

My face feels as if it's burning.

'You're having an affair?' I ask, trying to sound calm and hoping she hasn't noticed my consternation.

'*Affair*?' She gives a scornful, cynical laugh. 'I wouldn't call it an affair. That would be too grand a description. Although that's what I once thought it was: a great, passionate affair. Well, that's what it was for me, but not for him. For Hugo, it's more like one of those friendships with benefits – is that what you call them? Except I'm not sure what the benefits are for me.'

Her voice has taken on a note of bitterness. Her mouth has twisted into a smile that isn't mirrored in her eyes.

'So you think it's a convenience for him, but it still means something much bigger to you?' I venture.

She nods, a rueful look on her face.

'I must seem pathetic to you.'

'No, not pathetic. Not pathetic at all.' I'm fumbling for words. 'I . . . can understand.'

'You can't possibly understand. Not yet. You might when you meet him. Have you ever met someone for the first time and found yourself ready to give up everything for him there and then?'

Oh, yes, I have. I remember that first time I saw him. I remember thinking thoughts exactly like the ones you're telling me about.

I nod.

'Well,' she says, 'that's how I felt when I met Hugo. I had to have him.'

'How long . . .?'

'Oh, it's been going on for years. Hugo is what you might call the love of my life.'

'What about Arnaud? Does he know?'

'Arnaud? Bless him, he doesn't have a clue. He has absolutely no imagination. Not a shred. It never occurred to him that Hugo and I were jumping into bed every chance we got when he came to stay with us.'

'And now . . . are you still . . .?'

'In theory, yes. But we haven't for a while. You see, I told

135

him last year how I felt. I said I'd leave Arnaud. Big mistake. He didn't want to know. He said why change a perfectly good arrangement. Those were his words – *a perfectly good arrangement*. So I've become something I never wanted to be, something I've always despised. I've become one of those pathetic women desperately hoping the man of her dreams will see her as the woman of his. Because I want more than a perfectly good arrangement and that's something I'm not going to get.'

'You . . . you might, though. Maybe—'

She holds up a hand.

'Don't even *try* to encourage me, Nan. You're really helping me by just listening to me. Hugo doesn't do permanent. He does constant all right, but he has his own definition of constancy. I'm pretty certain he has other women and he's constant with them too. I'm convinced he's had something going with that sister-in-law of his for years. They were an item once, way back in the seventies. I think everyone thought they'd get married, but she gave up on him and married his brother. He could seduce anyone; he could seduce a nun. It's never really bothered me too much before because Hugo . . . well, it's just the way he is. And I really did think he and I had something special.'

She pauses, as if reflecting on what she has said.

'But this painting of you – I knew about it already because Marie-Laure told me about it, but I hadn't seen it until this week. And when I did see it and then met you,

I had a feeling, a kind of premonition, that I was going to lose him to you.'

'But . . . he doesn't know me. We've never met,' I say, my voice weak as it struggles to carry the lie.

'No, but you will. And I'm feeling jealous. Without trying to sound dramatic, I'm eaten up with jealousy and I hate myself for it. And I'm trying to hate you too, but I can't.'

'Oh, Alice, don't be ridiculous. Your imagination is running away with you. And don't forget that my husband died just two years ago. I loved him. There's no place for anyone else and there never will be.'

'Sorry. I didn't mean to suggest that you . . . It's just that I know Hugo so well and I wanted to tell you about him before you meet him and he charms you into thinking you're something special too.'

Oh, Alice, I know more about Hugo than you'll ever realise. I loved him once too. At least, I thought I did.

16

Hugo

Alice has left several messages on my phone and a similar number of texts, all asking me where I am and urging me to call her. The gist of the messages, delivered lightly in her trademark husky voice, is that she wants to discuss arrangements for the wedding. But I know she wants to talk about much more than that. Alice is far from stupid. She will have begun to wonder whether Nan and I have met before. I would prefer not to lie to Alice if she asks me about Nan, and so I ignore her calls and messages.

Loyal and faithful Alice. Well, loyal and faithful to me if not to poor old Arnaud. She has been quite a fixture in my life over many years, providing a great deal of uncomplicated pleasure and comfort when I needed it. I had not intended to seduce her, and certainly not on that first visit when I was there solely to discuss their wine, although I did find her more than a little attractive with her tall, lithe body, her tanned skin, sapphire-blue eyes and long blonde hair that several years of scorching French summers had bleached almost white. She was most definitely my type. If anything, it was she who seduced me, making it clear through unspoken messages delivered by her eyes and through more overt signals that came when her hips brushed against mine, swaying lazily while keeping the contact, that she wanted to sleep with me.

I did have some reservations about bedding the wife of the man with whom I hoped to do business, but I reasoned that because Alice was making all the moves, it would be discourteous not to go along with whatever she wanted. And, of course, she was dazzling. So much so that I had no alternative but to give in to the temptation that was becoming overwhelming in its intensity. Our initial couplings, played out in the small house on the estate where she and Arnaud accommodated business guests, more than rewarded several hours of anticipation. I did wonder whether Arnaud had any inkling of what his wife and I were up to every moment we could snatch together during those few days I spent with them, but if he did, he gave no indication.

What I hadn't expected was that what I saw on that first visit as a delightfully unexpected bonus would be repeated again and again over many years. What I also hadn't expected was to discover something that became apparent by the time I left to return to London: that Alice was the driving force behind the business and Arnaud, by dint of his family's ownership of the estate, was merely the facilitator.

About a year ago, she told me she planned to leave Arnaud, and suggested that she and I might try living together. I told her I was no good at living with anyone and that if we did live together there was a danger that our relationship would disintegrate. We had something that worked supremely well, I said. Why spoil it? She was disappointed, but she seemed to take it well, telling me I was probably right and that she had just given in to a moment of madness.

She still jokes about leaving Arnaud and joining me in London. She pretends she's just teasing me. But I know her too well; I know that beneath the jocular tone she's still looking at a future in which she moves into Paradise Place. I am very fond of Alice, but I cannot imagine having her around all the time. I don't tell her this, of course. When she makes a joke about running away from Arnaud, my response is always to remind her of that well-worn saying about familiarity breeding contempt. If she presses the point, I ask her how she thinks Marie-Laure would feel about her mother running off with her godfather; that tends to sober her up.

I have never come close to marriage. Nor have I ever been remotely interested in the kind of relationship that places two people in close proximity to each other day in, day out, whether married or not. My mother spent years hoping and plotting in vain that Caroline and I would tie the knot, move to Leicestershire, run Ravenby, the family estate, and produce the grandchildren she so desired. When I told her and my father that I had no intention of either marrying

Caroline or taking on the estate, they didn't take it well. And, despite my younger brother happily accepting the burden of maintaining Ravenby for the future generations he planned to sire on their behalf, they never quite forgave me.

Caroline remains in my life, but as my brother's wife and, these days, at a distance. I must confess that it did feel rather strange to stand with him as his best man as he tied the knot with Caroline, in whose bed I had spent much of the previous night. About seven years and two children – boys, of course; an heir and a spare – into their marriage, she became bored and we resumed seeing each other whenever she came down to London, which was about once a month. I recall those times fondly.

As I may have noted already, Caroline and I were equals. Our trysts had less to do with emotional attachment than with familiarity and physical enjoyment, and I must add here that her unexciting marriage to my deeply conventional brother had made her up her game in the physical department when she was with me. She was insatiable. But, like many women, Caroline eventually lost interest in sex over the years, even in sex with me, and the frequency of her trips to London diminished. I hardly ever see her now; whatever physical energy she has goes into the horse or donkey sanctuary – I can never remember which – she set up years ago.

I have never discussed any of my other dalliances with Alice, who has always known better than to ask whether there are other women in my life. Perhaps she assumes that my appetite has waned as my age has increased. It has not. I am sixty-three now and, as my doctor told me after my recent annual check-up, ridiculously healthy despite what I have gone through.

I have not quite worked out what I want from Nan. Certainly, an acknowledgement that she caused me years of pain. And revenge. But something else nags at me, a desire for something more. What *more* means, however, I confess I don't know. I frightened her when I spoke to her from the shadows of Paradise Place and I frightened her again when I came out from my hiding place and showed myself. I frightened her when she answered the telephone in her room at the hotel. I cannot deny having gained some pleasure from those moments, but nor can I deny that I also felt a sensation of – yes, desire. That word again. To complete what we began that night forty years ago. That, perhaps, would give me what the Americans call closure.

17

Now

People talk about closure all the time these days, about coming to terms with something terrible that has happened and then moving on with their lives.

I will never come to terms with Chris's death, which the coroner described as 'an unfortunate accident' and 'an accident waiting to happen'. I remember wanting to shout out that it was either one or the other, that it couldn't be both. I listened, numb, to the evidence.

The conclusion was that the new front wheel, which was found far from the jeep, had come off, causing the accident. But the coroner said it was impossible to say whether the wheel had simply come loose or had not been tightened properly in the first place. My grief was compounded by the sheer waste of it all.

We had been together so long and had gone through so much. We had built a good life together, brought up a son. I had lost him once through my own foolishness and had found him again – or, rather he had found me. At the worst time in my life, he had been there for me, offering the hope I so needed. But it wasn't just hope he had given me; he had given me love and stability and fun. Yes, we had had fun together. He made me laugh. Best of all, he was kind. I shudder now when I think what my life would have been without him.

I had thought, even assumed, that Ben would be there for me, to mourn with me and to ease me into the new life I would have to live without Chris. He had returned to York-shire immediately on hearing that his father was in hospital and had sat with Chris for hours on end, determined to be with him during those short periods when he was conscious. But between Ben and me there was a distance, and I knew why. It had been there for a long time, since my failure to visit the exhibition of his paintings in the Mayfair gallery. Chris had made the effort, but I hadn't, and Ben hadn't forgiven me for it.

Now, as I look back at the final days of Chris's life, I can see clearly that Ben was trying to deal with even more than the terrible knowledge that his father wasn't likely to recover, that he was trying to make sense of Chris's cryptic comments to him. I can see now what I should have seen then but didn't. If I had, if Ben had even hinted to me that Chris had been saying strange things that didn't make sense, I would have tried to talk to Chris while he was still clinging to life. I would have been able to put things right.

Chris knew part of the truth, but not all of it, and over time it became unnecessary to speak of it as we settled into the life we were building for ourselves and for our son. But he had broken a promise by talking to Ben, even if he didn't tell him very much, even though he was dying. I can't forgive him for that.

The funeral remains a blur in my memory. I recall that there were a lot of people in the church and in the graveyard, but I don't remember their faces. Ben gave the eulogy but I don't remember a word of what he said. There were drinks and sandwiches afterwards in the parish hall. I have no recollection of how that came about. Perhaps it was Ben who organised it.

I never did get around to asking him, because by the end of that terrible day, Ben had left the house, slamming the door behind him. I remember hearing his car drive away. I remember looking at the clock and thinking he had probably gone for a drive to let off some steam and that he would be back in an hour or two.

I waited up for him, my ears on alert for the sound of his car. But the hours went by and he didn't return.

He had asked me questions and I had refused to answer them.

He had heard Chris, in a semi-conscious state, say some strange things. Chris had spoken as if he were addressing me. *You have to tell him . . . gone on too long . . . know the truth.*

I recognised those words so well. They were like a mantra,

spoken by Chris at intervals over the years. But now they were being flung at me by my son, who was demanding answers – answers I couldn't give him because I couldn't even deal with them myself.

Ben's final words to me, before he walked out of the house and drove away, were, 'When you're ready to talk to me, let me know. Until then, I don't want to hear from you.'

I called him time and time again on his mobile, but he never answered. I left him messages telling him I loved him and I missed him. But I could never leave him a message telling him that I was ready to answer his questions. And at some point, he changed his phone number, so I couldn't tell him, even if I had been ready.

The way I'm feeling now, I don't think I ever will be ready. But my biggest fear is that I may no longer have any control over what Ben learns or what he is told. I'm afraid that if he finds out that everything I have told him is a lie he will hate me and I will lose him once and for all.

I will see him this evening. He and Marie-Laure will collect me from the hotel and take me to Paradise Place and we will sit around the table with Alice and Arnaud, and I will try to behave as if everything is normal. Nothing is normal. Hugo is in charge, controlling us, manipulating us as if we were puppets and he the puppet master. I wonder whether he will turn up for this dinner, or whether he will continue to pull the strings from a distance. I don't know how I will behave if he's there; I can't bear to think about it.

The others don't realise it. They go along, for their own reasons, with whatever he wants; Alice because she's in love with him, Arnaud probably because it suits him not to have to make decisions, Marie-Laure because he's her adoring godfather and Ben because of Hugo's patronage. They have no idea what Hugo is up to. But then, I think with a shudder, neither do I.

18

Then

Lying on her bed, kept indoors by the rain that lashed against the windows, Nan was thinking about Hugo.

He was downstairs now and he was playing something classical on his record player. A symphony or something like that, with lots of loud, crashing bits. He had put the volume up high. He often did that. She wondered for a moment whether he played loud music to drown out the presence of his tenants, to make it impossible for them to intrude into his world when he wanted it to be off-limits. The music was so loud and she was so deep in her thoughts that she almost didn't hear the knock on her bedroom door.

She knew Eddie was at work. Her heart beat faster. It must be Hugo. He had never come to her door before. She jumped up from the bed and hurried to the door, hoping her excitement and pleasure wouldn't be too obvious. But when she opened the door, her smile turned into an open-mouthed expression of disappointment.

'Chris! What are you doing here?'

'What do you think I'm doing? I've come to see you. I took the train.'

His eyes narrowed momentarily, as if he was trying to work something out, and then he said, 'You've changed the colour of your hair!'

He held out his arms to her but she moved back into the room. His hair and clothes were drenched. His face, normally bright and open, had a look that she couldn't fathom. She knew she should kiss him, or even just hug him, but she couldn't bring herself to touch him.

'You'd better come in,' she said, making a small gesture with her hand. 'You should have told me you were coming. I might have been out.'

'You probably would have made sure to be out if you'd known I was coming,' he said.

Chris looked around the room and then sat on the bed. Nan thought about sitting on one of the floor cushions so that she didn't have to be so close to him that he could read every blink of her eyelid, every small movement of her fingers, but she sat beside him on the bed. When he spoke again, Nan heard a brittle sound in his voice.

'So this is where you and Ilaria sleep,' he said. 'I would have thought there'd be two beds but there's only this. It must be very cosy.'

She hung her head, unable to look directly into his eyes. 'Ilaria . . . she moved out.'

'You're a liar, Nan. Ilaria never moved in, did she?'

'No,' Nan said quietly, shaking her head.

'I just don't understand, Nan. I asked you if you wanted a break and you said no. You said you wanted us to stay together. But I don't believe you, because when you opened the door just now you looked at me as if I was the last person in the world you wanted to see.'

'It's not that,' she says. 'I'm just . . . going through a bad patch. Things aren't great at the college.'

'Is that the best you can come up with?' He turned his head towards the door. 'And what about him downstairs?'

'What do you mean?' she asked, lifting her head.

Chris stared at her. She felt uncomfortable under his gaze, as if he was dissecting her, taking her apart.

'So that's it,' he said. 'That's why you've been so weird with me. You're sleeping with him, aren't you? I can see it in your eyes.'

'No-o-o,' Nan said miserably. But even as she uttered her denial she was conscious of all the longing for Hugo that that single word, elongated into something that was more like a wail than a denial, seemed to express. And she saw that Chris was conscious of it too, because his eyes had filled with an unbearable sadness and his face had collapsed. His whole body seemed to have deflated.

For a few moments, he sat quietly. And then he stood up and walked to the door.

'Chris,' she called out to him. She didn't want it to end like this. 'Don't go. Please.'

'Is there any point in my staying?' he asked, turning to look at her.

What should she – could she – say? She bit her lip and looked away, as if trying to find inspiration.

She heard him say, in a voice so quiet that she could just make out his words, 'No, I didn't think so.' When she looked back, he was closing the door behind him.

She sat for a while, numb. At some point, the enormity of her decision – and she knew that allowing Chris to walk out of the room amounted to a decision – hit her. What had she done? She had thrown away her future, and for what? Yet she knew she couldn't run after him because she had nothing to offer him. All she could do was weep, and she wept for what seemed like hours.

Later that evening, when she had cried so much that there were no tears left, she went downstairs. Hugo was in the kitchen, chopping onions.

He threw her a kindly glance. 'I'm making spag bol. Like some?'

She nodded. Shouldn't she feel even a little bit happier now that Hugo was asking her to eat with him? Maybe she should, but she didn't. She felt miserable and filled with guilt because of what she had done to Chris. And she knew, anyway, that Hugo wasn't remotely interested in her.

He didn't say much while he prepared the food, but when they were finally sitting down at the table and he had poured both of them a glass of red wine, he asked, 'Boyfriend trouble?'

'I suppose,' she said. 'I don't think he's my boyfriend any more.'

'Ah. Sorry to hear that. It can't be any fun being dumped. At least he came to see you. He didn't do it on the phone.'

'It wasn't him, really. It was me.'

'Ah,' he said again, and she wondered what that *ah* meant. Did it mean that he had cottoned on to her feelings for him?

'Eddie?' he asked.

'Eddie? You mean . . .? No, there's nothing between me and Eddie.'

'Oh? I thought there might be something brewing between you two.'

'There sort of was, a while back. But it's not going to happen. Not now. Everything has changed too much.'

'How are things at the Byam Shaw?' he asked. 'Are you enjoying your course?'

'Not particularly,' she said. And then, with a laugh, added, 'I think I may have overestimated my talent.'

'What makes you think that?'

'My stuff is . . . well, I suppose it's straightforward and

traditional. It's boring, if I'm honest. I draw and I paint, and I can be fairly abstract if I try. But I don't seem to have what the others have.'

'And what do the others have?'

She thought about this for a few seconds but couldn't come up with anything specific.

'They're just better and more talented than me. And they're more confident.'

'That's not a good enough excuse. You must have shown talent to get in. Maybe you need to stop thinking about how talented everyone else is and concentrate on your own work.'

His tone was devoid of sharpness but it was firm and she was so taken aback by it that she opened her mouth to respond but no words came.

'Nan, it's a foundation course. It's the beginning, not the end,' he said gently. 'Make the most of it. Don't give up. Now, I'm going to clear the table – no, you stay where you are – and then I'm going to make us some coffee. And when I sit down again, you're going to tell me what you've been working on. Okay?'

She watched Hugo put the bowls in the sink and run the tap. His back was to her, so she felt safe staring at him. She couldn't help it. Her eyes lingered on the way his hair wound itself into soft tendrils at the nape of his neck, the way his shirt moved as his body shifted. Her eyes moved lower, to the slim hips and long legs and she couldn't help but imagine those legs entwined with hers, his body on top of hers, his mouth on hers. And then she made herself look away, because she was afraid that if he turned around she wouldn't be able to disguise the naked longing she knew her eyes would betray.

19

Now

At home, I am organised. I have schedules. I know what I am meant to be doing at any given moment. But here in London I have no grasp of time. Have I really been down here for little more than twenty-four hours? How can so much have happened in so short a time?

I'm waiting for Ben and Marie-Laure to pick me up from the hotel. I'm more relaxed than I was earlier because I won't have to face Hugo. Marie-Laure called about an hour ago to remind me that they would come to the hotel around seven o'clock and to tell me that Hugo, unfortunately, would not be able to attend after all.

'It's a shame, because we really wanted you to get to know him before the wedding. And he really wants to meet you,' she said.

'He's obviously a very busy man,' I said, doing my best to sound nonchalant. I wonder what she would say if I told her how much I dreaded seeing him, dreaded hearing the sound of his voice.

'*À bientôt!*' she trilled.

Now I'm sitting in the lobby, my eyes trained on the main entrance to the hotel. Marie-Laure comes through the door and walks towards me, smiling so generously that I feel slightly guilty about my disappointment that it's her I see and not Ben.

'I hope you haven't been waiting here too long,' she says, giving me the obligatory kisses. Three of them. 'Ben is outside in the car.'

Marie-Laure insists that I sit in the front, and as I lower myself into the seat I smile hopefully at Ben, who rewards me with a guardedly cheerful, 'Hi.'

The expression on his face changes to one of momentary concentration as his eyes dart to the rear-view mirror before he pulls away. I know that look so well. As a child, he could sit endlessly in front of a jigsaw puzzle, his eyes focused only on putting the pieces together to complete the picture. And now, as I'm reminded of his powers of concentration, I wonder whether his wedding to Marie-Laure will merely put off for a while his determination to force me to supply the missing pieces of the jigsaw that is my past.

'I've been trying to work out where your flat might be among all these buildings,' I say. 'Maybe I can drop in tomorrow. I'd love to see where you live.'

'Sure,' Ben says evenly, as if he's talking to an acquaintance rather than his mother. 'It's not actually in the main Wharf area, but it's close enough. It's not the most stunning apartment ever but it has great views.'

'I thought it might. Have you painted scenes around here?'

'Yes, but I paint in a studio rather than the flat. I go there when I have time, which isn't very often at the moment, what with work and the wedding. I'm working towards an exhibition at Lucinda's gallery next autumn. Lucinda, if you remember, is the woman who gave me my break.'

'The exhibition is going to be called "Urban Islands",' Marie-Laure says enthusiastically. 'It's a wonderful title, don't you think, Nan?'

'It is. Ben, I'd love to see what you've done so far. Would . . . would that be possible?'

'I don't see why not. I'll talk to Hugo.'

'Hugo? Why?'

'He's storing them for me. There isn't room in our flat and I'm a bit reluctant to leave finished work in the studio. It's in a pretty dodgy area and there have been a few break-ins. Lost a couple of paintings a while ago.'

'They were stolen?'

'No. Just vandalised. So the only stuff I leave there is stuff I'm still working on, and I lock that in a cupboard when I leave, and everything I finish I give to Hugo for safekeeping.'

'The paintings you've finished are at Paradise Place?'

He nods. 'In the cellar.'

'But isn't it damp down there?'

'Not at all. It might have been damp once – I have no idea whether it was or not. But he did some major work on it years ago to turn it into a temperature-controlled store for his wine. I'm sure the paintings are fine. He's already bought most of them, anyway. He's not going to let any harm come to his investment.'

'Maybe we can look at them this evening?'

'Not this evening. Hugo keeps the cellar locked because the wine is worth a fortune. He has his main storage place out near Hounslow, but the cellar in the house is where he keeps the really top stuff. So maybe in the next day or so, we can show them to you. But even if it doesn't happen this trip, you'll see them soon enough. The exhibition is next September.'

I don't like the extent to which Hugo seems to have control over every aspect of Ben's life.

A question plants itself in my mind. Did Hugo cultivate Ben, buy his paintings and promote him, only in order to get to me? And if he did, will he discard Ben now that he has found me, punish my son to get revenge on me? Surely not, because that would hurt Marie-Laure too?

The one thing I *am* sure about as Ben eventually parks the car on a single yellow line in Pembridge Crescent and we walk the short distance to Paradise Place is that there won't be any nasty shocks waiting for me in the dark this evening. Hugo is away and Ben and Marie-Laure are beside me. Nevertheless, I still feel a shiver run through me as we turn into the passageway and emerge in front of the house.

Inside, Alice rushes in from the kitchen, where she has been cooking, Arnaud pours drinks and we all sit down.

'We're having something very simple,' Alice tells me. '*Pappardelle* and wild venison *ragù*.'

'It doesn't sound very simple to me,' I say. 'It sounds wonderful.'

'In that case, maybe you'd like to come to the kitchen and we can finish it off together?'

'I'd like that. I've never been adventurous in the cooking department.'

I have a sense that Alice wants to continue talking to me in private, away from her husband and daughter and Ben, so I stand up and follow her.

In the big open-plan kitchen, the table has already been set. I count only five places and feel reassured. Alice talks loudly about the *ragù*, how easy it is to prepare and cook, how the meat will have become incredibly tender after two or three hours of slow cooking. And then she lowers her voice and moves closer to me.

'I know I don't need to say this, but I thought I should. Just in case. What I told you this afternoon, about Hugo . . . Marie-Laure doesn't know and I don't want her to find out. She absolutely adores him. But she loves her father and would be devastated to think that I'd betrayed him, especially with Hugo. It would be a double betrayal. I just – I just don't want her opening that can of worms. It would be too awful. For everyone.'

'Oh, Alice, I wouldn't dream of saying a word to Marie-Laure. Or to anyone. Everything we talked about is between us.'

'Phew!' she says, taking a gulp of wine. 'Thanks. It's not that I thought you'd go straight to Marie-Laure and tell her what I told you, but on the way back here I began to worry that I'd said too much. It's one of my personality faults – I tend to say too much, especially when I've been drinking.'

'Yes,' I say, without really thinking. And then, when a look of embarrassment floods her face, I add, 'What I mean is, don't we all?'

'Not you, obviously,' she says. 'Maybe I should take the pledge and be a teetotaller like you.'

We are both laughing at this when Ben wanders in briefly to take a bottle of wine from the fridge.

'That smells good,' he tells Alice, nodding towards the casserole dish in which the meat is falling gently apart in the rosemary-and-juniper-enriched liquid. As he leaves, he pats my shoulder and my heart soars. I catch Alice's eye and we smile at each other; she has noted Ben's gesture and looks pleased for me.

Later, just as the meal gets under way, Marie-Laure hears her phone ringing in the sitting room and runs to answer it. '*Ah, quelle belle surprise!*' I hear her say. Still speaking animatedly in French, she comes back to the table and holds her phone out towards us.

'It's Hugo!' she says, her face bright with pleasure. 'He

wants to say hello to us all and especially to you, Nan, so that you will start to know him a little bit before the wedding.'

She's holding out the phone and I have no choice but to take it from her. I feel everyone's eyes are on me. How am I going to get through this? What is he going to say? I'm about to lift the phone to my ear when I realise that I can see his face. It's a video call.

I stare at the screen. I'm trying to act normally, as normally as a woman who has to talk to a man she has never met but is looking forward to meeting might act, but I'm not succeeding. I can't speak, can't say a word.

'Nan,' he says eventually, breaking what seems like several minutes of silence. I register the long vowel, the rich honeyed sound of his voice. 'How delightful to meet you at last, albeit, sadly, not in the flesh.'

I know I have to say something but my mouth has gone dry and when I try to speak I end up spluttering and coughing.

Ben takes the phone from me and as I rush away from the table, I hear him say, 'Sorry, Hugo, Mum is having a coughing fit. I'll pass her back to you in a couple of minutes.'

The short loss of breath gives me a bit of time to compose myself. I inhale and exhale, slowing down the thumping beat of my heart. I wonder what the others are thinking. When I return to the table, Ben gives me the phone and I come face to face with Hugo again.

'I can see the resemblance between you and Ben,' he says.

'Perhaps he inherits not only his good looks but also his artistic talent from you?'

'I hardly think so,' I respond. I hear how calm my voice sounds. I see that my hand isn't shaking. But inside I feel as if I am under attack from a thousand knives. My stomach lurches under a wave of nausea. The others look at me as if everything is normal, as if I am normal.

'Ben tells me this is your first visit to London. I hope you're enjoying it and have managed to see some of the sights. You must take a walk along Portobello Road. It starts just a few hundred yards from the house. And there's a lovely old pub nearby that you must visit. It's called The Rising Sun. You must have passed it. It was one of my favourite watering holes in the seventies when I first came to live here.'

'I'm having a lovely time,' I say, still struggling to keep my composure. I feel like a pig on a roasting spit, being turned by Hugo's distant hand. But, suddenly, something changes inside me. I've had enough of being his plaything, of letting him satisfy some warped need to torture me in front of an audience. I need to take control.

'I look forward to meeting you properly,' I say, doing my best to sound firm. 'And now I'm going to hand you back to Marie-Laure.'

I look around the table, anxious about what the others may think or say. But Alice is butting into the conversation now going on between Marie-Laure and Hugo, and Ben and Arnaud are discussing the relative merits of New and Old

World pinot noir. I breathe quietly but heavily. I am coping, but only just. I can't stay here. I have to get away, back to the hotel, where I won't have to make polite conversation as I fall apart.

'I'm so sorry,' I begin, folding my napkin and starting to rise from the chair.

They all look at me in surprise.

'Are you all right?' Marie-Laure asks.

'Not really . . . I'm not feeling very well. I think I should go back to the hotel and get an early night.'

Ben gives me an anxious look and I quickly say I must have the bug that has been doing the rounds at home.

'Maybe you should go upstairs and lie down for a while?' Alice says.

I smile weakly. I'm standing now.

'I think it would be better if I went back.'

'I'll call a cab,' Ben says. 'Will you be all right on your own or do you need one of us to go with you?'

I would love nothing more than for Ben to come with me, but I shake my head and give another weak smile. 'Don't worry. I'll be fine.'

20

Hugo

I should hate her.

Yet when I spoke to her this evening I found myself struggling to feed off the desire for revenge that has sustained me since I came across Ben's portrait of her. I had taken a risk, for I knew that putting her in the position of having to talk to me could expose myself as well as her. And, indeed, when she took the phone from Marie-Laure she looked as if she had been caught in the headlights of an oncoming vehicle. I feared that she might overreact and turn into a trembling wreck, something I did not want as it would have made the others question why I had had such an effect on her. But I confess that I also felt some pity for her, so stark was the look of anguish on her face.

I felt a shimmer of relief – for her sake as well as mine – when she ended the conversation and gave the phone back to Marie-Laure.

For the next minute or so, Marie-Laure chattered away to me. Then Alice took the handset and asked me when I was planning to put in an appearance.

'Where are you anyway?' she asked, a touch of belligerence in her voice. She looked tired, but that could have been down to the quality of the video connection.

'St Ives,' I said.

'Visiting a client, no doubt,' she said.

'Several clients,' I said. 'It's all taking rather longer than I expected. But don't worry – I'll be back well in time for the wedding.'

'You'd better be,' Alice said sourly, at which point Marie-Laure grabbed the phone, thanked me for calling and wished me sweet dreams.

Sweet dreams. I have had many nightmares over the years, but few dreams that I would describe as sweet. Yet I have to acknowledge that I have slept particularly well over the past few days.

Nan has no idea of the lengths to which I have gone in order to bring her to London. She has no idea that I have watched her for a long time, that I have driven to Yorkshire on many occasions, just to see how she lives.

The first time I drove up, not long after discovering the portrait at Lucinda's gallery, I didn't catch sight of her at all, which was disappointing. I was, however, pleased to see that her home, reached by a lane but visible from the road, was a rather attractive grey stone house that sat beautifully in its rural surroundings. I had feared that she might have succumbed to ordinariness. There were no cars outside and after several passes I thought I might take a look around. I peered in through the windows and saw rooms in such a state of orderliness that I could only suppose they were either freakishly tidy or away.

I spent the night in Hebden Bridge and the following morning ambled in to the Browns' garden centre, feigning interest in the various flowers and plants and shrubs but keeping an eye out for Nan and her husband. I knew nothing about him apart from his surname, although I did wonder whether she had taken up again with the boyfriend who had come to the house so long ago and married him. I had to be careful; despite the passage of years, I knew she would recognise me, and I had no intention of presenting myself at that point. But, among the few staff bustling around, there was no sign of Nan.

A buxom woman with a big open face approached me eventually.

'Need any help?'

'I most certainly do,' I said.

I gave her my best smile, the one denoting the affable but slightly helpless male, and launched into the spiel I had prepared.

'My garden, such as it is, faces north and it doesn't get a great deal of sun. I'm afraid rather a lot of plants and flowers have perished under my care. I should be extremely grateful for your advice.'

'North's not so hard when you know what will work,' she said. 'What have you tried?'

'Just about everything over the years. Most recently, I've tried honeysuckle. I really do like the idea of a scented climbing plant. But . . . well, it's time to put the poor thing out of its misery.'

I shrugged helplessly as I said this and she responded with a smile.

She pursed her lips and scrunched her eyes into slits, as if giving deep consideration to my plight. And then she smacked her lips and declared, 'I have the very thing for you.'

I followed her to a shed, outside which several tall plants covered in white, scented flowers stood in big pots.

'*Trachelospermum jasminoides*,' she said smugly, showing off her knowledge. 'Star jasmine to you.'

She proceeded to bore me rigid with the merits of the plant. It liked plenty of sun but could do all right with a bit less than plenty, she said. I listened patiently, trying to appear deeply interested, but after a while I had had enough and cut her off. Politely, of course.

'Well, you've certainly convinced me,' I said. 'I'll take two.'

She took me to a counter and rang up the purchase on the till.

I paid in cash. It was a shame that I was going to have to dump the plants somewhere on the side of the road. Perhaps I would pass a care home on the way and leave them there.

She lifted the plants on to a trolley and as she wheeled it towards my hired Range Rover, I continued to chat.

'Have you had the business for a long time?' I asked. 'Your knowledge is terribly impressive.'

'It's not my business. The owners are away on holiday for two weeks. Luckily it hasn't been too busy.'

'I wonder,' I said, stopping to look back at her as I opened the driver door. 'Do you, by any chance, offer a garden planning service? It occurs to me that, if you do, I should avail myself of it. You see, I also have a large garden at the back of my house, and now that I've talked to you and seen all these wonderful plants, I'm beginning to think I should take more care of it. I'm embarrassed to say that it's a bit of a wilderness at the moment.'

'We do have a planning service, as it happens. All you need to do is make an appointment and we'll set up a visit and tell you what's possible. I can do that for you right now, but it'll have to be for a couple of weeks' time, when they're back.'

I gave her another smile.

'I'm having to travel rather a lot at the moment, and I'm afraid I left my diary at home. But I'll certainly be in touch,' I said, heading for the Range Rover.

'Do you want to leave your name, so I can make a note of you needing a visit?'

'Of course. Yes. It's Edward.' I was tempted to say Edward Martin. That would give Nan something to think about if Sally mentioned my visit to her, but I knew that was a bad idea. I thought quickly of a surname, looking beyond her to the rose section. 'Edward Rose.'

Mission accomplished. I had seen where Nan lived and where she worked. I was excited. What would I do next? I could make an appointment for a visit from Nan and give her the shock of her life when she turned up to talk about flowers and plants at whichever rented address I might provide. I could imagine her as a garden designer, putting her artistic flair to practical use. But what if her husband came instead of her? What would I say to him? I had a great deal of thinking to do, but I had made progress. Of that I was sure.

21

Then

Despite Hugo's pep talk, she hadn't been to the school for a week. She couldn't face it. She couldn't bear to witness at such close quarters the superior talent of the other students. It leaped out at her from their canvases, their sculptures, their drawings, even from the way they talked about art. Her absences began with her skipping the odd class. Then it became most classes, and now she wasn't attending any classes at all.

At the back of her mind was the feeling that she just wasn't good enough and never would be, that everything had been a mistake. But she didn't want to leave London and return to Yorkshire either. If she went home, she would be admitting to everyone – her parents, Chris, those girls in the village she had once been friendly with – that she was a failure. Worst of all, she would be letting Miss Sheringham down.

And there was Chris, or rather the absence of Chris from her life. She hadn't heard a word from him. Several times a day, she sat by the phone, staring at it, willing herself to pick up the receiver and dial the number of his digs in Cirencester, but always stopping short of making the call. What was she going to say to him? That she had made a mistake and realised how important he was to her, that she was miserable and missed him? It was true that she was miserable; she had never been so miserable in her life and it surprised her. It was true, too, that she missed him, which also surprised her. She missed his face, his quiet demeanour. But she knew, deep down, that she hadn't made a mistake and that it would be unfair and dishonest to try to win Chris back, to keep him dangling, when she was still infatuated with Hugo.

The fact that her parents seemed to have no idea that they had split up suggested to her that he hadn't entirely given up on her. Maybe he was staying quiet about the change in their relationship because he thought she would come running back to him. Would she? She didn't know.

She was confused. She had acknowledged that she missed Chris and that she still nurtured some kind of hope that they would get back together. But she also knew that if she did make it up with Chris, he would want her to move out of Paradise Place, and right now she couldn't even think about doing that. She was besotted with Hugo and couldn't bear the thought of never seeing him again. And she was still hoping, in spite of everything common sense told her, that he would fall in love with her.

Her relationship with Eddie, meanwhile, seemed to be getting back on to an even keel. He seemed less resentful of her painfully obvious attraction to Hugo – probably, she thought, because he knew she hadn't a hope in hell of it going anywhere. And she had started to like him again, to enjoy his company. He had made himself available to her almost every afternoon of the previous two weeks.

Sometimes they went for a wander around the area, stopping for a coffee at one of the little cafés on Moscow Road or Queensway, and she noticed that girls looked at him in an appraising way. Sometimes they just sat in her room, where they were now, chatting. She was grateful that he didn't mention Hugo. And, in return, she didn't ask about Olivia.

She talked to him about her loss of confidence in her art.

'You see, if I was a real artist, I wouldn't be feeling like this, would I? I'd just get on with it because I'd believe in myself and I wouldn't care what anyone else thought of me,' she said.

'Everyone's different,' Eddie said. 'Look, I know you're not feeling great about things at the moment, but I don't think you should be skipping classes the way you are. It's a waste. It would be different if you had just a little bit of talent, but you've got so much of it.'

He pointed at a canvas she had propped up against the

wall just inside her bedroom door. 'I mean, look at that iris. I've never seen anyone paint an iris like that.'

'Exactly,' she said with a shrug. 'It's rubbish. It's not even *like* an iris.'

'But that's where you're so wrong, Nan. It's ... it's ... You've made that bloody iris something extraordinary. I can't explain it, but I *know* you're good. You can't give up!'

The energy and passion in his voice made her turn to him. She was aware that she was lifting her head and he was bending his and it was as if neither of them could alter the course of the movement that brought their lips together.

It had been a mistake. Eddie was furious with her and she was furious with herself. But when it came down to it, to taking what they had started all the way, she couldn't go through with it. She squirmed with shame as she remembered every second of their encounter, how they had lain back on her bed, how they had taken each other's clothes off, how they had caressed each other. Until she had gone rigid and told him they had to stop. She remembered the look of confusion on his face that turned to something darker as he disengaged from her and fumbled around for his clothes.

'I'm sorry, Eddie ... it's just that I was with Chris for so long ...'

'But you're not with him any more,' he said angrily. 'You know what I think, Nan? I think you were just using me.

173

You can't have Hugo, so you thought you'd try me after all. Well, you can fuck off. I can't bear the sight of you.'

She turned her face into the pillow and kept it there until she heard Eddie's feet stride heavily across the floorboards and then the sound of the door banging behind him. She lay there for a while, listening for the muffled sounds of Eddie's anger that came in bursts through the wall – thuds and thumps and clatters that told her how much she had hurt him.

She thought about what he had said and reluctantly acknowledged to herself that there was more than a grain of truth in it. She had needed comfort and had turned to Eddie. And Eddie had hit the nail on the head when he said, *You can't have Hugo.*

She thought back to that evening just a few weeks earlier when she had been upset over Chris breaking it off with her and Hugo had been so sweet and kind and had cooked for her. Even then she had known deep down that she didn't have a hope with Hugo, but she had also realised that the extent to which she wanted him was frightening, and that she had to counter it with something. Or someone. Eddie had been the nearest thing to that someone and he had wanted her. And today he had said all the right things, which had made her want him for just that short while. Except that she hadn't really wanted him at all.

I'm a monster, she thought. *I've hurt Chris and now I've hurt Eddie, and I've lost both of them. And for nothing.*

22

Hugo

On my trips to Yorkshire, I discovered that Nan and her husband followed the same routine with little deviation. They drove away from the house together around eight o'clock every morning, and from my lookout position behind a distant tree I was able to observe them through binoculars without being seen.

She looked older, of course, but the combination of several decades and many fine lines had sculpted the country-girl plumpness that I remembered from her cheeks to give her a hint of the kind of beauty that can remain hidden in youth but emerge in age. Most of the time, she wore her hair pulled back into a ponytail or swept back off her forehead under a wide hairband. It wasn't unattractive, but it was nothing like the thick, dark auburn Pre-Raphaelite locks that I remembered, hair that fell loose about her shoulders or sat in a precarious pile on top of her head, looking as if it might tumble down at any moment.

I remembered – I still remember – that night when I reached my hand up and removed the little clasp that had miraculously held her hair up.

How different she looks now, with her short silver hair.

Her husband, who I recognised from the visit he had made to Paradise Place several decades ago, had one of those weathered faces you often see on country people. Given that he probably spent most of his life outdoors, this was hardly a surprise. I would not have described him as particularly handsome, but he looked pleasant enough and I found myself feeling almost sorry for him. I wondered whether he really knew the woman he had married, whether she had told him what she had done.

That question is in my mind now as I accept the glass of red burgundy from Elizabeth, who says she will be back shortly. I am staying at a new boutique hotel in Holland Park, near enough to Paradise Place to enable me to go there quickly and far enough removed from it to be reasonably certain that I will not be seen by Nan or any of the others. It's a comfortable place that will do well. The owners, Elizabeth and Rodney, who have refused to let me pay for the room, are a couple in their late forties who became clients of mine when they opened their first venture a few years ago in Brighton.

I feel restless and impatient, but the endgame is only

days away and I must maintain my concentration. I remind myself that I have been working towards this for a long time; I can deal with my impatience for a few more days. The most difficult part of my – there it is again, that word which isn't quite the correct word – plan, the part that might not have come together, has been accomplished, and since then everything else has fallen into place.

All I have to do is be patient.

23

Then

Ilaria had fallen in love and Nan felt envious, because her friend's romance at least had a chance of going somewhere.

'I didn't sleep at the hostel last night,' Ilaria had announced a week earlier. There was something declamatory about the way she spoke, as if what she would say next demanded a long pause during which her audience – Nan – would wait with baited breath.

Nan had indeed waited, eyebrows raised, eyes wide open.

'I have met my future husband,' Ilaria said, again with a great sense of drama.

She had been walking along Bayswater Road and had overheard him on the first day of his holiday in London trying to ask a woman, in incomprehensible English, how to get to Portobello Road. Hearing his Italian accent, she had looked around and leaped straight in with directions.

'He is very good-looking. Of course, I would have helped

him even if he had not been nice looking. So, I told him I would take him to Portobello, and we walked all the way up to the bridge and he asked me where were all the antique stalls and I told him not in the week. And then we went to a pub and then we went to have dinner and then – well, then we went to his hotel.'

Nan gawped. Was Ilaria really telling her she had spent the night with a man she had met just a couple of hours before?

'And did you . . .?' She left the question unfinished.

'*Certo*. Of course,' Ilaria said, matter-of-factly. 'We did everything.'

'What's his name? What does he do?'

'His name is Matteo and he is a chef. And,' she smiled a big, broad smile, 'he is from Firenze. Like me. He works in the restaurant of his parents. I know this restaurant. It has a very good reputation.'

'Does this mean you won't be able to come to the cinema this evening?' Nan asked, although she reckoned she already knew the answer.

The sides of Ilaria's mouth turned downwards.

'Do you mind? We have such a short time together, just a few more days.'

'No, of course not,' Nan said.

She did mind. She would miss the film, because she didn't want to go to the cinema on her own. But she was unhappy for another reason. Her brain was already thinking ahead. Ilaria was in London to learn English and her English was already excellent. It had to be possible, it was even likely, that Ilaria would end her course early and return to Florence to continue her romance with Matteo.

And now, a week later, Ilaria and Matteo had spent the last night of his week-long holiday together. He was on his way back to Italy and Ilaria had hinted that she might not come back to London after the Christmas break. Nan felt bereft. She knew that, although Ilaria was still going to be around for a while longer, she was losing her best friend in the world.

Partly to console herself, she had begun spending a lot of time in the kitchen at Paradise Place, calculating that she would come across Hugo more often this way. She told Hugo she needed to learn to cook and she hoped he didn't mind her using his kitchen. She would use only ingredients she had bought herself, she assured him.

'Oh, please use whatever you like,' Hugo said, smiling. 'There's loads of stuff in the cupboards that needs to be used. Olive oil, mayonnaise, you name it, it's in there somewhere.'

Nan had never used olive oil in her life. At home, they cooked with lard or dripping or vegetable oil. Olive oil was something her mother occasionally bought in small bottles from the chemist for unblocking waxed-up ears. And they used salad cream, not mayonnaise.

But despite Nan's plan, she saw no more of Hugo than she had previously, and after a couple of weeks she abandoned the kitchen. Hugo gave no indication that he had noticed.

To tackle the guilt she felt at having let Miss Sheringham down, she began making more of an effort to engage properly with her art course and was now going to the school every day. She discovered she liked the printmaking sessions; perhaps that was because they were so practical. Could printmaking be the direction she would take? And if it was, would Miss Sheringham be happy?

24

Hugo

It sounds rather pompous now, even to me, but during my time at Oxford I saw myself as a kind of modern-day Renaissance man, passionate about music, poetry, literature, architecture. And when I came down, I had no intention of pursuing any of the *proper* (my mother's adjective) careers in banking or diplomacy upon which some of my friends were embarking. How that word *career* used to fill me with dread, because I saw it as just another label for a job that would tie me down and eventually bore me to tears, no matter how much I might initially like it.

But my artistic passions, including my failed attempt to become a professional singer, were not providing me with a living and my parents were issuing repeated threats to cut off my allowance. Had it not been for the drastic change in my circumstances forced upon me by Nan's violence, I might have meandered indefinitely among the lower foothills of penury. Indeed, I must admit that to some extent I owe some of my present wealth to what happened to me forty years ago.

I am a rich man now, but when I finally returned to Paradise Place after months in hospital, a stint in a convalescent home and then what seemed like years in Leicestershire in the bosom of my family, I was almost broke. My parents had withdrawn support when I refused even to think about taking on the estate.

My chief, indeed my only, pleasure – despite having been advised to avoid alcohol – came from making my way steadily through my remaining supply of decent wine. Inevitably, this supply dried up and one evening, having finished the last bottle, I took myself to the off-licence down the road to pick up a couple of bottles. It was a deeply uninspiring place, so unlike Berry Brothers, which hitherto had been my main source of fine wine. But, as I was still inclined to fatigue after my ordeal, a trip to St James's was out of the question. In any case, my funds were limited.

So, as I surveyed the harshly lit shelves for something cheap but passable, I found myself thinking about how I would turn that shop into something inviting.

It was then that I began to understand the extent to which the *incident*, as I sometimes refer to what happened, had changed me. Two years earlier, I might have thought for no more than a few moments about how that shop could be improved and then I would have put it out of my mind. But

I became driven, obsessed. Over the next few days, I thought of nothing but going into the wine business. I explored the idea of opening an off-licence. I would need financial backing to deal with the prohibitive up-front costs, so I talked to my bank manager, who found my proposal highly entertaining but rejected it outright. I then approached my father, who told me he wouldn't put a bet on me if I entered an egg-and-spoon race.

It was Caroline who came up with the suggestion that started off my wine business.

'Why don't you do something here?' she said, mildly exasperated after listening to yet another volley of complaints about my father's unwillingness to help me.

'What do you mean, do something here? Are you suggesting I set up a wine stall in front of the house?' I retorted, my voice laden with scorn.

'No, Hugo darling,' she said. She spoke gently, but I sensed the hurt in her voice.

Caroline had learned to tread on eggshells around me in the aftermath of my trauma, and it seemed that nothing I dished out, regardless of how rude or even cruel, could faze her. In fact, I credit her for turning me into a human being again. But I digress. She had made a suggestion and I had responded discourteously.

'Sorry, Caroline,' I said. 'I'm being a beast. Go on, then. Tell me.'

'You may think this is a silly idea, but what about buying

a few cases of very good wine – at a discount, of course – and then selling it in single bottles to your friends. You would pass on some of the discount, but only a tiny bit, and you'd make a small profit. And you could put that profit back into buying more wine. Little acorns, and all that.'

I could see all sorts of obstacles, a very obvious one being the question of whether I had a hope of persuading my friends to fork out the money for good wine when they could continue to get pissed on basic plonk.

Again, Caroline had the answer. 'Hugo, they're all starting to settle down, getting married, buying flats and houses in Kilburn and Clapham and Balham and having dinner parties and babies. Because that's what you do when you've grown up and you don't get pissed for the sake of it any more. They're ready to move beyond the cheap rubbish. They're ripe for—'

'Exploitation?' I offered with a cynical laugh.

'No! The word I was about to come out with is *education*,' she said. 'Seriously, I think this might work. No one in our set knows more about wine than you. And I'm sure everyone would want to support you by buying a few bottles regularly.'

'You've forgotten one crucial thing, my darling Caroline. Where am I going to get the money to stock up on a few cases? My father has pretty much told me to bugger off.'

Caroline smiled and opened her handbag, from which she extracted her Coutts chequebook and a fountain pen.

'You can pay me back when you get things going,' she said.

Each time I look back at that moment, I really do ask myself whether I made a grave error in not marrying Caroline. She was beautiful, kind and clever. She was an angel. Had it not been for her, I might not be in the position I now enjoy.

She was right about everything. With her money, I bought several cases of wine directly from wholesalers, sold them to friends and bought more cases. After a while, I was selling to friends of friends and making money. Eventually, I began to deal directly with vineyards. Over the decades I have built a reputation as a knowledgeable and reliable supplier.

Today, I am a rich man. I can have, within reason, whatever I desire. *Within reason* are the key words in this context, however, and for so many years the one thing I desired was not available to me. Revenge. Now it is, although I must admit to myself that I am not quite certain as to how I should proceed.

25

Then

It was 17 December and Christmas was just a week away, but the weather was ridiculously mild. Nan hadn't seen her parents since the end of the summer, and although her first term had finished she was still in London, finding one excuse after another to explain to them why she hadn't immediately dashed back up to Yorkshire.

One reason had been her break-up with Chris. Her parents appeared to be unaware of it still, but they would expect to see him over Christmas and New Year and would start asking questions if they didn't. She hadn't yet worked out a story for them.

Another reason had been Ilaria, who had now definitely decided that she didn't want to spend any more time apart from Matteo and would not return to London after Christmas; Nan wanted to spend as much time as possible with her friend. But that reason would disappear the following day, when Ilaria would fly to Italy.

Nan wasn't quite sure what she was waiting for. Sometimes she allowed herself to fantasise about a time in the not-too-distant future when Hugo would suddenly understand that he had merely been filling in time and that, really, he had loved her all along.

She created different versions of how he would come to this conclusion. In one version, he fell ill suddenly and she nursed him back to health. In another, she went back to Yorkshire for the Christmas holidays and on New Year's Eve there was a knock on the door and she went to open it and there he was, telling her that her absence had made him realise he couldn't be without her. It was childish, fairytale stuff, she knew, but she indulged in it anyway.

In any case, the painful truth was that the likelihood of anything happening between her and Hugo was tiny. The steady stream of girlfriends staying overnight in the house had made that clear. She just had to accept it. And yet . . .

She hadn't got over her crush on him. She speculated that all the girls he brought back, some of them more regularly than others, were some kind of distraction for him. In a funny way, she had been relieved to discover that Caroline wasn't the only girl he was sleeping with. If he had all these other girls, he couldn't possibly be in love with Caroline. Or with any of them. Ilaria said Hugo was a Casanova, but Nan couldn't accept that. He just hadn't met the right girl.

She knew some of them by name. There was Caroline, of course. Philippa, Harriet and Isabel also turned up regularly. Others came and went without making an impression. But all of Hugo's girls had one thing in common: they were beautiful and they were blonde and they looked like models. Caroline had aspirations in that direction, but Nan had heard Hugo tell her that models tended to be in their teens and that at twenty-two she was far too old to dream of a catwalk career.

Nan wondered whether Caroline, who was the most regular of the regulars, knew about the others. She tried not to address any of them by name for fear of coming out with the wrong one and stirring up trouble.

After the unfortunate episode in her room, Eddie avoided her for a while, walking out of the kitchen if she came in when he was there alone, or quietly ignoring her if he was chatting to Hugo. Now, though, he seemed to be more like his old self, the Eddie she had first known, and she was glad about that because she hated the feeling of having hurt him and of having lost his friendship. But while she felt that things were on a more even keel with Eddie, she knew the friendship was still fragile and had some way to go before it recovered completely. She wasn't sure it ever would.

Now she and Ilaria were at The Rising Sun for what would be their final outing for a long time, perhaps for ever. She felt sad. Maybe she would go home tomorrow, after all; she had already bought an open return ticket for the train and could make up her mind at the last minute.

Nan loved Christmas, loved the gaudy decorations and the warmth and the colours of it, the reds and the greens and the golds, and all of that was here at the pub. Someone, a big man with a Santa Claus hat and false white beard, broke into an impromptu rendition of 'O Come, All Ye Faithful', and everyone joined in, including Nan who became bolder in her singing with each verse until people turned to look at her and smile and cheer her on.

Eddie was somewhere behind the bar, but she hardly saw him all evening, so big and deep was the crowd. At ten o'clock, Ilaria looked at her watch and told Nan she had to go back to the hostel to pack for her flight the following morning. Ilaria was excited at the thought of seeing Matteo again.

'I think I'll go now too,' Nan said, not wanting to stay in the pub on her own, although she had had plenty of glances from the crowd that suggested she wouldn't be alone too long if she chose not to leave with Ilaria.

She walked with Ilaria to the hostel and they hugged for a long time.

'I'll miss you,' Nan said, bursting into tears.

'You will come to visit me at Easter,' Ilaria said. 'And, Nan, please don't waste your heart and your life on Hugo. He is not for you. Will you promise me?'

'I promise,' Nan said, wiping her tears on her sleeve. 'Well, I'll try, anyway.'

She walked back to Paradise Place. As she emerged from

the passageway, she saw that the house was lit up, which meant that Hugo must be there: she remembered switching off all the lights when she'd left earlier. He had probably brought a girl home and she steeled herself for the quietest possible entry into the house and up the stairs – which wouldn't be easy, given her inebriated state. She let herself in, clumsily and noisily, and, realising that the fire was blazing in the front room, moved quickly on tiptoe across the tiled hallway. Just as she put her foot on the bottom stair, Hugo came out of the room.

'Oh, Nan. I heard some odd sounds and thought there might be a burglar. I'm relieved to see that it's only you,' he said.

Only you. She couldn't help but grimace. *Only you.* Those two words said everything he thought about her.

'Are you all right?' he asked, clearly having noted the expression on her face. 'Has anything happened?'

'I'm fine. It's just . . . I'm just a bit tired. I'm going up to bed.'

'But it's Christmas!' he exclaimed. 'You can't go to bed so early. Come and have a drink with me. You can tell me what's been going on in your life. We never seem to be here at the same time.'

We do, actually, but you've always got some girl around.

But she didn't say that. She took her foot off the stair and smiled. 'Okay,' she said, and as she walked into the room and saw that there was no one else there she couldn't help but feel elated and hopeful, even a little excited.

191

They sat facing each other across the room, the liquid in their glasses sparkling in the firelight. Hugo had opened a bottle of champagne, a drink she had tasted only once or twice in her life. At home, they drank Babycham at Christmas and birthdays. Her father drank beer. Her mother liked the occasional glass of sherry. Until her move to London, Nan had rarely touched alcohol.

'How's it going at Byam Shaw?' he asked.

'It's fine. I'm glad I didn't give up completely. I skipped a few weeks but . . .'

'But you're back on track? Good!'

She shrugged, not quite sure what to say next. She was almost struck dumb, sitting alone with him like this. She wished she could impress him with a witty flow of conversation. She was worried that she was staring at him in adoration and that he would think she was an imbecile. And then he asked her more questions, as if he really was interested in her life. He asked her about her family, how they would spend Christmas, what she missed about home, whether she thought she would like to return to Yorkshire when she had finished her course.

He asked her about Chris, whether she had heard from him or seen him, although he referred to him not by name but as her boyfriend.

'No. That's over,' she said emphatically. She didn't want to talk about Chris.

'Hugo, have you ever had a job?'

It was a clumsy attempt to move the conversation away from herself, and she quickly apologised.

'Sorry. I've had a bit to drink. It's none of my business.'

Hugo smiled. 'No, I've never worked. I'm not proud of that, actually, but I haven't quite decided what to do with my life. Teaching Latin and Greek is an option but not a very attractive one. My mother would like me to start learning how to run the estate before my father croaks, so I suppose I may have to move back to Leicestershire at some point. And I dare say that once I do that, my mother will have lined up a few potential wives. But I have no intention of doing anything like that in the immediate future.'

A mixture of elation and gloom hit her, but she tried not to show it.

'Caroline is very nice,' she ventured.

'Caroline is an absolute angel. And my parents see her as the ideal brood mare.'

'So it's all settled,' she said. 'You and Caroline will get married and you'll go back to Leicestershire and live on your estate.'

'Steady on! I'm only twenty-three, hardly ready to get married and settle down.'

That cheered her up a bit. And then the other question she had been longing to ask was forming in her head. 'Hugo,' she began, relishing the feel of his name on her tongue, 'the girl who had my room before – Olivia. Were you . . .?'

'Was I what?'

'Were you and she . . .?'

'What?'

'Were you involved?'

'God, no. Why do you ask?'

'I just wondered why she moved out. I mean, it's a very nice room. And the house is wonderful and the rent is cheap. I thought . . .'

'You should ask Eddie why she moved out. He knew her better than I did.'

'I *have* asked him. But he gets cross when I do so I've given up. Anyway, *he* told me I should ask *you*.'

Hugo didn't respond immediately. He spent a couple of seconds looking at the champagne in his glass. When he did speak, the expression on his face said, *I shouldn't really be telling you this*.

'It's not a big deal, really. Eddie had a bit of a thing for her and she didn't reciprocate. So she left.' He shrugged and gave Nan a wide smile, but his lips were closed. It wasn't a real smile. She had a feeling he wasn't telling her everything.

'Did she come here through you or through Eddie?'

'Through Eddie. He knew her from the pub and she was looking for a room.'

Something wasn't quite right. She remembered Eddie having told her that Olivia had already been living in the house when he moved in. But who was lying, Eddie or Hugo?

'And . . . did anything . . . bad . . . happen?'

'Bad? Good God, no. They had a bit of a thing going

194

but Eddie took it more seriously than Olivia did. He can be a bit intense, our Eddie, but he's pretty harmless. He's told you, of course, that his uncle was a gardener at my boarding school?'

'No, he hasn't,' Nan said. She thought about this for a moment. 'Does that mean you and he knew each other then?'

'We didn't exactly know each other, but when he came here to see the room he recognised me and then I recognised him.'

'So you were friends?'

'Well, no. We weren't friends. Eddie sometimes helped his uncle in the gardens.'

She wondered why Eddie hadn't told her this. Maybe it hadn't occurred to him. More likely, though, was that Eddie didn't want her to know he had been the village boy helping his uncle in the gardens of a school he could never have aspired to.

And she understood now, more than ever, that Hugo was well beyond her reach. Because Hugo himself was effectively saying that the son of an upper-class landowner couldn't be friends with the nephew of a gardener. She needed to move the conversation away from Eddie and Hugo and their contrasting origins back to Olivia. She still wasn't entirely convinced that there hadn't been something between Hugo and the girl who had lived in her room. He seemed too cagey.

'Where is Olivia now?'

'I have no idea. South London somewhere. Don't tell Eddie

I told you any of that, by the way. Now, let me get you some more champagne.'

Hugo got up and refilled her glass from the bottle of champagne, which he had left in an ice bucket on a small table. But this time, instead of returning to his sofa, he sat down beside her. She told him how sad she felt that Ilaria was going back to Italy for good, how lonely she was going to feel without her closest friend. Hugo listened, his eyes soft and full of sympathy.

And, as she continued to unburden herself to him, she realised that he had put his finger on her wrist and was moving it ever so gently up and down her arm so that it felt like the softest breeze on the fine down of her skin. She didn't know how to respond, so she kept talking and talking, to the point where she wasn't quite sure whether anything she was saying made the tiniest bit of sense. And then she wasn't able to talk nonsense any more, because Hugo had bent his head towards her and his mouth was on hers, and everything she had wanted for so long was happening at last.

26

Now

Back at the hotel, I stand by the window, staring out over the water, not knowing what to make of Hugo's sudden manifestations. What will he do next?

I should probably try to sleep but it's only nine thirty and my nerves are so on edge that I know I'll be lucky to get any rest at all tonight. I look towards the minibar, tempted by what lies inside it. I haven't even opened it to take out a bottle of water since I arrived, instead ordering large bottles of water from room service. I haven't touched a drop of alcohol in forty years, not even at my wedding. There have been times when I've longed for a glass of wine, or even just a thimbleful of port or brandy, but I've always been able to resist the temptation, knowing that one sip would be dangerous. I'm having to fight hard now not to open that little door, because I'm so tense that every part of me aches and I'm thinking that one little calming glass of brandy, one tiny sip, would help me to relax, would help me to forget.

Drink befuddles the memory, and, yes, I had been drinking that night.

We had all been drinking, all three of us, because Eddie turned up from his shift at the pub and joined us. Hugo and I were still wrapped around each other on the sofa when Eddie came in. It was all innocent enough. We were still fully clothed and I don't think I was really expecting things to go any further. My head was too full of wonder that Hugo was kissing me at last, that his arms were around me, his hands moving around my body. When I heard Eddie's key turn in the door, I pulled away from Hugo, but not in time to prevent Eddie, who had walked into the room, from seeing how close we were on the sofa, how dishevelled were my hair and clothes, my midi skirt riding up my thighs. I couldn't read the expression on his face but he must have been embarrassed because he began to back out of the room.

I was mortified, but Hugo was unfazed.

'Eddie,' he called out. 'Come and join us. Have a drink.'

As Eddie moved forward again, I looked away, embarrassed, trying surreptitiously to button up my shirt to hide the fact that my bra was exposed. I didn't want Eddie seeing me like this. I didn't want his eyes on my breasts, but I knew he was staring at them. I prayed that he would go to his room and stay there. But he came back, poured himself a glass of wine – by now, Hugo and I had gone through at least two bottles of champagne and had moved on to red wine – and sat down on the sofa opposite. I had managed to edge my way to the end of the sofa, as far from Hugo as it was possible to be without getting up, and was trying to act nonchalantly. Eddie's face was different now, no longer dark crimson. It was as if he too had made a big effort to act as if nothing had happened.

'Remind me what you're doing for Christmas, Eddie,' Hugo said. 'Going back home to Norfolk?'

Eddie shook his head. 'No. I'll be working all over Christmas. I'll be here. I suppose you'll be going up to Leices-tershire?'

Hugo rolled his eyes.

'Of course. No choice. It wouldn't even enter my head to stay away. My mother would have a fit if I didn't show up for Christmas.'

'You'll be seeing plenty of Caroline, I suppose,' Eddie said.

As he spoke, he had a smirk on his face. He didn't look directly at me, but I knew he meant that remark for me. He was reminding me that I was just another girl as far as Hugo was concerned and that he and Caroline, with their family connections, would always find their way back to each other.

My embarrassment gave way to anger and jealousy – anger that my supposed friend was doing everything he could to upset me, jealousy that raged through me as I thought of Hugo and Caroline together at Christmas. I wished fervently that Eddie would go up to bed and leave us. But, as if he could read my thoughts, Eddie seemed to have decided he was going nowhere. He stayed stubbornly on the sofa and, before long, Hugo was opening yet another bottle of wine.

Emboldened by the alcohol and wanting to get rid of Eddie, I moved back towards Hugo. I sat so close to him that I was virtually on top of him. Almost absentmindedly, he put his hand on my knee and left it there. But that was all he did. I glared at Eddie. He smiled back and seemed to settle deeper into the sofa. His smile said he was glad he had ruined my evening.

I don't remember how many bottles of wine we drank that night. I became sleepier and sleepier and, eventually, I lost the battle with my eyelids, which were determined to close. I don't know how long I slept. When I woke, I was stretched out on the sofa. Someone – it must have been Hugo – had placed a plaid blanket over me. The room was dark, except for the dimmest firelight. Still half-asleep, and still horribly drunk, I tried to focus my eyes. I looked across to where Eddie had been sitting on the opposite sofa. He wasn't there any more. He had finally gone to bed. And then, hearing a sound, I moved my head slightly in the direction of the fireplace, where a figure was bent over the grate, stoking the dead coals with a poker.

Hugo.

I heard myself murmur his name and I closed my eyes, willing him to come back. Inside me, I felt the fire stirring again.

I felt him come to the sofa and kiss the top of my head. I moaned, my eyes still closed. Then he kissed my forehead. And then he kissed my mouth. I put my arms around his neck and drew him down towards me. I was feeling everything I had never felt with Chris, wanting what I had never wanted from Chris.

I shake now, thinking about it. Things might have turned out differently if Eddie had gone to his room and hadn't come back downstairs. But he did come back downstairs. And each time I reach involuntarily back into my memory I see it all happening again. And I close my eyes, and I clench my fist and tense every muscle in my body, because that's how I shut off that terrifying parade of images. But each time it happens, my ability to stop the parade in its tracks becomes weaker and pieces of memory push their way forward. I am afraid. Ben wants me to tell him everything, but how can I when I can't even tell myself?

27

Hugo

It's a strange thing to die and then come to life again. Of course, I did not really die. When I opened my eyes I knew something big, something traumatic, had happened but I didn't know what. The pain in my head threatened to send me back into blackness and for several seconds I struggled against it. Then I remembered that there had been some kind of fight – Eddie, Nan, me, all three of us tangled violently together. Nan screaming. But that was the limit of what I could remember then. Later, strange and jagged memories like jigsaw pieces came back to me one by one, leaving me confused and distraught. And then one day, I realised that I was beginning to put all the pieces together. But that was a long time later, and when I think back to that night, the strongest feeling I have is of pain and utter helplessness.

I touched my head and felt I was going to be sick. Every time I tried to move, nausea swept over me. And then I looked at my hands, wet and sticky with blood. I closed my eyes and lay still for a long time. It was the only way to dispel the nausea. And while I lay, my brain seemed to be encased in a dark cloud, a fog of nothingness. It was as if I no longer existed, and yet I could feel the floor. It was as if my spine and every one of my limbs had been stretched and flattened and I was now no more than a shape without any depth to it, a scattering of crushed skin and bone and ligament.

Eventually I opened my eyes again and spent a few minutes adjusting to the darkness that was diluted by light from the hall that snaked in through a gap between the door and the frame. After a while, and after several attempts, I succeeded in dragging myself off the floor and on to the sofa. It was then that I saw the poker lying just a couple of feet away from where I had lain. It was caked in blood. My field of vision widened and I saw pools of dark, viscous liquid on the carpet. Everything began to come back to me then in painful, ugly detail.

It took me two days – at least, I think it was two days – to clean up. I scrubbed the poker with steel wool drenched in bleach and restored it to its position by the fireplace. The carpet was ruined, so I cut out the bloodstained sections and threw them into the bin. What was left I rolled up and threw down the steps into the cellar. I would deal with it – I would deal with everything – another time.

I had just locked the cellar door when I began to realise that something was badly wrong with my head. I still do not know how long it took me to get myself to the Casualty department at St Mary's in Paddington. Time moved into a different mode and I was unable to measure it in any normal way. I staggered along the passageway on to Pembridge Road, where I saw the yellow light of a taxi glowing in the near distance. At the hospital, I said I had been attacked outside my house a couple of days earlier and had thought I was recovering but that I had suddenly begun to feel strange. The hospital summoned the police and I repeated the story: *I was standing outside my front door, taking my keys from my pocket. Someone hit me from behind. I didn't see my attacker, but I think he might have followed me when I turned into the passageway from Pembridge Road. I think I may have been unconscious for a few minutes. When I came to, I discovered that £200 had been removed from my wallet. Whoever attacked me didn't go into my house.*

I didn't mention either Eddie or Nan.

I was admitted to the hospital for observation. I had concussion, I was told. It was important to ensure that I did not develop complications as a result of my head injury. With a bit of luck, one of the doctors said jovially, I would be discharged in a couple of days. In the event, I remained in hospital for rather longer than a couple of days, for the injury to my head had caused blood to build up between my skull and the surface of my brain – a subdural haematoma, which had to be removed.

The operation I underwent was called a craniotomy. The surgeon removed some bone from my skull in order to expose my brain and suck out the haematoma. He then replaced the bone. It sounds simple and straightforward, but it was not. It was crude. I now have a metal plate holding my skull together. My recovery took the best part of two years, during which time I struggled to believe that I could return to a normal life. My powers of concentration diminished; indeed, I could barely read a few lines of text from a book or newspaper. I was so weak that I wondered whether I would ever again be capable of walking more than a few yards.

Despite my despair, I did recover. I spent some time in a convalescent home, for which my parents forked out the substantial fees. This was followed by several months at home in Leicestershire, during which time I became almost comatose with boredom. By the time I returned to Paradise Place, I was more or less myself again and impatient to make up for the two years of my life that had been taken from me. But, as a direct result of what Nan did to me, I am subject to occasional epileptic seizures and remain at risk of a number of unpleasant things, including stroke, heart attack, even another haematoma. The list is long. I do not let these risks influence the way I live my life. Indeed, I defy them by living my life to the full. I play tennis. I swim. If I die, I die.

But before I die, whenever that is going to be, I want to bring the past forty years, during which time Nan has rarely been out of my mind, to a resolution.

28

Then

She stared at her hands, stopping under streetlights every so often to examine them. What did she expect, rivulets of blood dripping from her fingers? But there was no blood. Maybe she had washed her hands, changed her clothes, but she couldn't remember having done either. Maybe it hadn't happened. Maybe nothing had happened at all. She was still drunk, or in the middle of a nightmare in which she was imagining that she had killed someone. That had to be it. She was having a vivid nightmare and she wasn't really walking through London's dark streets, trying to find her way to King's Cross on foot because the tube had long shut down for the night and she couldn't make head nor tail of the night buses. But the late-night sirens blasting out from speeding police cars and ambulances were too loud and too real. Every time a police car passed, she tried to shrink into herself, convinced it was looking for her.

She made it to King's Cross eventually. No one had stopped her. No one had looked at her. She was just another piece of the human detritus that moved around through the night, mostly unnoticed, only occasionally coming into relief under the harsh light of a street lamp.

In spite of the late hour, the area around the station was busy. But, gradually, the number of people wandering around became smaller and smaller until the only ones remaining were the drunks and the dropouts.

She was exhausted, desperate for sleep, but her mind was frantic, replaying the nightmare over and over in her head, compelling her to relive every second of it. At the same time she tried to convince herself that she was in the middle of a nervous collapse; she was imagining something that wasn't and couldn't be real. Frequently, she gave an involuntary moan, a low sound that seemed to come all the way up from her belly and lodge in her throat, where it reverberated before escaping, diminished, into the cold air in front of her. And in the replaying of the nightmare and the groans, she checked her bag frantically to make sure she still had her ticket.

Only when she boarded the first train of the day for Leeds and sank into a seat did her eyes finally close. But even as she gave herself up to oblivion, she knew that the respite would be short.

She found a public telephone at Leeds station and called her father, telling him she would take the next train to

Hebden Bridge, from where he could collect her and take her home. She made a superhuman effort to sound like her normal self but knew she had failed when her father told her to stay where she was and he would drive to Leeds to fetch her.

When her father saw her, he took his coat off, wrapped it around her. He held her so tightly that she felt she was going to break in two, but she didn't want him to take his arms away, because as long as they were around her, crushing her, she felt safe.

'You're freezing, lass,' she heard him say. 'Why aren't you wearing a coat?'

She hadn't noticed until now that she was wearing just a pair of jeans and a jumper. Hadn't she been wearing different clothes the night before? An image of the skirt and the thin blouse flashed across her memory and then faded. Maybe she had left her coat on the train. Maybe she hadn't taken it with her when she ran from the house. Her father asked the question again. She shrugged. She couldn't feel anything, not even the cold.

Her father didn't ask her any more questions but took her to the station café where he made her drink a cup of milky, sugary tea. He tried to coax her to eat something. Scrambled eggs on toast? Just toast, even? But she shook her head, her stomach heaving at the thought of food. And then they were in the Morris Traveller and her father told her to try to sleep. She closed her eyes and kept them shut all the way home but didn't sleep. She felt that his eyes were often on her, worried, puzzled.

Her mother fussed and fretted and Nan retreated into herself. 'I just want to go to bed,' she mumbled, over and over again.

She went to bed and stayed there. For how long she didn't know. She kept replaying the nightmare in her head and sometimes her groans turned into screams that brought her mother running upstairs. And then the doctor visited and the nightmare stopped. She didn't like the fog in her head but it was better than the nightmare. Chris came sometimes and sat by the bed. She let him hold her hand and she made an effort to listen to what he had to say. But she couldn't concentrate; she just let his voice wash over her. She found it comforting, the sound of his voice saying words that had no meaning for her. She didn't speak, because she had nothing to say. She didn't have plans. She couldn't see a future beyond the walls of her room. Perhaps she would stay in her bed for ever.

And then, one day, her parents bundled her into the back of the Morris Traveller and took her on a journey. She didn't ask where they were going and they didn't tell her, but she had a feeling she wouldn't be coming back for a while because they had packed some things of hers into a case and put it into the back seat beside her.

She spent the journey looking out of the window but the rain had turned everything into a grey blur so that she didn't recognise any landmarks. Not that she cared. She was beyond caring. When the car finally came to a stop, the rain was still falling. People – she wasn't sure how many – came to the car and her parents got out, leaving her inside on the back seat.

The people talked quietly to her parents and then they helped her out of the car and towards the big grey house. She didn't look back at her parents. Only when she heard the noise of the car starting up and the sound its wheels made on the gravel did she understand that they were leaving. But she still didn't look back. There was no point in trying to make sense of where she was and why. There had been a past she wanted to forget. There was no future. The present was about understanding that the dreams she had once had were over. Finished. Just like her.

29

Now

My thoughts are interrupted by the room telephone. I pick it up nervously.

'Mrs Brown, we have a delivery of flowers for you. May we send them to your room?'

'Flowers?'

I'm not expecting flowers. Who can be sending me flowers so late in the evening? Do florists deliver late at night? Maybe in London they do. My heart beats slightly faster as I wonder whether the flowers are from Ben. My stomach gives a twist at the thought that they could be from Hugo.

A few minutes later, the porter arrives at my room with an enormous bouquet of red roses. They are beautiful, but the tall velvety stems have no scent. Nervously I take the small envelope and pull out the card that will tell me who has sent me the flowers. But when I read the message I recoil.

How wonderful you looked this evening. We will meet properly soon.

There's no signature, but I know the flowers are from Hugo.

'Would you like me to put them in a vase?' the porter asks.

'No, no . . . thank you.'

I give him a tip. Then, when he pulls the door behind him, I hurl the bouquet across the room, as far away from me as possible. But when it finally hits the floor, the roses are facing me. Once, red roses meant something good, something fine. Now Hugo has made them ugly and base.

I sit on the bed and stare at the broken flowers, remembering another time I was given red roses, contrasting my feelings then with what I feel now. But maybe my memories, even the ones I want to remember, are not to be trusted.

I have only impressions of that time in the hospital, impressions of a life behind a dark curtain that was too heavy to lift. People emerged sometimes from the shadows, stayed a little while and then faded back into the dimness. I don't remember the precise point at which the curtains lifted, but when they did Chris was there, waiting to welcome me back.

We had an understanding that we wouldn't tell Ben I had once spent time in London, that something bad had happened. Talking about London, even thinking about it, would have opened a door that had been kept locked. I told Chris I wouldn't be able to cope with the opening of that door. It was in Ben's interests, I argued, that the door should remain closed and that the only way to keep it firmly shut was to say nothing for as long as possible, preferably for ever. Chris reluctantly agreed. Our pact extended beyond Ben; we didn't talk to our parents about it, or, most of the time, even to each other.

There were some difficult times. For his twelfth birthday, Ben begged for a trip to London. Such an innocuous wish, but I couldn't deal with it. I told him as calmly as I could that we would think about it but that it might not be possible to get away from work to go all the way to London. And then, upstairs in our bedroom, I crawled beneath the covers and had quiet hysterics. Chris came to the rescue. We would book a trip to London and then, at the last minute, I would feign illness and Chris and Ben would go to London without me.

'I wish you were coming, Mum,' Ben said when he came to see me to say goodbye. He was so excited that a tiny part of me wished I was going with them.

When they came back, he was full of what he and his father had seen and done – Buckingham Palace, the Tower, the Natural History Museum, the National Gallery, the riverboat trip.

'I'm going to live in London when I grow up!' he declared. And he looked so happy that I somehow managed to keep a grip on myself and give him the biggest smile I was capable of.

That night, when dinner was finished and Ben was fast

asleep in bed, Chris sat me down by the fire with a mug of Horlicks. He poured himself a glass of whiskey, which was unusual for him as he rarely drank spirits, preferring beer. I thought we were just having a quiet drink before bedtime in the glow of the flames. The trip had been a success but it was over and done with. Life was back to normal.

'I love evenings like this,' I said, curled up in the big armchair, my hands cupping the mug. 'Ben safe and sound in bed. You and me by the fire. All's right with the world.'

But the way Chris looked at me told me things were not all right with the world. Or, at least, not with him.

'Don't you want to hear how the trip went?' he asked.

'But I know how it went,' I said, my voice unnaturally bright. 'Ben told me. He talked about nothing else all evening.'

'I have a perspective on it too. Don't you want to hear what it was like for me?'

I shook my head and put my hands over my ears.

'No! I don't! I don't want to hear any more about it! Can't you understand?'

I stood up and began to walk out of the room. Chris followed me, took my hand and drew me towards him.

'All right, all right,' he said in a soothing whisper, and I allowed my head to rest against his shoulder. 'We won't talk about it. But some day we're going to have to. We can't run from this for ever. We have to tell Ben.'

I stared at him and pulled away. 'You're wrong, Chris. We don't have to talk about it and we're not going to. Not ever.

You agreed. And we're not going to tell Ben what happened. He doesn't need to know.'

Chris didn't answer. It was *my* past. He couldn't make me talk about it. He had no rights over me.

After that, things were quiet for years. By the time Ben left for university, I had already become inured to the likelihood that he would end up in London. He had had offers from Edinburgh and Cambridge but had opted for Architecture at University College London. Chris drove him down to London. I couldn't face it and chose to stay at home.

'I'd rather say goodbye here,' I told Ben. 'Do you mind? I can't bear to go all the way down to London and then have to . . .'

'It's fine, Mum,' he said, giving me a big hug. 'I wouldn't want you to embarrass me with your wailing.'

We both laughed, and then I teased him about how I would still be able to embarrass him with the food parcels I would send him, the terrible jumpers and scarves and socks I would knit for him.

As I waved them goodbye, the tears that had stung my eyes became a waterfall, because I wasn't only watching my son disappear from my sight, I was also looking back into the past, seeing myself wave goodbye to my mother and my home, unaware then of the pain that lay in store for me.

I walk across the room to where the roses lie, still in their cellophane wrapping, and crush them with my foot.

30

Then

Chris gave her red roses when Ben was born. She still had them, dried and hanging upside down in their bedroom at home.

It was as if London had never happened, as if those months in the hospital had been a kind of slow-motion dream of which she could recall only a few blurred and hazy images. She had recovered well from her breakdown and her parents and Chris no longer hovered over her with the same level of anxiety. She should never have left Yorkshire. London had been an aberration, a mistake that had been corrected. She and Chris were married now and their marriage was everything it should be. Chris was a perfect husband, kind and loving. And he was a perfect father too, because now they had a beautiful baby boy.

She had fallen in love with the baby the moment she held him. She had had a difficult pregnancy and hadn't expected to be so overwhelmed with love for the little boy who lay so peacefully in her arms. When the nurse asked her whether they had chosen a name for him, she exchanged a glance with Chris, smiled at the nurse and said, 'Benedict. It means Gift of God.'

She couldn't stop smiling at her good fortune.

By the time they took the baby home, he had become Ben. He was such a good baby, almost saintly as he somehow slept through much of the night. She loved the way Chris doted on the little boy, loved being a father. He talked about taking him to football matches when he was old enough. And he talked about having another baby; maybe, if they were lucky, a little girl.

There were no more babies. They had tests, but the tests came up with no obvious reason as to why she wasn't conceiving and the doctors suggested that she and Chris try to be less anxious about it and let nature take its course. But nature didn't oblige. She was disappointed, Chris even more so. But they had Ben and they had each other, and at some point they accepted the likelihood that there would be no little sister or brother for Ben. God had given them Ben and Ben was enough.

She was surprised when Ben started to show a talent for art that she had neither expected nor encouraged.

She couldn't help herself; she worried about this. Something inside her, something like a wriggling little worm in her stomach, kept warning her that no good could come of it. When Ben presented her with remarkably good drawings of people and animals, houses and cars and trees, the over-riding emotion she felt was fear.

'You can't keep torturing yourself like this,' Chris told her. 'Kids love drawing things. It's just that Ben is better at it than most of them, which isn't surprising, because he takes after you. It's not a tragedy. He's not going to come to any harm just because he's good at drawing. He'll move on to Meccano and then it will be football. I know how this is bringing all that bad stuff back to you, but nothing is going to happen.'

So she tried to convince herself that Chris was right and she largely succeeded. Children liked to draw and paint; it was hardly surprising that Ben had inherited some talent from her. And it hadn't been her love of art and her desire to be an artist that had torn her life apart but something else, something that wouldn't happen to Ben.

Over time, Ben developed interests in other things. He was good at football and running. He was academically bright, too, and Nan started to nurture hopes of him going to one of the top universities and emerging with the kind of degree that would help him conquer the world. But he didn't stop drawing and painting. At the age of thirteen, he entered a regional competition and won first prize in his age group. At fifteen, he won the overall competition, beating seasoned adult painters.

When it was time to think about A levels and what he

wanted to do in the future, he told her he wanted to go to art college. She tried to dissuade him. He wouldn't make a living from art, she told him. Why didn't he think about architecture? Then he could put his drawing skills to work and make a living at the same time, a very good living. He was stubborn for a long time, and she was reminded of her own stubbornness when she had been Ben's age, her refusal to consider anything but art college. She had no choice but to give in. The direction in which Ben's future lay was all too clear.

And then the miracle happened. She was right, he told her one day. He wasn't sure he had enough talent to be a full-time artist. Instead, he would go for architecture and paint in his spare time. Nan gave thanks to God.

31

Now

It's one o'clock in the morning and I'm lying awake in the dark. Suddenly, I hear the sound of something being pushed under the door of my room. I turn on the light, leap out of bed and see the envelope. I tear it open and extract a single sheet of paper that has been folded over. It's from reception and tells me that Mr Edward Martin would like me to call him as soon as possible, no matter how late into the night, on the mobile number given.

Edward. Eddie. My fingers turn weak at the sight of the name and the sheet of paper falls away, skewing its way to the floor, where it lands wrong side up.

I back away and sink on to the bed, turning on to my side so that the note is in my line of vision. I stare at it, wishing I could turn time back just a few seconds and leave the envelope unopened. In all these years, Eddie has made no attempt to get in touch with me, even though he knew where I was from, so why is he trying to contact me now? He must be in touch with Hugo because, otherwise, how would he know where I'm staying? Has Hugo told him to call me?

I don't want to talk to him. I don't want ever to see or hear from him again because he's another reminder of that terrible night. The room is warm but I feel suddenly cold and start to shake. I can see it all, everything that happened that night, as if it were happening now. Image after image hurtles through my mind, so fast that I feel dizzy and it's harder and harder to stop the terrifying slideshow.

After a while, when there's nothing left but exhaustion, I look again at the note. I should tear it up, flush it down the lavatory. But I need to know what Eddie wants from me. So I slowly dial the number. It rings and I wait, unsure about what I will say when he answers.

The number rings and rings, but no one answers. Maybe I've misdialled. I carefully tap in the number again, and as it starts to ring, the beat of my heart is so fast and so loud that I think I can hear it outside myself, bouncing off the walls of the room. But there's still no answer.

I should try to sleep. But having decided to call the number, I can't stop trying to get through. A horrible compulsion drives me to keep redialling on and off through the night. I drift off to sleep, but after a while I wake up again and my hand immediately reaches for the telephone and I press redial. And each time it's the same, the relentless, empty ringing that stops only when I put the handset down.

And each time, as I drift back into restless, broken sleep, it's that ringing I hear in my head.

The following morning, I wake up to the sound of the hotel telephone ringing beside my bed. I pick up the handset and hold it to my ear. I don't speak. I wait for whoever is at the other end of the line to say something. The seconds go by and the caller doesn't say a word. Eventually, my nerves have frayed so much that I feel I'm going to unravel.

'Eddie?'

Silence.

'Who is it?' I croak.

The silence is unbearable. But behind the silence I think I can hear breathing. I ask again, my voice trembling, 'Who are you?' And again there's no response.

I wait.

'Is there anyone there?' I ask.

The line goes dead.

32

Hugo

I couldn't resist sending the roses. I didn't put my name on the card, but I didn't have to. The message would be enough. She would know who had sent the flowers. I almost sent a bouquet of red roses to her – anonymously, of course – when her husband died.

I knew about his death within days of it happening, as I had begun reading the various Yorkshire newspapers online as soon as I discovered Nan's whereabouts. The reports said that Christopher Brown, owner of a popular garden centre, had died following a road accident, the cause of which was not immediately clear. The basic information given was that his vehicle had left the road. He had suffered internal injuries and died four days later in hospital.

The papers also carried reports of the subsequent inquest, and here there was more detail. Evidence taken from the scene indicated that the vehicle had lost a wheel as it took a bend and had veered off the road, rolling over and crashing into a tree. The inquest did not apportion blame to any entity or individual, but it noted that the deceased had taken the vehicle to the garage several days before the fatal accident to have a new front tyre fitted and a damaged spare replaced. The inference was clear: the coroner was suggesting that the garage might not have properly fitted the new tyre.

It was also through the local papers that I learned the garden centre was up for sale. Poor Nan, I mused. The combination of bereavement and the running of a business must have been too much for her. I did toy briefly with the notion of buying the place – what a jolt that would have given her – but quickly abandoned the thought. It was far too soon after her husband's death for me to reappear in her life. I had waited the best part of four decades to catch up with her. I could wait a little longer. I should reiterate here that I had not spent nearly forty years thinking about nothing but tracking her down. After the initial few years, I had all but banished any prospect of ever seeing her again. But, as I now realise, my unconscious mind had been working in a different way.

When I came upon her son, Ben Brown, through Lucinda, I felt it was no mere coincidence. A karmic event, some might say. Whatever it was, I was able to discover where she lived and, through regular visits to Yorkshire, how she lived.

Ben became the unwitting link between us. Involving Marie-Laure had not initially been part of my plan; I merely wanted to commission a painting from Ben Brown and it occurred to me that a portrait of my goddaughter would kill two birds with one stone in that it would not only put Ben's portraiture skills to a new test but would also please Alice.

I put Ben and Marie-Laure in touch with each other and thought little more about it. I certainly didn't expect that they would turn up at Paradise Place before the paint was dry on the portrait to announce that they were an item, having fallen in love more or less at first sight, and to thank me for bringing them together.

I was slightly surprised that Marie-Laure had jettisoned her longstanding *amour*, an athletic and extremely handsome Breton called Valentin, for someone she had just met. She and Valentin had been together for quite some time, at least three or four years, and had seemed fairly content with each other.

I could, however, see immediately that there was some extraordinary attraction between Marie-Laure and Ben that went beyond infatuation and plain old lust.

And I realised, with no small sense of elation, that if Marie-Laure and Ben were to marry, Nan and I would be linked together for the rest of our days.

By the time they came to me to announce their status, Marie-Laure had already moved her things out of the flat she shared with poor Valentin in Marylebone and into Ben's in Canary Wharf. That they would marry was not in doubt. All I had to do was wait.

33

Now

I have a plan. I'm going to stand up for myself, force Hugo and Eddie into the open.

When I woke up this morning, I rang the number Eddie had left again. As before, no one picked up and I felt anxious and shaky. And then something broke through the helplessness I felt. I would not allow them to frighten me.

I had only one piece of information to go on, a name I found by digging deep into my memory. And then I typed the name into an internet search. It came up straight away. I repeated the search several times and each time the result was the same. There was a phone number. I could have rung it, saved myself the bother of going there, but I needed to be sure. And difficult conversations are best done in person.

I checked routes and train times. It would not be the easiest journey, three hours on the train, including a change, and then a taxi. But I would do it. I wasn't going to sit around and wait for them to think up some new way of unsettling me.

I was about to leave when Marie-Laure called.

'How are you feeling?' she asked. 'We were worried about you last night.'

'Much better, thank you. I had a very good sleep.'

'That's wonderful! Because Ben and I would like to have breakfast with you. If you're free, of course.'

'I'd love that. Are you going to come here?'

'Yes, we are nearby. But we want to take you to a very nice place. We will be with you in five minutes. Is that fine for you? Yes? Wonderful. *À toute à l'heure*,' she trilled, and rang off.

My trip could wait a couple of hours. I was excited about spending time with just Ben and Marie-Laure.

Now, as I wait for them in the lobby, I think about how we'll talk about their plans for the future. I even begin to see a future for myself, with them and the children I hope they will have. Until today, I haven't thought about how I will live my life. Now, I feel a sense of excitement about the plans I can make. I've already sold the garden centre. Why can't I sell the house too? I can move into a smaller place, maybe move to Leeds. I can even travel. I can get a passport and visit Ilaria in Florence.

They make a beautiful couple, Ben and Marie-Laure, as they walk into the hotel where I'm sitting on a chair in the lobby.

I notice that heads turn to look at them, the stunning dark-haired beauty and the handsome man with flecks of grey in his hair. I wish Chris could see them. He would be so proud.

Ben is smiling. He seems so much more natural now than he was that first evening. But of course he's more natural, I tell myself. I've promised to tell him what he wants to know. But I still haven't worked out what I'm going to say and when. The wedding is the day after tomorrow. Time is running out.

We walk to the restaurant where we are going to have breakfast through swarming crowds of office workers emerging from the tube station.

'Is it always like this?' I ask, struggling to stay close to them.

'Pretty much. It's the morning rush hour,' Ben says.

The restaurant is several floors up. It doesn't look out over the water but the views are still incredible to someone like me.

'It's like being in New York,' I say. 'Or at least like the pictures I've seen of New York.'

'We can go there together some day, the three of us,' Marie-Laure says.

'I'd love that,' I tell her, and I mean it.

'Mum, I'm really glad you've come down to London,' Ben says. 'I know you've had a thing about going anywhere and, well, it means a lot that you're here now, especially without Dad.'

He takes my hand and squeezes it and I can't help but give in to the tears that fill my eyes. But they're tears of happiness. I squeeze my son's hand back.

A few hours later, I'm in Norfolk. I had been nervous about getting on the wrong train from Liverpool Street and missing the connection, but I managed to get myself on to the Norwich train and then, after a wait of about twenty minutes, on to the Cromer train.

And now the final leg of the journey is ending.

I pay the taxi driver and watch him drive away before I turn and walk into the pub. The Florin. It's what I imagined it would be, quiet and dark.

I know I've come to the right place when I see the woman who stands behind the bar, drying glasses. She could be a female version of him.

'Hello, what can I do for you?' she asks. I think I hear apprehension in her voice; she will have heard the arrival of a taxi outside and is probably wondering why a lone woman has taken a cab to her pub. Perhaps she thinks I'm a tax inspector or someone from the brewery turning up unannounced.

'Do you have a brother called Eddie?'

She almost drops the glass she's holding.

'Yes,' she manages to say after several moments during which her face goes through a series of contortions. 'Have you found him?'

229

Her voice is pleading, desperate, and that's when I realise that my big decision to confront Eddie has got me nowhere. I've come all this way for nothing. I'm trying to digest this when she speaks again.

'Do you know where he is? Is he . . .?'

'No . . . I came here because I hoped you could tell me where to find him.'

'I thought you were from the police. I thought you had news. Who are you? Why are you looking for Eddie?'

The word *police* jolts me. My first thought is that Eddie did go to the police after all and told them what I had done. *I have to get out of here*, I think, and I turn away towards the door. But Ellen is behind me in a flash, holding on to my arm and refusing to let me leave.

'You can't just leave like that! You've got to tell me what's going on! I need to know what happened to my brother!'

She locks the door. Then she takes me behind the bar and through a door that leads to her living accommodation. She gestures towards a sofa and we both sit down.

'Who are you?'

'My name's Nan Brown. I knew Eddie in the seventies in London. Not for very long, just three or four months. He worked in a pub and—'

'Wait a minute,' she interrupts. 'When in the seventies?'

''Seventy-seven. I met him in September.'

'September? You're sure?' She looks surprised, even shocked.

'Yes, because I moved to London that month.'

'Okay, go on.' She leans back, folds her arms.

'I don't know what to tell you,' I say, not sure what she wants to hear.

'Tell me everything. From the beginning. How did you meet Eddie?'

'He was working in a pub just off Notting Hill Gate. That's where I met him. We became friends and then there was a room free in the house where he was living and I moved in—'

'Moved in? You mean you and Eddie were living together? You were his girlfriend?'

I shake my head. 'No, we were just friends. And then . . . Well, I wasn't there for very long. I left just before Christmas and went back home to Yorkshire. That was the last time I saw him. We didn't stay in touch.'

'You haven't seen him for forty years and you're looking for him now. Why?'

'I had a message from him last night.'

It's difficult to read her face, which has frozen into a pale mask.

'What did he say?' Now her voice is weak, barely audible.

'It was a message left with reception at my hotel asking me to call him,' I say, rooting in my bag for the piece of paper. 'Here, this is the number. I called it, I don't know how many times, but no one answered.'

Ellen Martin stares at the piece of paper and then jumps up to grab her phone. As she taps out the number, I see that her hands are shaking. She lets the number ring for a long time.

Finally, she puts the phone down and tears roll down her cheeks.

Ellen tells me that the last time she saw Eddie was in April 1977. Her parents reported him missing in February 1978, nearly a year later.

'That was when he dropped out of his course at university, April 1977. He said he was going away for a while to think about things. We never heard from him again. Not a word. We thought he was dead, that he'd killed himself or something. But you met him in September, so that means he was fine then. And now you've had this phone message. So all along . . . he just cut us off, couldn't be arsed even to let us know he was all right. The bastard! My mum and dad went to their graves not knowing what happened to him.'

Ellen pauses for another bout of weeping and then, wiping away her tears, tells me she wants to know everything, about the pub, about where he lived, who his friends were.

I tell her as much as I can – that he worked at a pub called The Rising Sun, that he planned to go travelling at some point, that he rented a room in a house nearby.

'Did he tell you why he left university?' she asks.

'I think he said the course wasn't for him. Something like that. Why?'

'I just wondered,' she says. She seems pensive for a few

moments. 'I'm glad you came,' she says eventually. 'If you talk to Eddie, will you tell him to call me?'

'Yes. If he calls back. But . . . you have the number now. You can try calling him.'

'Maybe he won't want to talk to me,' she says. 'After all, he's tried to get in touch with you and not me. Anyway, I'll give the number to the police and see if they have any luck.'

'The police? Why would you give it to the police?'

'Because we reported him missing forty years ago and he's still on their list of missing persons. Now there's something to give them that may help them find him, thanks to you.'

I'm a bundle of anxiety as I board the train for the return journey to London. I went to Norfolk because I assumed that Eddie's sister would be in contact with him and would know how and where I could find him. The trip has been a mistake, a very big mistake. Because now Ellen will tell the police I knew him at a time she and her parents thought he was missing, months after they had last seen him. Maybe the police will simply close their missing person file on Eddie without any further ado. But what if they find Eddie and he tells them everything?

I call Ellen from the train. Before I say a word, she asks whether I've heard from Eddie.

'No, but . . . Ellen, the thing is, I don't know for sure whether that number is Eddie's, whether it really was him leaving a message for me at the hotel,' I say. The nearest people are a few rows away, but I keep my voice down. 'It might be better to wait a while before telling the police . . . until we know for sure that it was Eddie. We don't want to waste their time . . .'

'Who else would it have been?' she asks. 'Why would someone else pretend to be Eddie?'

'I don't know, but just . . . just wait for a few days. Maybe I'll hear something.'

She agrees reluctantly.

My face is turned to the window, but I don't even register the changing landscape outside. I'm back in 1977, reliving that terrible night a week before Christmas, seeing it all as if it were yesterday.

Then

Hugo was on top of her, crushing her, and he was pushing her skirt up. He wasn't gentle now. His chest was on her face, leaving her unable to see beyond the fabric of his shirt that pressed against her. He was pressing her down and pulling at her tights and her underwear. Her mouth was contorted by the weight of him, but she heard herself say, *No, please, no*. And then she felt something inside her break and she let out a cry because of the sharp pain, but he kept going and she was too tired and too drunk to resist any more. So she stopped struggling against him and let him do what he wanted to do. Her vision was a watery blur from the tears that spilled from her eyes. It wasn't meant to be like this.

And then she found she was able to move her arms because he wasn't on top of her any more. And she managed to wipe away the tears and open her eyes and she saw that Eddie had Hugo on the floor and Eddie's fists were pounding him. And for some reason she didn't understand she was screaming, *No, Eddie, no, don't hurt him*, and Eddie turned his head around when he heard this and that was when Hugo grabbed Eddie's neck and pushed him down and now he was beating Eddie's face and blood was coming out of Eddie's mouth and nose.

Frantic, she looked around and saw the poker. Her balance was bad because of all the alcohol she had drunk, and her vision was blurry, but she managed to grab it and then she lifted it above Hugo's head and smashed it down as hard as she could. She watched as he slid to the floor. She felt nothing for a few moments. Then she started to worry that Hugo would be angry when he got up from the floor, but he wasn't making any effort to get up. Eddie was bending over him, his head close to Hugo's.

Eddie looked up at her and there was a strange look on his face.

'He's dead.'

Eddie said this in a whisper so low she almost didn't hear it. She didn't really understand it. Eddie was saying that Hugo was dead. How could he be dead? She straightened her underwear and pulled her skirt down.

'We have to call the police,' Eddie was saying.

'We can't.'

'We have to, Nan! He's *dead*! He's fucking dead! You hit him and you killed him. Do you understand?'

'I killed him? But I didn't mean to . . .'

'I'm going to call the police,' Eddie said, getting up from the floor.

She stared at Hugo and saw that he really was dead. She gripped Eddie's arm. She couldn't let him call the police.

'Don't, please don't, they'll send me to prison . . .'

'They won't. Listen to me. We'll tell them it was self-defense. They'll believe us. You'll have to admit you hit him but I'll tell them you were defending yourself because he was attacking you. He *was* attacking you, wasn't he? Wasn't he?'

He was holding her by the arms as he said all this, but she struggled against him. She couldn't let him bring the police.

When she got free of him she ran upstairs to get her bag with the train ticket in it. She knew the police wouldn't believe her. They would say she had led Hugo on. They would look at her skimpy blouse. And they would know she had had a lot to drink. All she could think of now was going home. But first she needed to clean herself, wash away the horrible red stains on her clothes and her skin. She didn't know how long she stayed in the bath, scrubbing at her skin, emptying the dark water and then opening the taps again.

When she went back down the stairs and opened the front door, she glanced quickly at the room. The door was only slightly open. She could just about see that Hugo was still in the same position on the floor. She couldn't see Eddie, though. Where was he? What was he doing? The house was quiet. She closed the front door behind her and ran into the darkness.

Hugo was dead and she had killed him. She repeated those words over and over. She understood what they meant but they weren't making sense. They were just words. If she could get away from Paradise Place, if she could just go back home, everything would be all right. She ran and she ran and she ran.

Now

Curled up like a foetus on the bed in my room, I struggle against the panic that threatens to overwhelm me. For so long I've kept my secret buried. But now, because I made a stupid decision to find Eddie through his sister, my world is going to be blown apart.

34

Hugo

I am acquainted with bereavement. My mother died at the age of sixty-eight following a stroke, my father six years later from a rare form of cancer. Her death was fast, his slow and painful. I grieved for them both at some level; they were my parents, after all. My eulogies at their respective funerals brought the other mourners to tears.

But I cannot say I experienced either of their deaths as a loss. I have a pragmatic approach to death, which is that it is inevitable and that there is, therefore, little point in indulging in long periods of mourning.

The nearest I have come to deep, unremitting grief was during my childhood, when a favourite dog died.

I was ten and couldn't remember a time when Badger, a black and white Border collie, had not been at my side. He was a clever dog. Affectionate and playful. He died suddenly one June day, struck down by a seizure, when I was out riding my pony.

Badger and I had a special relationship. If my father issued a command to him, the dog looked at me as if to seek my approval for what he was being told to do. I can still recall the guilt I felt at his death, thinking that had I not been cantering across the fields, I might somehow have saved him.

We buried him in the little cemetery where we buried all our small pets. My brother performed the rites, because I was too upset to speak. I remember it all: my brother's eulogy, the soft rain that filtered like dew through the canopy of leaves, and my mother telling me in that straightforward, no-nonsense way of hers that I would have another dog soon, a dog just like Badger.

She had meant to soothe me, I am sure, to tell me that life would go on and that another dog would help me get over Badger. But I didn't want another dog; I wanted Badger, the dog I should have been able to save.

That night, before I slept, I wrote down in a lined copybook two sentences that expressed all my grief and all my guilt.

We buried Badger today and I cried. I don't think I will ever be happy again.

It was the beginning of a habit that has been a mainstay of my life, albeit a spasmodic one. Writing down my thoughts and memories, as I do now, has helped me to make sense of life and of everything that has happened to me. In that way, Badger's death was a catalyst. Perhaps it was a catalyst in another sense too, one that distanced me from my parents and eventually led me to renounce the estate. For, by renouncing Ravenby, I was also renouncing the obligations that would be heaped upon me, the most daunting of which would be to produce heirs that I could not hope to care for properly. I have never wanted children. A psychologist might ask me to consider whether this stance was linked to that summer day when I was ten years old and my dog died and I would probably concur. I had not been able to keep Badger safe; how could I hope to keep a child safe?

If I did have the misfortune to bring a child into the world, I would accept my responsibility towards it. I would cherish it and look after it. I cannot imagine the kind of situation in which Nan and Ben find themselves. Perhaps the state of their relationship, which at best can be described as difficult, is Ben's fault, but I find that hard to believe. Which leaves me with a question: what did Nan do to upset him so much that he ran away from her?

35

Now

I'm waiting for Alice outside Green Park station. Across the road, on the other side of Piccadilly, the Ritz is bathed in light, standing out against the dark. I look for Alice's face among the endless stream of people swarming towards me from all directions. I still haven't worked out what I'm going to say to her, how I'm going to tell her that I may become part of a police investigation, that I lied when I told her I had never been to London before and that I had never met Hugo—

'Sorry I'm late!' Alice's voice breaks into my thoughts. 'Had to wait ages for a tube.'

'Thanks for coming, Alice. I'm sorry to spring this on you at the last minute, but I need to talk to you about . . . about something that's bothering me. That may . . . bother you.'

She gives me a look of concern. 'Is it about Ben?'

'Sort of . . . well, yes. But it's not just about Ben.'

'Oh . . .'

'I'll tell you when we're sitting down.'

We walk to a restaurant that Alice knows on St James's Street. I exhale quietly in relief when we are shown to a table by the window, slightly apart from the main dining area.

A waiter asks whether we would like to order drinks and Alice, surprisingly, asks for sparkling water.

'I think you're going to need something stronger,' I tell her.

She gives me a worried look.

'Christ, it must be serious stuff if you're telling me I need to drink! Dare I ask – will you be joining me?'

'No. I'll stick to water.'

We order drinks and food at the same time so that we can keep interaction with the waiter to a minimum.

'Okay, I'm listening,' Alice says when the waiter has delivered everything we've ordered.

After a few false starts, I tell her what Hugo did to me, watching her face collapse as she takes it all in. When I finish, she shakes her head slowly.

'I can't believe I'm sitting here and you're telling me all these terrible things about Hugo. I can't believe he would ever do anything so evil, that he would rape you. That's not Hugo – I know him and I hardly know you. Why should I believe any of this?'

Anguish is spread all over Alice's face. Tears threaten to spring from her eyes but she's got them under control.

She doesn't want to believe me, but she will. She questions everything I've told her, dates, times, places. What I remember about the house. What I remember about Hugo.

'He had a girlfriend. Caroline. She was beautiful, very blonde and tall. Like a model.'

'His sister-in-law is called Caroline,' she says. 'She's blonde and tall and very good-looking. But you're saying that before she married his brother she was his girlfriend?'

'She was *one* of his girlfriends. Probably the main one, but there were lots of them.'

'And this Eddie – you say he's in cahoots with Hugo in some way, that the two of them are trying to scare you?'

I nod.

'But why would they want to do that? It makes no sense, Nan,' she says. 'It's – it's crazy. I just can't believe this.'

'Oh, Alice, it's true, every bit of it. I didn't want you or anyone to know, but I made a mistake in going to see Eddie's sister. Maybe it won't come to anything. Maybe she's already talked to Eddie and won't go to the police because she'll just be happy to be in touch with him again. But I had to tell you because I need your help. I have to talk to Ben – in case this all blows up – and I don't know how I'm going to do it.'

'Is this why Ben stopped talking to you? Because he got wind of it, but only some of it?'

'Not exactly ... it's a bit ... complicated. I'm not sure what Ben knows. Chris was saying things when he was ... dying in the hospital. I didn't hear what he said but Ben could tell there was something we'd been keeping from him. When Ben put me on the spot, I just couldn't talk about it. We had . . . a big row and he walked out and until this week I haven't seen him since then. I've been trying to get the courage all week to talk to him. I asked him the other night to give me a little more time. Now I don't have that time.'

'Maybe you don't have to tell Ben all this straight away. And even if the sister goes to the police and they want to talk to you, you don't have to tell them . . . what you say Hugo did to you. You didn't tell her any of that, did you?'

'No, I didn't, but—'

'Well then, no one knows anything but you and Eddie. And I've just thought of something else. This – this rape is supposed to have happened forty years ago. If it really had happened, wouldn't you have reported it at the time? Wouldn't Eddie have reported it?'

I try to respond but I'm lost for words.

'You see, Nan, I just don't believe Hugo did what you say he did. Even if the police get in touch with you they won't believe you, but maybe they'll do an investigation. Think of what that will do to my daughter and your son.'

As I search for a response, she continues to speak.

'What's the point in telling Ben all or even any of this just before his wedding? Don't you realise how terrible it will make him feel?'

Her voice is low and pleading, but it's strong, and her eyes

244

bore into mine like lasers. She takes my hand and squeezes it. I take my hand away. I haven't finished talking. There's another part of the story that I'm steeling myself to tell.

'I didn't know I would love him so much,' I begin.

36

Then

She didn't mind the tablets. The nurses handed her the pills and watched while she put them into her mouth and then drank water from the plastic cup to wash them down. The tablets kept her safe and quiet. The tablets told her that time was passing. But, even then, she had no sense of time apart from a vague awareness that light turned to darkness and back to light. She had no sense of the seasons, whether it was winter or spring or summer or autumn. She had no sense of her body, whether her hands and arms and feet and legs were where they should be as she lay, soft as a rag doll, in her narrow bed.

And then, one day, she began to feel things again – pain, discomfort, dread. She began to understand that something had changed. Her body was different. Her belly was round and as hard as a football. She thought she must be dying. She had cancer. That was it.

But she wasn't dying. One of the doctors came to talk to her. He told her he had had to stop giving her the medication that kept her quiet and calm and peaceful because of the harm it could do to the baby. She was puzzled.

'*What baby?*' she asked.

But before the doctor could answer, she understood.

She screamed and wept. She turned her hands into fists and pummelled her hard belly. The doctor pulled her fists away, gripping them firmly in his and calling for the nurses.

'Please get rid of it,' she begged.

But the doctor told her it was too late for an abortion and that she would have to deliver the baby. 'You don't have to keep it,' he told her. 'You can put it up for adoption.'

She hated the baby, the *thing* inside her. She would gladly have jumped out of a window, stuck a knife into herself, to get rid of it. But the doctors and nurses watched her closely. They never took their eyes off her.

Her parents visited once a week. They tried to talk about the baby, asking her whether she really wanted to give it up for adoption. Shouldn't she talk to Chris? Shouldn't he have a say? But she refused to listen, putting her hands over her ears and closing her eyes.

When it was time for the birth, she became impatient. At last, she was going to be rid of *the thing*. She would push it out of her and it would be taken away and given to some couple and that would be the end of it. But she wasn't prepared for what happened when, her eyes closed after the exhaustion and her body covered in sweat and blood, she became aware that the nurses had lifted her arms and put something into them. Something soft, something faintly moving.

She moved her head to look and there he was. She felt a moment of disgust for the creature and for the fact that the nurses, knowing how much she hated it, had done this to her. But then everything changed. The disgust left her. She looked at the baby, at the dark downy hair on its head, the scrunched-up eyes, the tiny fingers, each one perfect, and in that instant she fell in love.

When her parents visited, she told them she wasn't going to have the baby adopted after all, that she was going to keep him. She watched them exchange worried glances, could read their faces, which asked how they were going to look after not just one but two fragile creatures.

'Don't worry,' she told them, beaming with positivity. 'Everything's going to be fine.'

Chris came to visit. He didn't tell her he was worried about her or the baby. He told her she looked like the most natural mother in the world. He admired the baby and asked to be allowed to hold him. She smiled, put the baby into his arms and watched happily as he cooed at her son.

And then Chris told her he had a proposal. He still loved her and he thought she could learn to love him again. He would love the baby, too – indeed, he already did, he said with a smile.

'Think about it, Nan,' he said, getting up to leave. 'We can be a family, the three of us. Look, in case you're wondering, I never said anything to my lot or yours. They think . . . they think he's mine.'

She thought about Chris's proposal. It would be good for the three of them. And when he came back the following day she smiled and told him, 'Yes.'

Chris left agricultural college and the wedding took place a month later. His parents sold some land to fund the purchase of a garden centre and a house as a wedding present; their farm would eventually go to Chris's brothers. Nan's parents had nothing to sell, as they rented the land on which they farmed.

Both sets of parents became enchanted with their new grandson. They knew nothing of the baby's real provenance.

Nan and Chris made a pact. Some day, when he was old enough to understand, they would think about telling Ben the truth about his birth. For both of them at the time, 'some day' was a long way off. But, at some point, the day arrived for Chris. It never did arrive for Nan.

Now

Alice looks as if she's going to collapse. Her face is pinched and pale, her eyes red and strange.

'Alice, are you all right?' I ask anxiously, touching her arm. A stupid question. Of course she's not all right. I've told her things that have turned her world upside down. I've told her that Ben's biological father is the man she has loved for decades, the man she still desires.

She shakes her head, her eyes closed now.

'I think I'm going to faint,' she says weakly.

I summon a waiter and ask him to bring more water, which we persuade Alice to sip slowly. Colour slowly comes back into her face.

'I'm so sorry I haven't been able to tell you this before. I know how you feel about Hugo,' I say.

'What I feel about Hugo doesn't matter now. What you've told me – it changes everything.' She scrambles for her bag and gets to her feet. 'They can't get married. We have to tell them now.'

'But why can't they get married?'

'Haven't you guessed? Nan, I thought you'd figured it out.'

Figured what out?

And then it hits me. I stare at Alice, looking for some sign that I've misunderstood but her expression tells me I haven't.

Neither of us is able to speak. We are both silent in the horrifying realisation that we cannot voice.

37

Hugo

I should have intuited that there was a problem by the number of missed calls from Alice that showed up on my telephone when I took it out of the locker after my swim, but I assumed that she was probably just in a nervous state ahead of the wedding the following afternoon. I would call her back, but not until I had left the club, which banned the use of mobile phones in public areas.

As I walked out of the club on to the street my mobile burst into sound. It was not a voice call. The screen crackled into life and I expected to see Alice, perhaps a little bit tipsy and emotional. But it was Marie-Laure's face that filled the screen. It looked distorted and strange. There was no sound at first. Then, a second later, her voice began to come through, but it too sounded strange and distorted. I was about to tell her that we had a bad connection and that I would call her back when I realised that she was wailing, her words barely decipherable through the dreadful sounds she was making.

'Marie-Laure, what's the matter? Has something terrible happened?' I asked her.

This brought more wailing and I was at a loss as to what to do, how to comfort her. I had no idea what had happened, but at that moment, I understood for the first time that what I was doing could have repercussions for her. I didn't mind if Ben suffered as a result of my plan for revenge on Nan, although I had become quite fond of him. But, incredible as it may sound, I had not remotely considered the possibility that my actions might inflict suffering on Marie-Laure.

'How could you? How could you?'

She kept saying this over and over, and although her voice became less shrill the sounds of her lower tones were like those of an injured animal. I was unable to extract anything comprehensible from her and eventually said, 'Marie-Laure, please try to be calm. I'm going to call your mother. Everything will be all right. I promise.'

I ended the call and tried Alice's number. She answered on the first ring. In the background, I heard Marie-Laure's hideous, disturbing weeping.

'What's wrong with her?' I asked.

'She knows everything,' Alice said, her voice croaking with weariness and distress. 'About you and me.'

I digested this for a few moments. So Marie-Laure now knew that her mother and I had had an affair. I could begin to understand why she might be upset that her mother had betrayed her father. But I couldn't understand why Alice had decided to tell her.

'But why on earth did you tell her? You must have known that she'd be upset.'

'I had to tell her. And I had to tell her what I'm going to tell you now. Something you should have guessed already. Marie-Laure . . . she isn't Arnaud's daughter. She's yours.'

I felt a flutter high in my chest. This was a surprise but it was not the bombshell Alice might have thought she was delivering. I had, in fact, often wondered whether Marie-Laure, who bore no resemblance whatsoever to Arnaud, could be mine. Although I had never particularly wanted children, the thought that Marie-Laure, who had been a captivating child and was now a delightful young woman, might be my daughter had pleased me. The provision I had made for her in my will, which excluded my brother's offspring, now seemed entirely justified.

'I see,' I said. 'Does Arnaud know?'

'He does now. He's not, shall we say, exactly delighted.'

'Alice, I'm on my way home and we can continue this conversation there. But, listen, we can get over this. She was bound to find out at some point, and, in fact, it's right that she should know. It's just rather unfortunate that she's finding out now, on the eve of the wedding.'

'There's not going to be a wedding,' Alice said. 'There can't be.'

She ended the call.

*

I took a taxi to Paradise Place and let myself into the house, where a suitcase stood at the bottom of the staircase. Alice and Arnaud came out of the kitchen and Arnaud, without acknowledging me, picked up the suitcase and walked out of the house.

'He's going back to France. As you can imagine, he's got a lot to think about,' Alice said. Her face was strained. Cracked. Anyone would think she had just been diagnosed with a terminal illness.

'Alice, you've been saying for years that you want to get out of your marriage and you've done nothing about it. Now you can, if you really want to. It isn't the end of the world.'

'It is for Marie-Laure.'

'It doesn't have to be. Arnaud may not be her natural father, but he's her father to all intents and purposes. They will work this out together. And I don't see why the wedding is being cancelled.'

'You don't? And I thought you were clever, you with your Oxford degree.' She threw the words at me with a sneer. 'You really don't get it?'

'No, I don't,' I said.

'Well, let me enlighten you. The wedding is off because . . .' Her voice trailed off into a wobble. I waited.

'. . . because she can't marry her brother.'

38

Now

Ben is slumped forward in an armchair in my hotel room, his head in his hands. For the past hour he has interrogated me, sometimes breaking off his questioning to walk away and bang his fists against the wall. Now he's exhausted. And I'm exhausted too. We are both broken. I move towards him and reach out my hand to touch his shoulder. But he pushes my hand away with force, and looks at me with such hatred that I feel afraid.

'You could have told me all this when Dad died. You knew he wanted me to know the truth about who my real father was, but he wanted you to be the one to tell me. You could have prevented this . . . this shitshow!'

'I know . . . I know I did the wrong thing. And I would give anything, I would give my life, to be able to go back to the beginning and tell you the truth from the first moment. But how could I have known this would happen, that Hugo could do something so *sick*? I didn't know about Marie-Laure until Alice told me today.'

'I wish I'd never been born,' Ben says. He looks like a child again, forlorn, tragic. I want desperately to put my arms around him and protect him. 'Why didn't you have an abortion?'

'You're the only thing I don't regret,' I tell him. 'Oh, Ben, I'd go through it all again a thousand times just to have you.'

He stares at me. '*You* would go through it all again. *You* don't regret having me. It's all about you. Everything has been about you. Oh, I'm not saying you didn't go through something terrible. You say Hugo raped you. You say you had a nervous breakdown and then you discovered you were pregnant. You say it was too late to have an abortion. You say you were going to have me adopted but you say you were smitten the moment you held me. It's all about you. What about me, though? You were going to let me go through my whole life not knowing who I was or how I came about. And what about Marie-Laure? You've ruined her life too, even if you didn't intend to.'

'I'm not without blame. I admit that. But, Ben, can't you see that it's Hugo who has ruined all our lives?'

'I'm not excusing Hugo. But you should have told me. When I told you the things Dad had said you should have told me then. I can still remember every word. *You have to tell him . . . gone on too long . . . know the truth.* Even when he was dying, he was keeping the promise he'd made to you, but he wanted you to tell me the truth. And you understood that but you chose not to tell me. You could have prevented all this from happening, because if you had told me the truth then I would probably have never met Marie-Laure.'

As he says her name, his voice cracks and he puts his head in his hands. 'Now I understand why there was something so special between us when we met,' he wails. 'And now I can never see her again.'

I have no words to comfort him. I can't even touch him because he won't let me.

His mobile pings and he looks at the screen.

'Hugo wants to talk to me,' he says, showing a text.

'Are you going to talk to him?'

'No. He may be my father but he's a rapist. Why would I want to talk to him?'

39

Hugo

I was, to use a word I dislike intensely, gobsmacked.

'Her brother? Ben is Marie-Laure's brother? That's ridiculous, utterly ridiculous!'

'Is it?' Alice asked, her voice laser sharp, her eyes angry and filled with hate. I had never seen her like this. 'I know about Nan living here in the seventies. I know about that night and what you did.'

And what you did. Her words were venomous, her voice ugly and cracked.

And what you did. I was momentarily confused, not sure what she was accusing me of. For once, I was speechless.

When I found my voice again, I asked her, as calmly as I could, what she was talking about.

'Surely you remember, Hugo, that you raped her? Hard to forget doing something like that, I would have thought.'

'*Raped* her?' I echoed. 'Of course, I didn't rape her. She's a fantasist. I have never forced a woman into sex and I certainly didn't force her. Alice, you know me. You probably know me better than most. Do you honestly believe me capable of rape?'

Alice opened her mouth as if to say something, then hesitated. For several seconds, she appeared to wrestle with whatever thoughts were going through her mind, and then she made a small side-to-side movement of her head. I exhaled in relief. She believed me.

'No,' she said. 'But you slept with her, didn't you? Something happened between the pair of you, and Ben is the result. You're his father, and yet you introduced him to my daughter – *our* daughter – and let them fall for each other. Maybe you even encouraged them.' She turned her face away from me. 'I can't bear to look at you.'

'Alice, you've got it wrong,' I said, moving towards her. 'Ben isn't—'

She pushed me away.

'Don't touch me, Hugo. You're sick, rotten to the core. And keep away from Marie-Laure. I'm taking her to a hotel. She can't go back to Canary Wharf and she certainly can't stay here.'

'Alice, I swear to you, I did not rape Nan. And Ben can't be the result of what happened between Nan and me because the truth is that nothing very much happened between Nan and me. I didn't even have sex with her. I remember that we had been drinking and that we smooched a bit on the sofa and then . . . Look, I did not have sex with Nan and I most certainly did not rape her.'

'This is very hard for me, Hugo. I believe you when you say that you didn't rape her. But I don't believe anything else. Nan is a liar. That's for sure. She lied about this being her first time in London. She acted as if she was seeing your house for the first time and she didn't tell us she knew you. That was some act she put on. But you lied too. You could have told us you'd known her in the seventies. Maybe you're telling the truth and you didn't rape her. But maybe you're lying about having slept with her. Maybe you knew Ben was your son. And maybe you had a good idea that Marie-Laure was your daughter. What were you up to, Hugo? What were you plotting? To ruin Nan's life by having her son fall in love with my daughter, his sister? Did that brain injury years ago turn you into a monster? Maybe we weren't supposed to find out. Maybe you thought of us as bit-part actors in your own revenge drama? But what did you want revenge for? What terrible thing can Nan have done to you to make you want to hurt her so deeply and destroy so many other innocent people?'

So many questions, so many accusations. I was racking my brain for clues as to why Nan should accuse me of rape and of being the father of her son. And then it came to me.

Of course! Nan had prepared her accusation decades earlier to use in her defence if the police ever came looking for her. I took a deep breath.

'Alice, I know why Nan claims that I raped her,' I said.

'That brain injury. I told everyone, including the doctors and the police, that I had been attacked by a stranger outside my house. But I was lying.'

Alice looked puzzled.

'I was lying then, because it wasn't a stranger who attacked me. It was Nan. I don't suppose she told you that she hit me on the head with an iron poker and left me for dead?'

It was obvious from the shocked expression on Alice's face that Nan had not told her this.

'I didn't rape Nan,' I repeated. 'And I'm not Ben's father. I can prove it with a DNA test.'

'But why did she hit you?'

Alice had put me on the spot.

'I'm sorry. I can't tell you that,' I said.

She gave a heavy sigh and began to weep. I tried again to touch her, to show that I did care about her, but she held her hand up, warning me not to come close.

'A DNA test will prove that Nan's lying about me being Ben's father. You can't stop the wedding because of her crazy accusation.'

'We've already started telling people the wedding is off,' Alice said. 'Do you honestly think we can all get over this?' she went on, a blend of incredulity and bile dripping from every word. 'I'm beginning to wonder who's worse, you or Nan. Maybe you're both sick in the head. Maybe you deserve each other. Two things I know, Hugo. One, I wish I'd never laid eyes on you. And, two, I never, ever, want to see you again.

I'm walking out of this house now and I'm taking Marie-Laure with me. And don't try to talk to Marie-Laure – she hates you.'

She gave me one last look that was filled with disgust and then turned and climbed the stairs.

I knew it was unlikely that either Nan or Ben would speak to me on the telephone, so I sent him an email.

Dear Ben,

Despite what you have been told, I did not do what your mother claims I did and I am not your biological father. I know I cannot expect you to believe me because, in effect, I lied to you by failing to acknowledge that I knew your mother a long time ago. You will require proof of my non-paternity. I propose, therefore, that a DNA test be carried out.

If you are willing to be tested, please let me know as quickly as possible. You may not trust me enough to allow me to make the arrangements, in which case I will be more than happy to deal with a laboratory of your choosing. I will, of course, pay for the test.

Hugo

Ben's response came early this morning. He said he had contacted a laboratory and had made fast-track appointments for both of us in the afternoon. I wrote back and thanked him, adding that I was confident the test would show that we were not related.

Now, alone in my house, I have opened a bottle of Austrian

Pinot Noir and I am slowly making my way through it. I am thinking about the past four decades, reliving in my mind the good and bad times. I am thinking about Caroline, about Eddie, about Alice, and about Marie-Laure and Ben. I think briefly about Christopher Brown. Mostly, I am thinking about Nan and the effect she continues to have on me.

Thanks to her, I lost two good years of my life. Even when seen as a fraction or percentage of the total number of years I have so far spent on this planet, two years is a long time. Indeed, two years of one's youth is probably equivalent to ten years of one's later life.

And during those two precious, lost years I prayed day after day to a God I didn't believe in, imploring Him to restore my life and my faculties to me. And even as I prayed during those dark times, I cursed Nan and wished her a hell worse than death. My prayers were answered. I was restored. And over the years, the intensity of my need for revenge on Nan dissipated. Or, at least, it seemed to. It was only when I saw that portrait, felt the surge of excitement as I made the connection between her and her son, that I understood. The desire for revenge had never really left me; expediency had relegated it to a less conscious part of my being.

But something in me changed over the years. I have to acknowledge that. I once thought of myself as a broadly good person. I have to accept now that there is a part of me that is bad. I accept it, but I take no responsibility for it. Because the badness that is in me comes directly from what Nan did.

40

Now

Ben's voice on the telephone is low and solemn.

'The results of the test show that Hugo isn't my father.'

'Oh, thank God!' I exclaim, filled with relief. I've done nothing but worry all day, pacing around my hotel room. Ben can marry Marie-Laure. They are not related.

But then confusion overwhelms me. The test results are wrong. They have to be. Someone has made a mistake. Maybe one of the samples got mixed up with someone else's. Or, worse, Hugo somehow managed to give a fake sample.

I blurt all these thoughts out to Ben, conscious of how ridiculous I must sound.

'He can't have given a fake sample or made a substitution. The samples were taken by a technician.'

'He's capable of anything, Ben. You don't know him the way I do. You've only seen him laying on the charm.'

Ben sighed. 'Look, as far as I'm concerned the results are

conclusive. As Hugo is not my father, Marie-Laure and I can get married. But if Hugo isn't my father . . . you still have to tell me who my father is? I need to know. What are you not telling me?'

I feel strange, as if my body has become weightless. It's a frightening and disconcerting feeling. I lean back against the wall, needing to feel something solid behind me. I press myself into it and close my eyes.

When I open my eyes again, I have no immediate sense of what has happened. I'm on the floor, staring up at the furniture and the ceiling. Somewhere distant I hear the sound of a voice. What's it saying? Are you there? Are you there? It's Ben's voice. I lift myself into a sitting position and reach for the phone, which is lying just a couple of feet away.

'Ben?' I manage to say into the phone.

'What happened? Are you all right?'

'I'm fine. Sorry. I don't know what happened. I think I fainted.'

'Have you eaten lunch?'

'No . . .'

'Breakfast?'

'I didn't feel like it.'

'No wonder you fainted. You have to eat.'

'I know, I know. I'll order soup or something from room service. But, Ben . . . I just don't understand these test results. They can't be right.'

'The tests were done properly,' Ben says slowly, separating each word, as if speaking to a child. 'But if you keep insisting that Hugo made you pregnant when he – *if* he – raped you, and that some mistake must have been made, we can repeat them. And when the second tests come up with the same result, you're going to have to have an explanation. If Hugo isn't my father, and if Dad wasn't my father, I want you to tell me who is. I need to know. You can't keep lying to me for ever.'

Ben ends the call before I can say anything. I clamber on to my feet and, because I've promised Ben that I will order some food, I stumble to the room telephone and call room service. And then I lie back on the bed, bewildered and afraid. Ben is Hugo's son. I know that. I have always known that. There must be an explanation for the negative paternity test. Hugo has managed to fool Ben, but he's not going to fool me. I put on my shoes and coat and hurry down the corridor towards the lift.

Outside, black clouds hover ominously overhead. The wind is strong and seems to be coming from all directions. There will be a storm. I am tempted to take a cab but I know the tube will be faster. As I approach Canary Wharf station, I think about calling Ben or sending him a text. But by the time I have descended on to the platform, I have lost the signal.

41

Hugo

Despite my certainty that I am not Ben's father, I was nevertheless relieved when the DNA test result came back as negative. I had known this would be the case, and yet, at some deeper level, I must have questioned my recall of the events of that night forty years ago.

But while the test result gave some comfort, it did not necessarily mean that Nan would not pursue her claim that I had attacked and raped her. I allowed my mind to imagine the consequences of the police taking her allegation seriously and shuddered. My concern was not simply that I might be found guilty of a rape I had not perpetrated; it was that a court would look back over the recent years during which I had cultivated her son and might well begin asking questions I would prefer not to have to answer.

It is important for me to reiterate at this point that I did not rape Nan. Nor have I ever raised a hand against a woman; it is simply not in my nature to do so. But, since my brain injury in nineteen seventy-seven, and probably because of it, I have been conscious of some small changes in my perception of the difference between what is acceptable and what is not.

I had, for example, smiled when I read about the accident in which Nan's husband had been killed. And I smiled again when I read some time later that the coroner had described the accident as one that had been 'waiting to happen.'

But would a court dealing with a rape allegation make a connection between my coming into contact with Ben, insisting on buying the portrait of his mother and the subsequent death of his father? There is no paper trail of my visits to Yorkshire because I used cash for each transaction.

But what if someone up there is able to identify me? And what if my house is searched? For decades I have kept a journal of sorts, not a leather-bound diary but a collection of loose pages that I have built up over many years. My intention has been to burn the pages at some point in the future when I feel my health slipping away. I would not like them to be found and read; I am not a man who would want his private thoughts to be available to anyone, even when I am dead. But now, following Nan's rape claim, there is another reason to destroy them, and I am thinking of one entry in particular. I do not even have to go upstairs to my office to read it. I can almost remember it word for word.

Having found Nan through her son, I became obsessed

with her and her life in Yorkshire. I wanted to know more; I wanted to know everything. At some point I would make myself known to her but I was not immediately inclined to do so. I cannot recall exactly when I made the decision that Chris Brown would have to be removed. Perhaps it was when I first saw them together, coming out of their house, easy in each other's company. Was it then that I knew exactly how I wanted to make her suffer?

On one of my trips to Yorkshire, I was driving near Ilkley when I passed an isolated house with a *For Rent* sign outside it and a garden that needed attention. The house was not being offered through an estate agent but directly by the owner, an elderly farmer with no wife and no family. I gave my name as Martin Edwards and told the farmer I was writing a book set in Yorkshire and needed a quiet place for a month. The old boy started mumbling about how he wasn't sure there was any point in renting the house for just a month, but he agreed to let me have it when I told him I would pay up front, and in cash, with an extra two hundred pounds thrown in.

This was the weakest part of my plan; if things didn't work out exactly as I intended, and Chris's death was treated as suspicious, there was a chance that the police would find their way to the house and to the farmer. In theory, I would have long made my escape from the area, leaving nothing behind that could lead the police to me. But I couldn't be sure that I would be untraceable.

Putting the next part of my plan into action also had some

risk attached to it, but turned out to be easy. One night, about an hour after all the lights had gone out in their house, I quietly set about damaging one of the front tyres of the jeep. I used a sharp screwdriver rather than a knife, my intention being to make it look as though some sharp pieces of gravel had punctured the tyre. That took a long time and was exhausting because of the care I had to take to ensure that the damage gave no grounds for suspicion.

Dealing with the spare was much easier; I deflated it enough that it wouldn't be immediately noticed but would, when he came to use it, cause some concern as to whether it had a slow puncture. And I thanked my lucky stars that Chris drove one of those old jeeps that carried the tyre on the back and not some saloon or estate car that stored the spare under a floor panel in the boot.

Job done. I walked back to my rented car, which I had parked a good distance away, set my alarm for six o'clock and slept on the back seat for a few hours. The following morning, I moved closer to the house, watching it through binoculars. Shortly after seven thirty, Chris came out, climbed into the jeep, started the engine and drove it to the front of the house. I was too far away to hear their conversation, but just as Nan emerged from the house, Chris jumped out of the jeep and pointed to the tyre.

I watched the dumb show progress as I had hoped it would. Chris got out a car jack and removed the damaged tyre. I felt my breath quicken as he got to grips with the spare. It was obvious from the way he examined it that he realised it wasn't up to scratch. But would he be suspicious? I waited, aware that my heart was racing. And then I exhaled, my breath as slow and steady as the air escaping from the tyre.

When the spare had been fitted and the damaged tyre thrown in the back, Nan and Chris both climbed into the jeep and drove away. I managed to follow them from a safe distance, wondering whether they would drive to the garden centre or to a garage. They went to a garage. *Yesssss*, I hissed, driving on. Everything was working out beautifully. The jeep would come out with a new front tyre and a new spare. All I had to do now was go back to London for a few days before returning to Yorkshire to complete my plan.

I almost didn't return to Yorkshire. Not because I was having second thoughts but because of several days of appalling weather that was afflicting the north and parts of the Midlands. Still, I did ask myself once or twice whether I was really prepared to go through with my plan. Even if I was not going to kill Chris with my bare hands, I was still planning a set of moves that would, if all went well, leave him dead.

I waited for the weather to improve, and while I waited, I fantasised about what I would say to Nan when we eventually met. Exactly *how* we would meet I still had to work out. I could, once a few months or a year had passed after Chris's death, simply turn up on her doorstep. That would certainly give her a shock. Already, though, I was beginning to formulate a much more ambitious scheme to bring her to London.

A key part of my plan for Chris involved setting up an appointment for him to visit the house I had rented in order to talk about a garden design project. I could go about this in one of two ways. I could call the garden centre and ask to speak to him. The risk here was that he would almost certainly record details – name, address, and so on – and I wanted to avoid that. Instead, I could 'accidentally' encounter him in a shop or pub and persuade him to drive over there and then. This is what I did.

Having followed him several times when he left the garden centre, I established that when deliveries were made to customers, including flower arrangements for businesses, Chris always made them. I also learned that he tended to end these delivery trips with a short visit to a pub. Clearly, Nan wasn't given to sitting in hostelries so Chris made the most of his absences from the garden centre.

When I made my move, he was already sitting at the bar, lifting a half of beer to his mouth. I ambled up to the bar and, pretending to show interest in the beers on tap, asked him whether I should try what he was drinking.

'You could do worse,' he said amiably. And then, just for a moment, I had a sense of his eyebrows narrowing slightly, as if he had recognised me. But I quickly became confident that he hadn't – he had, after all, seen me only for a moment some forty years ago – because he gave me a half-smile and returned to his beer.

'I'm disturbing you. I'm sorry,' I said, moving slightly away. He said nothing.

The barman ambled over and asked what he could get me.

I was as pleasant as it was possible to be, telling him I would like something local.

He pointed at Chris's glass. 'You could try that,' he said.

'Two recommendations. I'll have a pint, please.'

While the barman was pouring the beer, Chris turned towards me. 'Sorry,' he said. 'Didn't mean to be rude. The pub is my quiet time. No offence.'

'None taken,' I said.

I hovered, not sure whether he was providing an opening for me to engage him in conversation or trying to send me away politely by telling me he had a lot on his mind. But I couldn't afford to lose this opportunity, so I decided to risk a rebuff by remaining at the bar. We drank side by side in silence. Until he turned to me again.

'You're not a local, then?'

'No. I've just been visiting my uncle. He's in his nineties, likes to eat lunch early and he's a teetotaller,' I said, rolling my eyes upward. 'I was desperate for a drink. In fact, just thinking about my uncle makes me want another drink before I hit the road.'

Chris chuckled. I called the barman over and asked for the same again for both of us.

'Thanks,' he said, pleasantly surprised by my generosity.

'Where are you off to then?' he asked me.

'A couple of miles this side of Ilkley.'

'Oh. Ilkley. I had you for a southerner.'

'Definitely not a southerner,' I said. 'Though I do admit that I lived in London for years. Until I retired a few months ago.'

We fell into conversation. He asked what I had done for a living and I told him I had worked in advertising but now wanted to try to write a novel I had been thinking about for years. 'That's what brought me up here. What about you? What's your line of work?'

'My wife and I have a garden centre,' he said.

It was easy from there on.

'What an extraordinary coincidence!' I said. 'I moved into my house quite recently. Everything needs work, but especially the garden. I've been meaning to hire a proper garden landscaper to come up with a design. I don't suppose you do anything like that?'

'It's what I like doing best, but we don't get these jobs every day,' he said. He fumbled in his jacket and produced a card.

I made a show of examining the card and then hesitantly asked, 'I wonder . . . I don't suppose you could come over today? I mean, I know it's short notice, but I'd really love to get going with this.'

He frowned. 'Not sure about today. It'll take the best part of an hour to get there and there won't be much daylight left.'

'Oh,' I said, disappointment dripping from my voice. It was only partly feigned. 'Oh, well, I'll get in touch.'

I drained my glass and stood up, extending my hand. Chris took it. His grip was light but then it tightened, and as I walked away I had a feeling he might stop me from leaving the pub.

'Hang on,' he said. 'Let me finish this and I'll come with you.'

'Are you sure? I really don't want to inconvenience you.'

'No, no, you're not inconveniencing me. I'll just call my wife and tell her.'

He took out his mobile and held it to his ear. When he began to speak, I understood immediately that he was responding to a recorded message.

'It's me. Just to let you know that I'm on my way to Ilkley to look at a possible garden job that's come out of the blue. I might drop in to see Dad on the way back.'

He ended the call and put his phone away. 'Right,' he said. 'Let's go.'

I led the way to the house I had rented, hoping he wouldn't know it or its owner. I was relieved when, as he got out of his jeep and looked around, he said, 'Nice spot, but I see what you mean about the garden.'

We walked around and he made observations and suggestions. I responded enthusiastically.

'Okay, give me a few minutes to think this out a bit more and then I'll do a sketch showing how it might look. Just a rough sketch. To give you an idea. We can refine it later.'

'Wonderful,' I said. 'I'll leave you to it and put the kettle on.'

Inside, I filled the kettle and plugged it in to boil and then quickly went out to the front of the house where he had parked the jeep. I opened the boot of my rental car, took out the extendable wheel brace I had bought at a car accessories shop before I left London, and set to work loosening the front right wheel of the jeep. And then I went back inside and made a pot of tea. The exercise had taken less than a couple of minutes.

And the rest, as they say, is history.

42

Now

The rain is coming down in torrents as I climb the steps from Notting Hill Gate station. I have no umbrella and within seconds I am drenched, but I don't care. I hurry to Paradise Place, pausing only for a moment to catch my breath before I make my way along the passageway to number 4.

I bang the knocker up and down several times. I bang it loudly. Hugo opens the door and says 'Why, Nan,' in that supercilious way of his. He thinks he can charm me. I don't wait for him to invite me in. I walk past him into the house and turn on him.

'What's going on, Hugo?' I demand.

He doesn't answer immediately and, as I wait for a response, I feel my grip on the rage inside me begin to loosen. *What now? What if he doesn't give me an answer?* I'm not in control. I thought I was but I'm not. I shouldn't have come here.

'You're soaked,' he says. 'Give me that wet coat. I'm going

to make some tea and then we can talk. Why don't you sit in here? I'll be back shortly.'

So now I hear the sounds of activity in the kitchen, the kettle heating up, a spoon against the metal sides of a tea caddy, the whoosh of water being poured into a teapot. Such normal sounds. And I am sitting in what would seem to anyone else a normal room. A room with a fireplace in which a fire blazes. A set of fireside instruments. A shovel. Tongs for moving the coals.

A poker.

Hugo comes back into the room. He holds a bottle of wine in one hand, two glasses in the other.

'In the end I thought the occasion called for wine rather than tea,' he says.

I look at the wine doubtfully. I need to be in control of my wits. But I say nothing. Time seems to have stopped and reversed. A dark night. A blazing fire. The same house. The same room. And Hugo.

He's bending forward to place the bottle and the glasses on a low table. His back is to me. I look again towards the fireplace and my eye settles on the poker. Is it the same poker? I imagine myself lifting it and I pause. This time, there *is* a moment during which I see across to the other side of the line that will make me a murderer. A *murderess* – how creepily old-fashioned that sounds in my mind. I will smash the poker down on his head and the force of the blow and the ones that follow will shatter his head.

I will do it properly this time. I will kill him and there will be consequences. I will be arrested, put on trial and I will go to prison. But then I think about Ben. There will be consequences for him, too. I don't care about myself, but I do care about my son.

But the moment for action is gone; Hugo is standing up straight and he's handing me a glass of wine. For a moment, I have an urge to throw it over him, to turn the white shirt he's wearing into a blood-red rag. I haven't drunk alcohol for forty years, not since that final night at Paradise Place. It has been easy over the years to decline the wine, the beer, the whiskey, but it's not easy now. I'm shocked by how much I need the drink that Hugo is offering me. I need to feel its warmth on my tongue and in my throat. I hold the glass to my lips and drink from it and when I put it back down on the table, I see that the glass is half-empty.

'It seems you needed that drink,' Hugo says. 'Are you feeling calmer now?'

His voice is mellifluous, solicitous, kind. I am weakened for a moment by this emergence of the old Hugo, the Hugo who had insinuated himself into my every thought, waking or sleeping. But I stiffen my guard. I won't allow myself to be seduced by him again.

'Is that your idea of small talk, Hugo? I don't need to drink, but maybe you think that by getting me a bit the worse for wear you can convince me that you didn't do what you did to me, that you didn't rape me. And I don't know how you faked that DNA test, but you're Ben's father. It wasn't the Angel Gabriel.'

'I didn't fake the DNA test. That would have been impossible,' he says evenly. 'And I didn't rape you, Nan.'

'You did. You took advantage of me. I was drunk. I screamed. I said *no*! But you went ahead and raped me. And Eddie was there. He's my witness. Why don't you call him?'

'Eddie? I don't think Eddie is in any position to act as your witness.'

'Why not? Because you've managed to blackmail him into taking your side?'

'Because Eddie is dead.'

I freeze, my mouth open in shock.

'But . . . but he left a message for me at the hotel. He left a phone number. I rang it . . .'

'That was me, Nan, not Eddie. I wanted to give you a jolt, remind you of what you did.'

'I don't need reminding. I hit you over the head with a poker. I thought I'd killed you but it turns out I hadn't.' I look at him with hate. 'I wish I had. You're bad, Hugo. You're sick.'

'I'm not a saint. But am I bad for wanting you to feel fear? Am I bad for wanting you to suffer for what you did to me? You destroyed two years of my life, Nan. Because of you, I had brain damage. But at least I survived. Which is more than I can say for Eddie.'

'What happened to Eddie?'

He gives me a look that is both patronising and inquisitive. His eyebrows raised, his nostrils wide and his mouth saying all sorts of things without speaking. His mouth, always so expressive without having to do very much.

'You really don't remember?' he asks, his eyebrows lifted in a show of incredulity. 'My dear Nan, you of all people should know what happened to Eddie. Your memory can't be that bad. Unless, of course, you've decided to be selective about what you remember. People do that, don't they, when they can't face up to the truth?'

'Wh . . . what do you mean?'

'Oh, come on, Nan. You can't really have forgotten what happened? What you did? Well, let me refresh your memory. But, first, let me give you some more wine. You certainly got through that first glass very quickly.'

I begin to protest. I need to be alert, in control of myself. But I need something to help me through this, so I watch, numb, as he fills my glass.

And then he begins to speak, taking me back to that night when everything that was good and wonderful about my life was taken away. And as I listen, I feel something gnawing at my stomach, pushing against my throat. Something is happening in my mind, too. Something is trying to get in. I'm resisting it, trying to block it, but I'm too weak to stop the onslaught of long-buried memory.

Then

She was straightening her underwear, pulling her knickers back in place, tugging her skirt back down below her calves from above her bottom. It wasn't easy because her hands weren't working properly. Eddie was crouching on the floor, saying something. She didn't hear him properly because he was whispering.

'What?' she asked. She was irritated. How did he expect her to hear him if he insisted on whispering?

'He's dead.'

She tried to ignore him but he kept saying the same thing, that Hugo was dead. How could Hugo be dead? He was pretending. In a moment, he would open his eyes and sit up.

'We have to call the police,' Eddie said, getting up from the floor. He pointed towards Hugo, who stayed very still. She looked at Hugo more closely. She saw the back of his head now. His hair matted in something dark and viscous.

'We can't.'

'We have to, Nan! He's *dead!* He's fucking dead! You hit him and you killed him. Do you understand?'

'I killed him? But I didn't mean to . . .'

She watched him get to his feet.

'What are you going to do?' she asked.

'I'm going to call the police.'

'But you can't ... I'll be ... Don't, please don't, they'll send me to prison!'

'They won't. Listen to me. We'll tell them it was self-defense. They'll believe us. You'll have to admit you hit him but I'll tell them you were defending yourself because he was attacking you. He *was* attacking you, wasn't he? Wasn't he? You didn't mean to kill him.'

Why was he using that awful word? *Kill.* She lifted her hands to her ears, covering them to block the sound of Eddie's voice, but she could still hear what he was saying.

'It's all right, Nan. It was self-defense. We're going to tell the police he attacked you and that you were protecting yourself. I tried to help you but he attacked me too. The police will believe us, because it's the truth. You know that, don't you? You know it's the truth and so you won't go to prison.'

He was holding her by the arms as he said all this. She pushed him away but he grabbed her again.

'Nan, calm down, please calm down,' he was saying. 'I won't let anything happen to you. It was an accident. Look, I promise, I won't call the police until you're ready. Let's talk about this first and work out what to do.'

She stopped struggling against him and felt his hands and arms loosen and then fall away from her. She was exhausted. She wanted Eddie to look after her but she couldn't trust him. She couldn't trust him not to call the police. He was just saying it so that she would calm down and he wouldn't have to restrain her and then he would go to the phone in the hall and dial 999 and she would be arrested and put on trial and she would go to prison.

She made the move without really thinking. The poker was still where she had dropped it. As fast as lightning, her hand grabbed the poker and she hit Eddie. He let her go and put his hand to his head. He shouted something at her too. She couldn't quite work out what it was he had said because she was in such a state, but she heard him shout something. And then she ran up the stairs and into her room. She half-expected Eddie to come after her, but he didn't.

She had to get out of the house, had to get home, where she would be safe. A few minutes later she crept downstairs and moved to the front door on tiptoes, terrified that Eddie would hear her and come after her. As she closed the door softly behind her, her big fear was that he had already gone to the police station on Ladbroke Road to report that she had killed Hugo.

Now

I stare at Hugo, my eyes and ears filled with the horror of what he says I did.

'You killed him, Nan. It certainly wasn't me. I was already unconscious on the floor. It was a bit of a shock to see him when I regained consciousness. You left both of us in a bloody mess, a bloody mess that I had to clear up.'

Why should I believe him? But I know somehow that he's not lying.

'I . . . I only hit him, to get away from him. He was going to call the police . . . I didn't know he was . . . dead.'

'He may not have died straight away but by the time I came to and discovered him he had definitely shed his mortal coil.'

I wince, imagining all too well the scene.

'There's one thing I don't understand,' I say. 'Why didn't you call the police?'

'They wouldn't have believed me if I told them that a little slip of a thing like you had managed to kill Eddie and had nearly killed me. They would have dumped it on me. The whole thing would have been very unpleasant.'

He's omitting the most important thing, so I remind him.

'You raped me, Hugo.'

He frowns and shakes his head.

'No, Nan, I most certainly didn't. I would never have dreamt of forcing a woman into sex. You're being selective again. Why don't you let me refill your glass and I'll tell you exactly what happened?'

43

Hugo

'I wasn't entirely disappointed when Eddie came in. I knew you had drunk much more than was good for you and I didn't want to take advantage. You weren't like Caroline and my other girlfriends. They were open about sex. They liked it for what it was. But I knew it would be different for you. I found you extremely attractive and I found the idea of having sex with you also highly attractive and even exciting, but that was the extent of it. You would have fallen in love with me and you would have clung and I would have broken your heart.

'You drank a ridiculous amount of alcohol that night. You probably won't remember, but you fell fast asleep on the sofa. Eddie and I continued drinking for a while and then decided to call it a night. We thought about carrying you to your room and tried to lift you, but you were a dead weight. And so we agreed that it would be better to leave you on the sofa.

'Eddie said he would fetch a couple of blankets from the linen cupboard and make sure you were going to be warm enough on the sofa, so I said goodnight, went to my room, got into my bed and fell asleep immediately. I have no idea how long I was asleep, but I was jolted awake by the sound of screaming. I jumped out of bed, rushed downstairs and saw Eddie on top of you. His trousers were halfway down his legs so it was pretty obvious what was going on—'

'Eddie? No, Eddie would never have done that!'

'No? Well, he did. And needless to say, I ran to your aid and pulled him off you. It was quite a fight. I should have been the victor, the gallant knight who succeeded in saving the maiden's honour. That's the way it's supposed to go, isn't it? But the next thing I remember is regaining consciousness and finding myself on the floor with a bleeding and very painful head.'

I paused for a moment. Her face looked anguished and twisted, as if she was wrestling with a mind full of thoughts and memories that were too much for her.

'And Eddie . . .?' Nan asked, her voice trembling.

'Eddie was lying on the floor a few feet away. Dead. His head was split open. Not a pretty sight. You killed him.'

'I didn't know . . . I heard him shout at me. I told you, I didn't know he was dead. It was an accident. I . . . I didn't mean to . . .'

The sound of her weeping distressed me. I have always hated to see women cry and I have hated even more to be the cause of their weeping. But I had to make her cry some more, because I needed her to admit the truth.

'Nan, you remember now that it was Eddie who raped you, don't you?'

'I was drunk . . . I thought it was you,' she mumbled, the sound of the words distorted by her sobs. 'I was so sure it was you I saw by the fire . . . But now . . . I don't know what to think. What did you do with . . .?'

She was unable to finish the sentence, so I finished it for her.

'What did I do with Eddie's body?'

She nodded, her mouth twisted downwards, her eyes pressed into a squint as tears gushed out of them.

'It wasn't exactly easy, but I managed to drag him down into the cellar that same night. God knows how I had the strength. I left him there for a few years. By the time I was ready to go down there he had pretty much disintegrated. Don't look so appalled, Nan. What else was I going to do?'

'Is . . . is he still there?' she asked, a look of horror on her face.

'God, no. I did think about scattering the bones here and there – in the river, in refuse tips, and so on, but I knew that would be rather risky. All it takes is for a chalky old shin bone to turn up somewhere and next thing there's a nationwide hunt for the other bits and pieces.'

She winced at this, closing her eyes, and I took up my story again.

'No, scattering them was out of the question. In the end, I took them up to my parents' estate and buried them in one of the dogs' graves – Badger's, if you're ever seized with the urge to visit. He was a lovely dog. At least Eddie's remains lie in good company.'

Her face was a picture of consternation. Actually, that was an understatement. Her face was a picture of absolute horror and distress. It made me think of one of those *Scream* paintings by Edvard Munch.

'Sorry. I don't mean to offend your sensibilities, but I often find that a bit of levity can provide a great deal of relief. Anyway, Nan, you have a choice. You can decide whether to go to the police and tell them what happened or you can leave things as they are. I'll go along with whatever you want to do. If you decide to go to the police, I'll go with you. I'll tell my side of the story, that Eddie was forcing himself on you and that I intervened, that you struck me by accident. But I won't be able to back you up if you tell them that you killed Eddie in self-defence, because I was unconscious when you killed him. I'm sure they'll believe you, though. Why wouldn't they? But before making up your mind, you should think about the consequences of going to the police with this, not just for you but also for Ben, who's still trying to find out who his father was.'

'Ben . . . oh, God . . .'

The truth finally appeared to be dawning on her. 'The DNA test . . .'

'Yes, Nan. You were so drunk you thought it was me. But it was Eddie who raped you and it was Eddie who made you pregnant. And you killed him. You killed your rapist, who was also the father of your child. That's a hell of a lot for Ben to take in, don't you think?'

She looked as if she was coming apart at the seams. Rather inappropriately, I thought of the painting upstairs, *Nan Mending*; she certainly could have done with some mending now.

'I'm sorry. I've been rather brutal. I should have been more sensitive in my choice of words,' I said softly, moving to sit beside her and placing my hand on her arm with the lightest touch.

She didn't push my hand away. With my other arm, I drew her towards me. Still, she didn't react. Then she did something surprising; she collapsed into me and sobbed her heart out.

I made the most of her anguish. I held her gently and told her everything was going to be all right, that I would look after her. We would go together to Canary Wharf and tell Ben the truth – or at least as much of the truth as either of us dared to tell.

We would tell him that Nan had had too much to drink that night and had been confused, that it was Eddie and not I who had raped her. We would not tell him that his mother had killed Eddie. We would not tell him that Eddie's bones were buried in a dog's grave in Leicestershire. It would be our secret.

'But what about Ellen?'

'Ellen?'

'Eddie's sister.'

She told me about her trip to Norfolk and her fear that Ellen Martin would talk to the police, that she might have already contacted them.

'Don't worry. I'll call her tomorrow. It's too late now. We'll tell her that Eddie moved out because he had found a new job in a different part of London. And if she has already contacted the police, which I think is unlikely, because she's still trying to call Eddie on that mobile number you gave her—'

'How do you know she's trying to call . . .? Oh, because you've got the mobile. But what if the police track it to you? What if they charge both of us with murder?'

'They won't. Nan, everything is going to be all right. If the police come, we'll talk to them together. They'll need a body to prove murder. And they won't find one. You're safe now. I *will* look after you, I promise.'

She sobbed for a while and I could feel the wetness of her tears soaking through my shirt on to my chest. Eventually, her tears subsided but she didn't pull away from me. And when I put the tip of my finger under her chin and raised her face towards mine, she didn't resist.

Later, I watched her for a long time as she slept. How odd the situation felt. It was as if we had travelled back in time to somewhere we had failed to reach a long time ago.

I thought back over the evening. I should not have been surprised to find her on my doorstep, violently banging the heavy cast-iron knocker. Ben would have told her already that the paternity test was negative.

'Why, Nan,' I said, opening the door to find her standing in front of me, drenched by the torrential rain that had been battering down for the past half-hour.

I confess that at that moment I found her more attractive than I had ever imagined I would, her hair soaked, her wet face glowing, her eyes blazing and her lips an improbable red. She was fifty-eight but looked at least ten years younger. An almost overwhelming urge to take her in my arms swept over me, but I dismissed it; it would be uncouth. I still had the utmost confidence in my powers of gentle seduction, even with someone like Nan, who had made a false accusation of rape against me.

She would not pursue her claim. Not now.

I thought about the question she had asked, why I hadn't gone to the police. I had answered her truthfully; the police would not have believed that a girl as slight and fragile as her could have killed one man and severely injured another. But perhaps there was another reason. Perhaps, even then, I was thinking about justice in kind rather than in law.

I ran my finger gently along her cheek but she was dead to the world and didn't stir. She looked so peaceful that I was loath to leave the bed. But I had things to do before I slept, the most important of which was the updating of my journal, which I would not now need to destroy. I pulled my dressing gown around me and left the bedroom quietly.

44

Now

I wake to a cold dawn light trickling in through a gap in the curtains. I wake in the full knowledge that I have slept in Hugo's bed, that we have been intimate with each other. Until last night, I had feared him, but that fear has left me because I know now that he tried to save me from Eddie. But what *do* I feel? Last night, his arms around me in this bed, he talked about a future in which we would be inextricably linked by my son and his daughter and by our new and 'long-overdue relationship'.

I feel faintly embarrassed. I'm fifty-eight. In two years I will be sixty. I had thought the physical part of my life was over. I couldn't have imagined responding like this to a man I had hated for so long. I know now that my hatred and fear were misplaced, that trauma had made me create a new version of the events of that night to protect myself. I accept now that somewhere deep inside me I must have known the truth but had kept it just out of reach. And the basic truth is that I had been so drunk I failed to distinguish between Hugo and Eddie.

I think back to that time in 1977 when I first saw Hugo, that time when I lived in his house and longed to be in the place of those beautiful girls he brought back. And I think of the years during which I tried to shut out the memories of that terrible night, memories that turned out to be unreliable.

And now here I am, lying in Hugo's bed in a tangle of sheets. But I feel no sense of elation, of having – as Ben put it when he talked about his feelings for Marie-Laure – come home. I feel overwhelmed and drained of emotion. And now I'm trying to make sense of it and asking myself what I want from Hugo – if I want anything at all.

There's a quiet knock on the bedroom door and Hugo comes in, a wide smile on his face. He's fully dressed but his hair is dishevelled and the skin around his eyes is still crinkled from sleep.

'Good morning,' he says, bending to kiss me.

I'm confused by how quickly and strangely everything has changed. I had feared him for so long but now I'm lying in his bed, his lips on mine, my skin still warm from the night-long closeness of his body. Once, I wanted this more than anything in the world. Now I have it. But it feels strange, too strange.

'How are you feeling?' he asks.

'A bit hungover. The wine – it was the first alcohol I'd drunk in years.'

'In that case, I think I should rustle up a full English. Nothing better for a hangover. I've got sausages and black pudding in the fridge, but I'll have to run down to the shops at Notting Hill Gate to pick up some bacon and eggs. Do you mind waiting twenty minutes or so?'

'No. A fry up would be lovely. I'll get up and have a quick shower.'

'Take your time. Towels are in the bottom drawer of that chest,' he says, kissing me again. 'I'll see you shortly.'

I help myself to a large bath towel and a smaller one to dry my hair. But before I step into the shower I have a sudden urge to look again at Ben's painting of me in Hugo's office. I examine it, looking for whatever made Hugo want so much to have it. It's a good likeness and it's a good portrait. And, because my son loved me then, it has something more, something that moves me so much that I feel tears well in my eyes.

Will my son ever look at me in that way again? Will he ever be able to forgive me?

I look too at the portrait of Marie-Laure and, knowing now the depth of his feelings for her, I begin to understand how much of her and of himself he has put into this painting.

And then I start opening the drawers in Hugo's desk. I'm curious about the liaisons that Alice thinks he continues to have and I'm wondering whether I will find evidence of them here. *Alice!* Oh, God, for a moment I'm plunged into a deep sense of guilt as I realise how devastated she would be right now if she knew I had slept with the love of her life.

The two small drawers at the top of the desk are home to a collection of pens and pencils, staples and staplers, paper clips, all neatly arranged. In the next drawer down there's a slim laptop and beneath it a large desk diary for the current year. I take the diary out and flick through it, looking for and finding the names of women written in here and there. Someone called Lucinda features quite a bit. I hate myself for feeling a pang of something akin to jealousy and I quickly banish it. There's an Emma, a Patsy, a Rosalind. But there's no Caroline; I wonder whether that relationship stopped when she married his brother, but I can hardly ask him. There's no mention of Alice, either.

I open the doors of a tall cabinet and rows of box files on shelves. I pull a couple of the boxes out, open them and put them back. They are ordinary business records.

And then I notice that one file has no label. I take it down. I don't know what I expect to find in it – photographs, perhaps, of the women in Hugo's life – but I know the moment I open it that there is something strange. I'm looking at a stack of handwritten pages torn from a lined A4 pad and on the top page my eyes immediately pick out my name, which occurs several times. The top page has yesterday's date on it. I glance through the pages and see that each one is dated but that some of the dates are weeks, months and even years apart. And I see that my name shouts out from each one.

Later, I watched her for a long time as she slept. How odd the situation felt. It was as if we had travelled back in time to somewhere we had failed to reach a long time ago . . .

I confess that at that moment I found her more attractive than I had ever imagined I would, her hair soaked, her wet face glowing, her eyes blazing and her lips an improbable red . . . An almost overwhelming urge to take her in my arms swept over me, but I dismissed it; it would be uncouth. I still had the utmost confidence in my powers of gentle seduction, even with someone like Nan, who had made a false accusation of rape against me . . .

Yesterday's date is written at the top of the page. He has recorded his thoughts about everything we did last night. But when? Did he get out of bed when I was asleep, or did he do it earlier this morning? I don't know what to make of it all. Perhaps I should be flattered, but instead I feel disturbed. And as I read on, I feel increasingly unsettled by the fact that he has devoted page after page of this very odd diary to his obsession with me.

And then I see Chris's name.

I wanted Nan to be without support. I wanted her to be isolated. Perhaps, too, I admit, I was mildly jealous of him. The coroner described the accident as one that had been 'waiting to happen' – as indeed it had been. And, happily, not too much waiting had to be done.

A wave of nausea hits my stomach but I force myself to read on. I am in tears, broken. I have slept with the man who killed my husband and I am filled with guilt and shame. But I make myself read more.

It was a painting that led me to her . . .

When Eddie brought her to see the room, I saw a young and unsophisticated girl. She was a pretty little thing . . . might even become a beauty once her cheeks, which made me think of a pair of early autumn apples, lost their plumpness. She didn't conform to my type. She was on the short side, no more than five-three or -four, and a brunette. I've always liked blondes, the taller the better. Nevertheless, she had some quality I couldn't quite put my finger on . . .

My hands trembling, I put the box file back into the cabinet and quietly walk back to the bedroom. In the shower, I try to wash him off my skin, but I still feel dirty when I emerge.

I hear the sound of the front door closing and Hugo's voice calling that he's back and that breakfast won't take long. I sit on the side of the bed for a long time, still wrapped in the towel. What am I to do? I want to confront Hugo but I know that wouldn't be a good idea, not now that I know how dangerous he is. I wish I had taken the pages from that box file and hidden them in my bag. Maybe there will be another opportunity to get back into his office. Maybe I can ask him to get something he won't have in his house and will have to go out to the shops for. But what?

But even as I'm scouring my brain for an excuse to send him out of the house, the hopelessness of my situation sweeps over me. Hugo has all the cards. He knows I can't risk having the truth come out about Eddie's death.

It's all too much for me. I can't make a decision because whatever I decide will have a bad outcome.

Hugo calls me to breakfast. I go downstairs reluctantly. The only decision I've made is to do nothing for now, show nothing. I can't eat; my stomach is still sick from what I read on those pages. I don't know what to do; the only thing I do know is that I dare not say anything to him.

'Has something happened?' Hugo asks. 'You look terribly pale.'

'I'm feeling a bit sick. It must be all the wine I drank.'

'You didn't drink that much.'

'No . . . but it was the first time I've drunk alcohol in years.'

'At least try the baked beans. The sugar in them will settle your stomach.'

'I'll throw up if I eat anything. I'm sorry. I'll just have the tea.'

'Maybe you need to sleep, go back to bed for an hour or two. And then, if you feel better later, I think we should probably go to Canary Wharf and talk to Ben and Marie-Laure.'

'What will we tell them? I'm a bit confused. I can't remember everything we talked about last night.'

'We'll tell them the truth. Or, at least, most of it – we won't tell them what happened to Eddie. It won't be pleasant for them but at least they'll be able to move forward. And I hope they'll be pleased when we tell them about us.'

'Us?'

'That you and I are together.'

He smiles at me and I force myself to smile back.

Together. I want to vomit.

'What about Ellen? If she's gone to the police and they talk to us. I know we talked about this last night, but . . .'

'Nan, you have nothing to worry about. You're a respectable woman who lost her husband two years ago after a long and happy marriage. I'm a respectable man from a respectable family. I've had no problems with the police and nor have you. As I told you last night, you need a body to prove murder and the police aren't going to find one because neither of us is going to tell them that Eddie's bones are buried in a dog's grave in Leicestershire. It will be our secret.'

I'm ready to leave. I have the pages, rolled up and hidden in the bottom of my bag. I'm trying not to show how anxious I am. I'm terrified that Hugo will discover what I've done.

Earlier, when he suggested I go back to bed, I came upstairs, stripped to my underwear and lay beneath the covers of the bed. A few minutes later, Hugo came in to say he had to go out for an hour.

'Will you be all right?' he asked.

'I'll be fine,' I said, faking a weak smile. 'I'm going to try to sleep.'

A couple of minutes later, I heard the front door close. I waited for another few minutes, just in case he had forgotten something and had returned to the house. When I heard the sound of heavy rain beginning to fall, I was afraid he would cut short whatever errand on which he had set off, so I had to be quick. I went back to the office, opened the cabinet and took the pages from the box file. I had no idea what I was going to do with them, but I knew it was important to have them. Thank God, I thought, that I had never been a carrier of elegant little handbags with no room for anything beyond a purse and a set of keys. Nevertheless, the pages took up a lot of space in my bag and I had to rearrange the contents to make everything fit.

I stayed in bed, still in my underwear, until I heard the sound of the front door opening again. I looked at the time on my mobile. He had been out for about an hour and a half. I waited for him to come up to the room, but he didn't, so I dressed and went downstairs.

'Are you feeling better?' he asked.

'I think so. I slept.'

'Good. Sleep cures everything, I find,' he said, taking me in his arms.

I had a feeling that something wasn't right, that somehow he knew what I had done. But how could he know? I was being paranoid.

He began to kiss me deeply.

I wanted to bite him, draw blood and spit it back at him. But I knew I had to respond as if I desired him, kissing him back as deeply as he was kissing me. I couldn't give him any reason to doubt me.

'Shall we go to Canary Wharf now? We should probably phone Ben and Marie-Laure to tell them we're coming,' I say.

I wanted to get away from Paradise Place. I had no idea what I was going to do with Hugo's horrible journal.

'Yes, I'll do that from my office,' he said. 'I have a couple of quick emails I need to send – business stuff.'

He's up there now. I feel panicky. What if he opens the box file and discovers that the pages aren't there? I wait nervously for him to come back downstairs and when he does, about ten minutes later, he's smiling. I feel some of the tension inside me dissipate, but there's still something that's bothering me and it's clenching my stomach tight, something I can't put my finger on, something that had unsettled me for a fleeting moment when he held me to him.

'Emails sent. And I called Ben and Marie-Laure. They're expecting us. Are you ready to go?' he says.

'I'll just grab my coat.'

'I'm afraid we're going to have to take the underground,' he says, looking apologetic. 'I called my usual driver but there's been an accident on the M4 and he's stuck in a traffic jam near Heathrow. I've tried a few taxi companies but everything is booked because of the rain.'

'That's fine.'

I'm relieved that we're taking the underground rather than using his driver. I will feel safer on the tube.

We walk out of the house and along the cobbled passageway. The rain is falling in torrents and it makes the cobbles slippery. The wind seems to be blowing in every direction and the big umbrella Hugo has opened up can't keep us dry. 'Dangerous weather,' he says.

My stomach twists. There's something in his voice that unnerves me. I say nothing. I'm probably being over-sensitive, over-cautious, because of what I have in my bag.

The steps down into Notting Hill Gate station have been made treacherous by the rain, the concourse even more so. A notice says the Central Line has been suspended because of a signal failure at Leytonstone.

'It will have to be the Circle to Westminster and then Jubilee the rest of the way,' Hugo says.

I pick my way behind him across the wet tiles to the ticket machines, and then through the turnstiles. As we walk down the steps to the platform, there's an announcement apologising for severe delays on the Circle and District lines caused by the weather and promising the imminent arrival of a train. Still on the steps, I can see that the entire platform is thronged with people and looks dangerously overcrowded. At that moment, another announcement advises passengers to take care on the slippery surfaces and warns against standing too close to the platform edge.

'Maybe we should wait for the crowd to thin out,' I say.

'Let's see if we can get through,' he says. 'Otherwise we may have to wait a very long time.'

He puts his hand under my elbow and steers me to the bottom of the steps and along the platform, pushing his way through the crowd until we're close to the edge of the platform. I'm frightened and I try to move back, but I can't because Hugo's grip on me has tightened.

'Hugo, please . . .'

I hear my voice come out as a hoarse whisper. I want to scream but I can't. I'm frozen, caught in his vice-like grip. I hear the sound of a train approaching. The crowd undulates and I feel myself pitching forward. Hugo steadies me and holds me even tighter.

'Careful, darling,' he says.

Darling.

I feel sick.

I look up at him and his eyes seem to have a cold gleam in them. *He knows.* And now I remember what it was that was bothering me back at the house before we left, what I couldn't put my finger on.

His hair and his clothes were dry when he kissed me.

He hadn't left the house.

He knows I took the pages.

Now I understand what he's planning. He will wait until the train is just a few feet away and then he will release me on to the tracks with a push so imperceptible that no one will know what has happened. I try to break away from him again, and again I fail because I'm not strong enough.

The noise of the approaching train is deafening, unbearable. They say that in the moments before death you see your life flash before you. It's not a myth. I know that now. But in those same moments I also see the future, that terrible moment when I will be shattered into thousands of pieces. And as I hear the thunderous sound of the train that's about to explode from the tunnel, the future and past collide in my brain.

Hugo

Last night, I thought I had found a kind of peace. At last, I understood everything that had happened four decades ago, that Nan had mistaken Eddie for me and that she thought she was attacking the man who had raped her. My need for revenge diminished. I even began to see a place for her in my life.

I woke early this morning, happy to see her sleeping beside me. I would have done anything for her.

But something had changed between last night and this morning. I went out to buy food for breakfast, leaving her to take a shower. When I returned to the house, her manner disturbed me. She was more distant, less emotional than she had been last night, and I needed to know what, if anything, had instigated the change. I told her I was going out, and made the appropriate door opening and closing sounds. But I stayed inside the house.

When I discovered that my papers were gone, I felt a cold anger at her treachery. I could have taken her bag from her and emptied it on to the floor. But, and this was so strange, I could not bear to make her afraid of me. I knew I had to let her walk out of Paradise Place. But what was I to do then?

I hear the sound of a train approaching and I feel Nan trying to pull back from me. But I can't let her walk away.

Nan

My ears are filled with the sounds of people screaming. I put my hands up over them, trying to block the unearthly noise. I open my eyes and look for Hugo but he's no longer there. I can't feel his grip on my arm.

People ask the same question over and over.

Are you all right?

Are you all right?

Are you all right?

Every muscle in my body is frozen. I can't move, can't speak. And then I start to shake and a man takes off his coat and wraps it around me. And I hear many voices.

She needs to sit down.

She's in shock.

Has anyone called an ambulance?

I lose track of time. At some point, I am taken to a hospital, where the doctors who examine me say I'm physically fine but in shock. I listen to them, although their voices seem distant, as if there's a sound barrier between them and me. Then the police talk to me, nicely, quietly, considerately. They want to know what happened.

I keep telling them I don't know, that one minute Hugo was there and the next he was gone.

'Were you with the gentleman?' a policeman asks me.

I nod.

'Where were you going?'

'We were . . . we were going to Canary Wharf. We were going to see my son and his fiancée.'

'Why were you standing so close to the edge of the platform?'

'Hugo wanted to make sure we got on the train. I wanted to wait for the next train, but he said we'd be late. I didn't want to stand so close to the edge. I was frightened because the platform was so wet and slippery, and I was afraid . . .'

'What were you afraid of?'

'That I'd slip. Or . . . or that someone would accidentally push me and I'd fall in front of the train.'

'But you didn't slip.'

I shake my head and close my eyes. And when I open them again, they're filled with tears.

'Is he . . . is he dead?' I ask.

The police officers exchange glances and eventually one says, 'I'm sorry.'

45

Now

I gaze out of the tiny window at the mountains below. They're covered in snow, their jagged peaks and ridges rising out of the clouds. These must be the Alps and I am flying above them. I have never been in an aeroplane before. I have never seen a horizon like this, a horizon that stretches endlessly into the heavens, even to heaven itself.

And as my thoughts drift, unanchored by any earthbound fears or obligations, I hear in my mind the sound of unearthly voices. They soar beyond those jagged peaks and the thick soft blanket of cloud. I am thinking now of that first time I went to Paradise Place and Hugo played Allegri's *Miserere* on his record player, of how he told me that this was what he thought heaven must be like beyond the clouds. For years, I turned off the radio whenever that piece was played, because for me it was a reminder of my suspension in a void, somewhere between Earth and Hell, with occasional glimpses of Heaven through my son.

I'm free of Hugo. That's what I tell myself. But I know I will never really be free of him. Even now, deep inside me, I can hear his voice, sonorous and mellifluous, the languid drawl of it dreamy and hypnotic. After everything that has happened, I still remember how, at the beginning of that terrible night all those years ago, he put his finger on my wrist and moved it so gently up and down my arm that it felt like the softest breeze on the fine down of my skin.

That night when I thought that everything I had ever wanted was happening at last. That night when my world began to fall apart.

Hugo is dead and I am reclaiming my life. I will live it, not hide away from it. I will travel. For the first time in my life, I have a passport. I am flying to Florence to stay with Ilaria, finally able to accept the invitation that she has extended to me year after year after year. Ben and Marie-Laure will marry next year. I pray I will be invited to the wedding, but I'm not sure they will want me there. Alice and Arnaud are still together. Ben knows most of the truth now; he's dealing with it and Marie-Laure – who has had her own anguish to deal with – is helping him.

Ben knows that Hugo was responsible for Chris's death. And he knows that I killed Eddie.

The world knows that I killed Eddie: the pages I took from the file in Hugo's cabinet provided an account that I hadn't noticed as I flicked through them but which the police, when they examined my handbag, couldn't ignore.

I was charged with murder. Eddie's sister was surprisingly supportive of me in her evidence. She said that when I visited her in her pub I had genuinely seemed unaware of what had happened to Eddie. She also said in court that Eddie hadn't left university voluntarily but had been sent down after a young woman complained that he had sexually assaulted her.

In the end, I was convicted of manslaughter and given a suspended sentence, the judge having taken into account my supposed mental state at the time and Hugo's part in my husband's death.

The newspapers had a field day for a few weeks during the trial. I tried not to look at them, but sometimes it was difficult to avoid seeing my photograph splashed across the front pages. Some tabloids speculated that Hugo's death might have been more than an accident, that I had deliberately pushed him to avenge my husband. I read all the lurid accounts of my life in a state of numbness, thanks to the medication I had been prescribed.

And then, almost overnight, I was old news.

I live in south-west London now, in a small flat in a gated development. It has only one bedroom, but it does have a communal garden that backs on to an artificial tributary of the Thames. I spend most of my time in my own little bit of the garden outside the French doors, planting and weeding. In summer, when the weather is fine, I take a chair outside and read a book. Swans glide by. Ducks waddle up, demanding that I feed them.

I've started colouring my hair again and I've let it grow. I don't look anything like the woman who appeared in court and on the front pages of newspapers. I threw away the red lipstick. That woman wasn't me, though I'm not sure, even now, who I am because so much has happened, so much has changed.

It has been hard for me, but harder for Ben. I should have told him the truth, or at least the truth as I saw it then, when he was still young but old enough to understand that Chris wasn't his biological father. We might have avoided all this. Though perhaps not, because what I might have told Ben then would only have been the truth as I saw it. Ben would have found Hugo and there would have been a DNA test and the truth, the real truth, would have come out. Because the truth always finds its way out.

Tell the truth or someone else will tell it for you.

The only thing that matters now is my son, my son who hates me. I slip my hand into my bag and run my fingers across the letter he wrote to me after the end of the trial. I don't need to look at it to remind myself of what he said. I see every word in high relief in my mind and every word feels like a knife wound. But it's the final paragraph that cuts deepest.

You say you wanted to protect us. But it was all about you, wasn't it? Dad and I were just extras in the drama you made of your life. We didn't matter. What we wanted, even what we needed, didn't matter. It was only ever about you and your version of the truth. And after everything that has happened, I'm still not sure that I know the whole truth.

He's right about not knowing the full truth, but it's the one truth I can still protect him from.

I still don't remember exactly how it happened, how one moment Hugo was beside me on the platform and how, a moment later, he was gone. What I do remember is the sound of the train coming through the tunnel, becoming louder and louder the closer it came. I remember the way his hand gripped my arm and how fear coursed through me.

And I remember the voice in my head telling me what to do. It said, *Just a push, just a slip.* It was Hugo or me. I made the only choice I could.

BETTWS